ACKNOWLEDGMENTS

Many thanks to my wife Edith for all her contributions, editing and patience. Thanks to Becky Veall for her help with the technical stuff and with the cover design. Also to Lauren Forester for her editorial expertise and contributions.

CW01502133

One

The morning of Monday, 4th April 1949 marked the end of one of the coldest Marches since records began.

Using a small wooden spatula, Archie Freestone gently scraped the ice from inside the window of the small apartment he rented in Beaumont Crescent, W14. He looked thoughtfully down at the busy street and watched as people hurried along the narrow pavements. The snow had finally melted and they could go about their daily lives safely.

Turning away from the window, he neatly folded his last shirt and carefully placed it in the already full suitcase. The trunk, full of his personal belongings, had already been sent ahead of him.

He slowly looked around the room, checking to see if he had forgotten anything. "No, that's everything," he murmured. Having forced his case closed, he put on his overcoat and hat, then carried the suitcase to the door.

He looked back, the apartment appeared empty and cold as though its soul had been stripped away. The smell of his pipe tobacco still filled the air, but little else of Archie remained. With a heavy sigh, he closed the door for the final time, locked it and posted the key back through the letterbox.

It hadn't been an easy decision to make. He had enjoyed the time he'd spent at the War Office and, while his decision to resign from commission wasn't an easy one, he felt it was time for a new chapter in his life. This had been his home for many years and deep down he knew he would miss it. There were numerous happy memories hidden within the four walls, memories never to be forgotten but maybe some to share with others in the future.

Down on the street, Archie stood shivering on the pavement, his suitcase by his side as he waited for a taxi to pass. The harsh wind blew through his dark wavy hair, his expensive suit doing little to shield him from the chill.

"Taxi!" he shouted at the approaching vehicle, but it failed to stop and drove past.

He looked at his watch. "I've still got plenty of time." he said quietly to himself, scanning the passing traffic, while being ignored by several cabs..

After a while, time was beginning to run short and Archie began to feel frantic, he stood in the middle of the road, hand stretched out in front of him, ordering the next taxi he saw to stop. Eventually, a cabbie slammed on his brakes, jolting to a stop just in front of him.

"Keep your hair on, mate. Are you trying to get yourself killed? What's the hurry?" The taxi driver stubbed out his cigarette, removed his cap and put the stub behind his ear. Getting out of his cab he lifted

Archie's suitcase and placed it in the front compartment. He got back into his cab, leaving Archie to climb in the rear and settle down on the soft black leather seat.

"Where to, guv?" asked the driver, his voice coming from the glass divide separating the driver from the passenger.

"Paddington Station." Archie shouted, finding it hard to be heard over the engine's roar.

"Are you in a hurry?"

"Well, I'm not really in a hurry, but the quicker the better. You see I'm meeting someone special."

At that, the driver yanked the gear stick into first and pulled out into oncoming traffic. The sound of horns bellowing and drivers shouting profanities came from behind them. The cabby waved his arm out of the side window and responded with expletives only ever heard on board a navy ship.

An embarrassed Archie sank into his seat and pulled his hat down over his eyes, in the hope no one would see him. All he wanted was to get to the station as quickly as possible, without too much fuss.

In no time at all, having cut up most of London's traffic, the driver pulled up outside Paddington Station.

"That'll be four bob, guv."

Archie fumbled around his coat pocket feeling for any loose change but only had one and six on him. As this was probably the last time for a while he would use a London cab, he got out his wallet. Feeling quite generous, he removed a ten shilling note and handed it to the cabby.

"Keep the change."

"Cheers guv, you're a gent." The cabby said as he lifted Archie's suitcase from the front of the cab, and placed it on the pavement.

"Not at all, it was an interesting experience."

After watching the cab disappear into the distance, Archie picked up his case and walked quickly into the station, passing under the half-glazed ark of the main entrance.

He hurried past the busy, shop-lined thoroughfare toward the ticket office. People were drifting around, some with their heads down, scurrying toward platforms, while others stood around waiting for their trains. A film of smoke mixed with early morning mist clung to the ground, creating an eerie atmosphere.

"The nine twenty-five for Birmingham is departing from platform four." Echoed the tinny voice of the station announcer, sending pigeons scattering high into the atrium.

After buying his ticket, Archie approached the small cafe opposite the ticket office. His face lit up. Sitting at a table in the window was someone who had become very special to him.

Lily, gazed out of the cafe window, watching the people passing to and fro. When she saw Archie coming towards her, a smile spread across her face and she rose from her seat to greet him.

"Lily, I'm so glad you could make it." Archie exclaimed, hugging her to him as he kissed her cheek.

"I wouldn't miss seeing you off, we've just got time to have a coffee. I hope you don't mind but I've ordered two already." she said over the noise.

The station cafe was crowded with several well-dressed city gents sitting on the high stools that ran along the tall counter. Drinking coffee and reading the morning papers, filling the room with clouds of smoke from their cigarettes.

The atmosphere was buzzing as couples reached across small round tables holding hands and saying their farewells along with salesmen, notepads in hand, planning their week's journeys.

As Archie and Lily sat talking and drinking, a voice came across the tannoy. "The ten-fifteen to Bristol will be departing from platform five in ten minutes. Archie's heart sank.

"Oh dear, that's my train. When will I see you again?"

Lily jumped up and looked at Archie with a broad smile."Can you grab my suitcase over there, that's my train as well."

Archie, bemused, looked around and saw two suitcases with Lily's coat draped over them hidden under their table.

"I don't understand." He looked at her cases, bemused, not sure what was going on.

"I'll tell you all about it on the train." Lily grabbed Archie's arm and ushered him toward the platform, as

Archie called for a porter to bring his and Lily's cases.

"All aboard." the guard shouted as they settled into an empty first-class smoking compartment. Archie stowed their luggage on the overhead rope rack then placed their coats and his hat on top. He reached into his jacket pocket for his beloved pipe, filled it, pressed the tobacco down with the end of his penknife and lit it. Drawing on the pipe he sent up plumes of smoke as he flopped down beside Lily and took her hand in his.

"Well," said Archie, "what's going on?"

Two

Archie turned towards Lily, leaning forward in anticipation of what she was about to explain.

"Well, what's going on?" he asked again.

A voice came from outside. "All aboard!" Then the sound of slamming doors and the shrill of the guard's whistle set the train in motion. With a gentle shudder, the train slowly left the platform, surrounding their carriage in clouds of steam and smoke.

"Well?" Archie eagerly pressed.

Lily squeezed Archie's hand as she turned to face him.

"I have been thinking about my future, although I have enjoyed my time at MI6, I think it's time for a change."

"What do you mean?"

"I have spoken to my department head and he has given me leave over the Easter Holiday to consider my future. I was going to Hastings to stay with Mum and Dad to think things over. But I've been talking to Emily, your mother, who suggested I come to stay with them. She believes Pewsey is such a peaceful place to be, it will give me the head space I need to think about my future."

"That's a marvellous idea," Archie grinned, hardly able to contain his excitement. Although somewhat surprised his mother had said nothing to him.

"Emily has my old room ready at the hotel and said I can stay for as long as I like, which is rather kind of her."

As they were talking a shadow darkened their compartment as someone passed along the corridor. Lily looked up and caught a glimpse of a man.

"Wasn't that your vicar, Reverend Ward from St Johns?" Lily asked.

Archie turned quickly to scan the corridor but the man had vanished.

"I didn't see, but if that was Ward he certainly gets about."

Just at that moment, a figure filled the carriage doorway.

"Do these seats belong to anybody?"

Archie looked up, a strange thing to say, he thought.

"No, none of them are taken," replied Archie.

The man was quite tall, over six feet. He had black Brylcreemed hair, slicked back and greying at the sides, making him look quite distinguished. He was wearing a very stylish navy blue pinstripe three-piece suit. Hand made Archie observed. The man stepped into the compartment holding a brown leather suitcase in front of him and a small briefcase tucked under his arm. Putting the briefcase down on the seat, he lifted his case onto the rack above with both hands. Before sitting down he took a book from a small attache case he was carrying and settled into the seat by the door.

Archie couldn't help but notice what the man was reading, Wage-Labour and Capital by Karl Marx. That is rather a strange book to be reading, especially in public, as the Cold War was creating a tense conflict between Russia and the Western Allies. Just sticking out of the attache case was also a copy of Paese Sera, a left-wing newspaper. *Is he a communist?*

Just at that moment, a young woman entered the compartment, wearing high-waisted wide-legged dress pants. Her tucked in blouse was half hidden by a double-breasted jacket and she carried a copy of The Daily Sketch tucked under her arm.

"Are these seats free, ducks?" she asked, looking at Archie.

"Yes, they are."

The lady seemed a chirpy character and from the sound of her accent, from the East End of London. She beamed and the smile seemed to fill the room. She sank into the seat opposite Archie and started to read her newspaper.

The journey was quiet, the man appeared engrossed in his book, hardly taking time to look around. The young lady just thumbed her way through her newspaper and occasionally appeared to stare vaguely out of the window, both seeming lost in their own worlds.

Archie and Lily held hands, drew closer to each

other and chatted quietly about the future. He had longed for this moment, they were to be together again, even though he didn't know for how long that would be, he was content with the time he had now.

In no time at all they arrived in Pewsey. A blast from the train's horn marked their arrival at the station and with a burst of steam from the engine the train shuddered to a halt.

Archie lifted the cases from the rack and helped Lily with her coat. Looking out of the window he noticed the Reverend Ward scurrying down the platform, grasping his small briefcase close to his chest and heading towards the exit.

"You were right, that was Ward you saw. I wonder what he's been up to?" he whispered to Lily.

"I'm not -"

"All aboard", the guard's voice cut off Lily's reply.

"We had better hurry or we will be going on to Westbury," Archie ushered Lily off the train.

On the platform, several people were making their way to the exit, among them was the tall distinguished man from their compartment.

"Archie, Lily, over here." A voice called out, trying to attract their attention.

Standing by the railing that ran alongside the station house was Tomasz Kazimierz, the manager of the River Hotel that Archie's parents owned. He was frantically waving to get their attention. Tomasz was from Poland. He had been a pilot during WW2, had stayed in Britain when the war was over, and had come to work at the hotel in 1945. He was enthusiastic, hard-working, and always ready to help everyone he met.

Tomasz had helped Archie when Inspector Noah Jackson was accidentally shot outside of the police station back in February. A rifle bullet had passed through a prisoner, who Noah was taking to a safe house in Milton Lilbourne. The projectile had entered the inspector's chest and, although serious, he survived.

"Hello Tomasz, it's so lovely to see you again," greeted Lily.

"It is good to see you too, how are you both?"

"Thank you for picking us up," Archie said, shaking Tomasz's hand vigorously. "We're very well thank you, how have you been?"

"How is Daisy?" asked Lily.

"Bardzo dobrze, thank you for asking. I don't see her anymore. Her father objected to our friendship, so it made it impossible for us. Can I help you with your cases?" Tomasz asked, taking both of Lily's suitcases from her as he guided them to the waiting car.

Archie's father's gleaming Morris Six Series MS was parked in the small station car park, still warm from the journey up to the station.

"Come on, let's get you home. Your parents are eager to see you both."

After loading the cases into the car's boot, Archie sat next to Tomasz while Lily settled into the back seat. On leaving the station Archie noticed the

Reverend Ward walking along North Street still clasping his briefcase close to his chest.

"Shall we offer him a lift?" Lily asked.

"Good idea," Archie replied, who was more interested in finding out where the reverend had been.

"Tomasz, can you stop the car?"

They pulled into the curb and Lily wound down her window.

"Reverend, would you like a lift?"

"Hello, that's very kind of you but I need to get some fresh air. The walk will do me good. But I hope to see you on Sunday?"

"Yes of course," Lily replied, closing the window.

At that, the reverend shuffled quickly along North Street staring at the ground. He was still clasping his well-worn briefcase with one broken clasp close to his chest, appearing a little flustered. Archie and Lily watched him as he made his way back to the rectory.

"That chap is always in a hurry, I wonder why he wouldn't accept a lift," Archie pondered.

"Yes, he is rather strange. For a vicar he never seems very friendly," Lily remarked.

Three

In no time at all they pulled up at the main entrance to The River Hotel. Although it was still daylight, the large copper lamp over the main door was lit, giving a soft glow to the impressive Georgian entrance of the three-story building.

Archie got out of the car, looked around, and breathed a sigh of contentment.

"Good to be home," he said, as he was joined by Lily who put her hand in his.

"Yes, it's certainly good to be back."

Archie, upon opening the hotel door, was greeted by an over-enthusiastic Maisie, his mother's black poodle, who was jumping and barking excitedly around them.

"Hello old girl, good to see you too." Archie bent over and ruffled Maisie's head. She immediately lay on her back with legs in the air waiting for someone to tickle her tummy.

Archie's mother, Emily, was waiting by the reception desk with a broad smile on her face. She was still leaning heavily on a walking stick having broken her leg earlier in the year.

"Darling, welcome home! It's so lovely to have you here and even better that it's for good this time," she smiled, with just the hint of a tear in her eye, "and Lily too. I'm so glad you decided to spend some time with us," she smiled as she took Lily's hands in hers.

"Thank you for inviting me Emily, it's very kind of you."

Archie hugged his mother and kissed her on the cheek.

"It's good to be back. I know I've made the right decision and I'm looking forward to helping in the hotel. How are you? How's your leg? It's good to see you up and about."

Just then Tomasz, laden with suitcases burst through the main door.

"Let me give you a hand with those," said Henry, Archie's father, who had just come out of the office.

Grabbing a case from Tomasz, he helped carry them into the hotel reception.

"Good to see you, Dad," Archie said, hugging his father.

"It's good to see you too, Archie. We've been waiting a long time for this day. Having you back will be like old times. Mrs Vincent has already lit fires in both of your rooms, so let's get you settled in. Your trunk arrived yesterday, Tomasz has already put it in your room."

"Thanks, Dad, thanks Tomasz."

Henry picked up two of the cases. "Are you sure you can manage them at your age, Dad?"

"Less of the cheek," Henry chuckled to himself as he and Tomasz carried the cases up the wide main hotel staircase.

Archie and Lily followed behind when Emily called out. "We've saved you and Lily a table in the dining room once you've sorted yourselves out."

"Thank you, Mum," Archie called. "Oh, and we must remember to give you our ration books when we come down." Archie turned around and said to Lily. "It really is good to be home."

***

Entering the dining room, Archie saw Lily waiting at their special table. *She is beautiful*, he thought, looking at her red wavy hair which fell onto her shoulders. She was wearing a pretty green flowered dress with a sweetheart neckline. Archie couldn't help thinking that she could have graced the front cover of Vogue Magazine.

"You look lovely," Archie said as he kissed her on the cheek.

"Thank you, Archie. You look rather dashing yourself." Lily replied, blushing slightly

"Are you ready to order?" a familiar voice interrupted their conversation. Ruth, the hotel head waitress and part-time receptionist stood over them with pen and notepad in hand.

"Hello, Ruth, how are you?" Lily asked, looking up at her.

"I'm very well thank you, Miss Forester."

"Do call me Lily. Yes, we are ready to order, I'll-"

"I'm sorry to cut in but isn't that the vicar's wife at the reception desk," Archie exclaimed, nearly falling over as he leaned back in his chair to get a better look.

"You're right. What is she doing here?" Lily turned in her chair to get a better view.

I wonder what has brought her here, wondered Archie, she does appear to be in distress, but why come to the hotel. I need to find out.

Four

Florence Ward, a tall slim woman wearing wire-rim glasses, was talking to Henry.

Archie got up and wandered to the dining room door, trying to hear what was going on.

"Archie, have you got a minute," his father called from the reception desk.

"Yes, of course, I'm just coming."

"Do you know Florence, the rector's wife?" Henry asked.

"Yes, we met when I was here earlier this year. How can I help?"

"Hello Mr Freestone, I know this is silly, but did you happen to see my husband on the London train this morning?" Mrs Ward asked.

"Hello Mrs Ward, yes, he got off at Pewsey with us. As we were driving down North Street we saw him and offered to give him a lift. But he said he needed some fresh air and would rather walk. Why?"

"It may be nothing, but he hasn't come home and that's not like him."

"Lily, can you join us?" Archie called over his shoulder before turning back to Mrs Ward. "Shall we go into the lounge? It's more private."

All three retired to the hotel lounge. Although the

room was empty there was a roaring fire burning in the hearth. Archie loved this room. It always reminded him of a smart London gentlemen's club, with its panelled walls and soft leather armchairs and Chesterfield settees.

Lily, leading the way, guided Mrs Ward to the armchairs by the fire. Mrs Ward sat down and pulled the hem of her skirt over her knees, making herself comfortable, then looked up. Archie, having put another log on the fire, turned to the vicar's wife.

"Would you like anything to drink?"

"No thank you, Mr Freestone."

"Do call me Archie."

Archie reached into his jacket pocket and took out his pipe. He filled it with tobacco, pressed it down and lit it, sending up plumes of smoke. He turned to Mrs Ward.

"Well let's start at the beginning, shall we? Firstly, have you spoken to the police?"

Florence hesitated. "He's only a few hours late and I didn't think the police would be interested." she said, her voice trembling..

"It'll be alright," Lily patted her hand in an attempt to reassure her, "Don't worry, we will find him."

Archie leaned forward in his chair, "Why have you come to the hotel?"

"I thought perhaps someone who was on the ten-fifteen from Paddington may have booked in here and I could ask them if they had seen a vicar on the train. Your father said that you were on the train and called you over."

"Can I ask," Lilly said, "what was your husband doing in London?"

"He was attending a seminar at Dean's Yard, near Westminster Abbey and stayed overnight. He was catching the morning train home."

"Do you know where he was staying in London?" Archie continued.

"No, he didn't tell me."

"Did he say what the seminar was about?" Lily cut in.

"No, I'm not that interested in that side of his work. It all sounds very political and that's never appealed to me."

"Have you spoken to him since he left on Saturday?" Lily continued.

There was a long silence as Florence seemed to consider her answer.

"He telephoned to say he had arrived at Dean's Yard, but that's the last I heard from him."

The sound of footsteps made Archie turn. The imposing figure of Tom Hopkins, the local police sergeant, stood in the doorway of the lounge.

"Archie, Miss Lily, I heard you were back. How are you…? Oh, I'm sorry, I didn't mean to interrupt. I didn't realise you were with Mrs Ward, hello" He smiled at her.

"Hello Tom, we're both well, thank you for asking, it's good to see you. In fact, this is an opportune moment, perhaps you can help. The Reverend Ward seems to have disappeared. We saw him about midday walking down North Street, but he hasn't arrived back at the rectory and that's not like him."

Archie looked back at Florence Ward, concern written on his face.

"Strictly speaking, he's not actually missing. Normally a person has to be reported missing for at least twenty-four hours before the police will act. But saying that, as it is unusual, I will make some discreet enquiries around the village."

"Thank you, Tom. Is there anything we can do?"

"I'll let you know."

As Tom was leaving he turned around and with a smile said, "Does this mean the old team is back in action?"

"What does he mean?" Mrs Ward asked.

"Oh, it's nothing," Archie replied with a wry smile.

"Maybe it would be better if you went home and waited for your husband there, he may phone you," suggested Lily.

"Yes you're right, he probably called in to see one of his parishioners and forgot to tell me. He can be very forgetful."

Archie helped Mrs Ward with her coat and escorted her to the door.

"If we find anything out we'll let you know, likewise if your husband turns up, will you let us know?" Archie asked, opening the door.

"Yes, I will, thank you, Mr Freestone."

"Archie, please."

"Yes, of course, Archie."

As Archie watched Mrs Ward disappear down River Street, Lily joined him on the hotel steps.

"Does this mean there's a case to solve?" she asked, jokingly.

"Maybe. Who knows." Archie secretly hoped that there was and that he would be working with Lily again.

"You must be starving, Lily," he stated knowing what her answer would be, she was always ready to eat. How she managed to stay so slim he didn't know. He was sure she could eat a horse if there was one around.

"Yes, I am rather," she replied as Archie took her by the arm and headed back into the restaurant, where Ruth was clearing the tables.

"Are we too late to order some lunch?"

"No, Sam is still in the kitchen and I believe there is some game pie left."

"Sounds good, thank you, Ruth."

***

After they had eaten Archie and Lily returned to the main foyer. Tomasz was at the reception desk booking several people into the hotel.

Two of the men were here for a golfing holiday at the local Pewsey golf course. One was middle-aged and rather overweight. He had wavy red hair and a well-manicured beard, he stood, one hand pushed into the trouser pocket of his dark blue suit. He pulled out a pocket watch from his waistcoat, checking the time, eye's constantly searching the room. The other was younger, slim and wore a collarless shirt, high-buttoned waistcoat, and dark blue suit. He was continually stroking his clean shaven chin, as if he was expecting to find a beard there. Despite being young, his dark brown curly hair was beginning to recede.

Watching them, Archie thought they were like chalk and cheese, an odd couple.

Tomasz handed the two men their room keys. Archie continued to watch them as they climbed the stairs carrying their suitcases. He turned to Tomasz.

"Hello, you look very busy."

"Yes, we are fully booked." Tomasz said as he looked up from his work.

While they were talking, a lady wearing a brown tweed suit, beige twin set and sensible brogue shoes handed Tomasz her room key. She wore her hair in a bun at the nape of her neck and oversized round glasses. Her appearance reminded Archie of his old Sunday school teacher.

"Thank you, Miss Hunt, will we see you later for dinner?" Tomasz inquired.

"Yes, would six o'clock be alright?" she said.

"That will be fine, I'll reserve a table for you."

As Miss Hunt disappeared out of the main door, Lily turned to Tomasz and asked if he knew what she was doing there.

"She's here for the week on a bird-watching holiday. Apparently, we have a wonderful diversity of birds including rapacious birds. Although I'm not sure what that means."

"Rapacious birds are birds with hooked bills, and sharp, strongly curved talons. There are three families, represented by the vultures, the falcons or hawks, and the owls." Archie confidently said.

Lily and Tomasz looked silently at each other with eyebrows raised, then at Archie. For once they were stuck for words.

"You really are a font of knowledge," remarked a surprised Lily.

"Well, you pick things up when you live in the countryside."

He took Lily gently by the hand and, smiling, he suggested they have coffee in the lounge.

They were both happy to be back in Pewsey and were looking forward to spending time together. As they were talking Ruth came over to advise them that she had reserved their special table for dinner at six o'clock, if that was alright.

"Thank you Ruth, that sounds perfect, if that's okay with you Lily."

"Yes, of course, six is fine with me."

***

Archie was already waiting in the dining room

when Lily arrived. He stood up and kissed her on the cheek.

"You look lovely this evening," he whispered as he pulled the chair out for her.

"Thank you, you look quite the man about town yourself," she smiled.

As they were ordering their meal, Tomasz appeared at their table.

"Archie, someone is waiting to see you in reception."

"Thank you, Tomasz, I'll be right there." I wonder who that can be, has the reverend been found, is he alright, has there been any trouble, he pondered as he made his way to reception.

Five

Archie followed Tomasz into the main foyer and was greeted by his old friend Noah Jackson. Noah had worked with Archie at the War Office during the war and more recently on the murder of Frolov, a Russian spy. During that case, Noah had been shot and badly injured but was now on the road to a full recovery.

"Noah, it's good to see you up and about old chap," Archie grabbed Noah by the hand, pumping it up and down with pleasure at seeing his old friend looking so well.

"Why didn't Tomasz say it was you? Do join us in the dining room, Lily would love to see you."

"I told him I wanted to surprise you. I'm glad you're back, I hear it's for good this time," Noah smiled. "Sorry I can't join you though, I'm here on business, hopefully, you and Lily will be able to help me."

Archie called Lily to join them in the foyer.

"Hello Lily, it's lovely to see you again. For good I hope."

"It's wonderful seeing you looking so well. Unfortunately, I'm only here for a short break to decide my future."

"How can we help you?" Archie asked.

"You know the Reverend Ward hasn't turned up at the rectory? Well he's still missing. I wondered whether you could remember anything about the journey from London that could shed some light on his disappearance."

"We only caught sight of him leaving the train at the station, we passed him in North Street and offered him a lift but he declined saying he wanted some fresh air. Sorry, not much help I'm afraid."

"Can you think of anything or anyone acting strange on the train?" Archie asked,

"No, it was quite a normal journey, nothing stood out," Lily remarked.

"Although we were somewhat focused on each other and didn't take a lot of notice of anybody else," Archie confided with a smile.

"It's probably nothing and he will turn up sooner or later," Noah said. "Perhaps we can meet for coffee tomorrow morning and catch up."

"Yes, that would be lovely. Shall we say here at ten thirty?" agreed Archie.

"Perfect, I'll see you then."

Noah was making his way to the main door when Tomasz called him back.

"Inspector, there's a telephone call for you."

"Thank you, Tomasz."

Noah made his way back to the reception desk, then picked up the receiver.

"Jackson here."

"It's Hopkins, sir. John Strong, the local farmer,

has just telephoned. When he was getting his cows in for milking, something caught his attention, tucked in the hedgerow was a small brown briefcase and beside it was the Reverend Ward's ration book. I told him to leave them until we get there."

"Is that Manor Farm dairy?" Noah asked.

"Yes sir, on the Salisbury Road."

"Thank you, sergeant. Make your way there and I'll meet you in about ten minutes."

Putting the telephone down he turned to Archie and Lily and explained what the sergeant had said. "Would you like to join me?"

"Try stopping us," Archie burst out, almost vibrating with enthusiasm

As they were leaving, Archie's father came into the reception area carrying a crate of beer on his way to the bar.

"Oh, Dad, we are just popping out with Noah to help examine an incident at John Strong's farm. Can you ask Ruth to keep our table for us please? We shouldn't be too long."

"Yes of course. Is this history repeating itself?" his Father asked with a wry smile.

"I don't know what you mean, Dad. We're just going to see if we can help." replied Archie innocently.

Pewsey was quiet. It was still freezing and the smell of log fires permeated the air. North Street was almost empty as the three made their way quickly to the police station to pick up Noah's car.

Manning the front desk at the station was Jack Jones, the young police constable.

"Hello Jack, good to see you again," Archie smiled as they entered.

"Hello Mr Freestone, Miss Forester, welcome back, it's good to see you both."

"Call me Archie."

"And do call me Lily, Jack."

"I will, Archie and Miss Lily," a slightly embarrassed Jones replied.

"Jones, can you get my car keys? I think they're on my desk."

"Yes sir."

Jones soon returned and handed Noah his keys.

"Thank you, Jones, if anybody needs me I'll be at Manor Farm with Sergeant Hopkins. Archie and Lily are joining us to see if they can help."

"Is something going on sir? Another murder?" Jones eagerly enquired, unable to hide his excitement. He had enjoyed working with Archie and Lily back in February on the Frolov case. But it was tainted with a little sadness as he was about to embark on a residential course at Mill Meece in Staffordshire. Although not living in the county, Noah had managed to secure a place for him on a police training programme.

"We're not sure yet, I'll keep you up to date on what's happening. Meanwhile, carry on here at the station "

John Strong was leaning against the farm gate, one Wellington clad foot on a cross bar, the other planted firmly on the ground, with both elbows balanced on the top. He was a well liked man, known as much for his good nature as he was for the long brown raincoat and well worn trilby hat that he habitually wore.

He was talking to Sergeant Hopkins. As the three approached, he pushed open the gate to let them into the farmyard. He smiled as he suddenly recognised Archie.

"Archie Freestone, I heard you were back, what are you doing here?"

"Hello Mr Strong, I've decided it was time to move back home and help Mum and Dad in the hotel, as they're not getting any younger. This is Miss Forester, a very close friend of mine. We are here to help Inspector Jackson."

"Nice to meet you, Miss Forester." He smiled as he shook her hand.

"Hello, Mr Strong, nice to meet you too, you have a lovely farmhouse."

"Thank you. Please call me John, Mr Strong makes me sound like my father."

She laughed, "You have a lovely farmhouse, John."

The building bathed in sunlight, looked old and comfortable in it's setting. The smell of the farm permeating the air was unfamiliar to Lily having come from the city, but she liked it.

"This is Inspector Noah Jackson, he is in charge of the case."

"Nice to meet you, Inspector." They shook hands.

"Nice to meet you too. Sorry, it's not under better circumstances."

"This way, I found the briefcase and ration book over here."

Archie, Lily, Noah and the sergeant followed the farmer to the back of the farmhouse. Farm machinery was parked ready to be used as was needed. The farmyard was orderly and well kept. The hedgerows that boarded the yard were now in leaf. The birds that were sheltering in their branches suddenly took flight as they approached.

Six

"They're just over here," John Strong pointed to a somewhat overgrown hedgerow.

Hidden, almost out of sight, was a small brown briefcase that had been pushed into the bushes as if someone had attempted to hide it in the thick undergrowth. Beside it was the Reverend Ward's ration book, just appearing from beneath the foliage.

"Thank you, Mr Strong, we'll take it from here," Noah said.

"Sergeant, can you check the other side of the hedge and see if you can find anything?"

"Yes sir."

"I don't suppose anyone has brought a camera?" Noah enquired.

"No, I didn't," Archie replied.

"I have one. I always carry a camera with me, you never know when it may come in handy," grinned Lily, removing her pride and joy, a Jiffy Kodak Six-16 from her handbag.

"Thank you, Lily. Would you mind taking some pictures of the scene."

"We need to search the area around the hedge and along the bank. Archie and I will start at the farmhouse end. Lily, when you finish taking photographs can you help Tom on the other side of the hedge?"

"Yes, of course. I won't be a jiffy," Lily replied.

Soon all four were meticulously scrutinising the surrounding area, hoping to find clues as to the whereabouts of the reverend.

"Over here," Lily's voice breaks the silence.

Archie and Noah headed around to the other side of the hedge. Tom and Lily were standing, staring at something lying half-hidden in the hedge.

"What is it?" Noah asked.

"It looked like a cigarette packet," Tom replied.

"Let me have a closer look," Archie said, pushing forward.

"You're right. Have you taken a photograph of it yet, Lily?"

"Yes, I've taken several."

Archie bent down, carefully removing the leaves that covered the packet and picked it up, careful to only touch the edges just in case there were any fingerprints to be found.

"My God, it's a packet of Kazbek cigarettes, a Russian brand. You can't buy them in England. What are we dealing with here?" Archie stepped back, staring at the packet in his hand.

The memories of the spy ring and Parkhill Garrison, of Frolov, Baptiste, Doherty and Colonel De Villiers-Blyth came flooding back.

"Let's hope it's just a coincidence."

"We don't believe in coincidences," Lily said,

smiling at Archie.

"No, we don't, do we?" Although he smiled back at her he shivered at the memory, it must be getting cold he thought to himself.

"Sergeant, can you bag everything up and take them to the police station?" asked Noah, "I'll meet you there."

"Yes sir."

Noah turned to Archie and Lily, "As it's getting dark, there's not a lot we can do here. I think that's probably enough for today. Let's head back."

"I don't know about you but I'm starving," Lily said as she grabbed Archie by the hand, eager to get back.

Noah dropped Archie and Lily off at the hotel's main door then drove on to the police station where Sergeant Hopkins was waiting for him.

"Still no sign of the reverend, sir."

"No, I'm sure he'll turn up sooner or later. Where's his briefcase?"

"It's in your office, would you like me to go and get it for you?"

"If you would, thank you."

Sergeant Hopkins brought the briefcase from Noah's office and the two examined it. Unfortunately, it was locked and, as they didn't have a key, they decided to take it to someone who had a particular skill in picking locks.

"I'll pop along and see him later. There's not much more we can do this evening, you might as well go home. We'll carry out a full search first thing tomorrow, that's if he hasn't shown up."

***

After they had finished eating, Archie and Lily joined his mother, Emily, in the lounge for drinks.

"Hello darling, how has your day been? Have they found the reverend yet? And how are you Lily darling, have you managed to eat anything, is your room alright?"

"Mum, one thing at a time. We've had an interesting day and no the reverend hasn't shown up yet, and yes we have eaten."

"And I'm fine. The room is perfect, thank you," Lily smiled.

"Oh, I'm so pleased. It is lovely having you here Lily."

"Where's Maisie this evening Mum? It's very quiet."

"Dotty has taken her out for her evening walk, she should be back soon."

Dotty, Mrs Vincent, lived in the old coach house with her husband Bob and their adult son Arthur, an old friend of Archie's. She was the hotel housekeeper and had been since time began and was like part of the family.

While they were talking, a very excited Maisie came bounding into the lounge and made straight for Lily. She laid submissively on the floor in front of her, paws in the air waiting for her tummy to be tickled.

"Hello Maisie old girl, how have you been? I've missed you," Lily said, bending down to give her tummy a rub.

"It's so perfect having you both home," his mother said with a hint of a tear in her eye.

"It's so good being home and-"

"Archie, the inspector is here to see you. Shall I show him through?" Tomasz interrupted as he appeared at the lounge door.

"Yes, if you would. Thank you, Tomasz."

Noah, briefcase in hand, stood excitedly into the lounge.

"I'm sorry to spoil your first evening, but I have a small problem that needs your expertise, Archie." He says as he seats himself next to Archie and Lily.

"No problem old chap. Would you like anything to drink, a whisky perhaps?"

"Well, just a small one would be welcome," said Noah, taking a packet of Woodbine cigarettes from his overcoat pocket. Taking one out, he lit it and took a deep breath, inhaling the smoke.

"I'll leave you three to it," Archie's mother said as she got up to leave.

"Thank you, Mum. We'll pop up and see you before we retire. Now Noah, sit down and tell us the problem?"

"Well, so far we haven't got much to go on except the reverend's briefcase. Unfortunately, it's locked and we can't open it, I need your particular talent to pick the lock." Noah explained, sitting down by the fire.

Archie had always prided himself that there hadn't been a lock invented that he couldn't pick.

Noah handed the briefcase to Archie who, slightly confused, stared at it.

"Interesting, I've not come across this make before. I don't think it's English. Lily, you wouldn't happen to have a hairpin would you?"

"I do as it happens," she said, taking a pin from her hair and handing it to Archie.

"Let's see," Archie started wiggling the pin carefully to the left and then to the right of the lock.

"This is a tough one." He continued to move the pin gently from side to side, searching for the right spot until it eventually popped open.

"What have we here? I didn't expect that," Archie said, peering into the briefcase.

Seven

Archie reached into the case and, sitting amongst a pile of papers, he pulled out a well-worn copy of Wage-Labour and Capital by Karl Marx.

"Where have I seen this before?" Archie mumbled to himself.

"On the train, you remember, that chap sitting in the corner."

"Yes, you're right Lily. What's it doing in the reverend's briefcase?" Archie lifted the case to examine it more closely. "I'm not sure this is his. It appears too new and both the clasps appear to be in good order."

"It looked more like the one the man had on the train," Lily frowned.

The three looked at each other puzzled, wondering if this could be a new case for them to work on.

Noah broke the silence. "What else is in there?"

"Let me see," Archie rummaged around. "Hang on!" Taking his penknife out of his pocket, he opened the blade and, using the tip, he levered up a panel from the bottom of the case. Secreted in the bottom was a pistol. He lifted it out carefully so as not to destroy any evidence. "Well I never, who is this chap?" he asked.

"Let me see!"

Archie handed the gun to Noah.

Examining it, Noah remarked. "It looked like an Enfield No. 2 Mk I .38/200 caliber revolver, army issue."

"I think you're right. But, more importantly, why is it hidden in his briefcase? What about the papers, do they tell us anything?" Archie remarked.

"There are a few with notes scribbled on them but I can't make out what they say. It looked like a spider with wet feet had crawled over the page. There's also some Lloyd's of London bank statements addressed to a Mr John Allen from London."

"Do we know anything about this chap?" Noah asked.

"If it's the man from the train, he was fairly unassuming. Kept to himself. The last we saw of him he was walking down the platform here in Pewsey." Archie replied.

"What did he look like?"

"Well, he was quite tall, I'd say over six feet, dark hair, greying at the temples."

"He did look rather distinguished," Lily interrupted Archie, who gave her a sideward glance.

"He was wearing a very stylish dark blue three-piece suit, probably handmade. Oh, and carrying a small attache case, if I remember rightly - looked quite new."

"I wonder where he's staying. Can you check with Tomasz and see if anyone with that description has registered here? Meanwhile, I'll get Tom to check the pubs and boarding houses in Pewsey."

"I'll go straight away." Archie left them to see what he could find out.

The foyer was bustling. Mondays were always the busiest day of the week but this Monday seemed even busier. As Archie approached the reception desk, he found Henry talking on the telephone.

"Thank you for calling, we look forward to seeing you on Friday," he said, placing the handset on the receiver. "Hello Archie, what can I do for you?"

"Hello Dad, it looked busy tonight." Archie commented.

"Yes, a lot of extra people have booked in this week. Massey Ferguson, the agricultural manufacturers, are in Pewsey and have planned several events at the Bouverie Hall to promote their new range of tractors."

"That's marvellous Dad," Archie said, smiling. "Can I help you with anything?

"No we're fine, thank you, Tomasz will be here in a minute."

"Dad, can I ask, did you have a gentleman register earlier? He is about six foot and quite distinguished looking, dark hair greying at the sides."

"Right, well we've had quite a few people register who sound similar, but there is one in particular that fits the bill. Let me look at the register," He fumbled around behind the desk before pulling out a thick blue book. "Ah, here he is. John Allen from Parfett Street,

Whitechapel in London. He's in room seven. His key is still here, so he must be out. Do you need to take a look in his room?"

"No, not now, thank you Dad. It's getting late and Lily and Noah are waiting for me in the lounge."

Archie left his father and returned to the lounge where Lily and Noah were deep in conversation.

"Well, how did you get on?" Noah asked as Archie approached them.

"There was a chap who registered, he does fit the description and his name is John Allen, from Whitechapel, so that would match the papers we found in the briefcase. He's out at the moment, so there's not much we can do."

As the evening progressed there had been no sign of Mr Allen returning. Noah decided it was time he went home and that he could speak to him in the morning. They said their good nights to each other, agreeing to meet the following day. He picked up the briefcase and left Archie and Lily to their evening.

Archie pushed some tobacco into his pipe, lit it and settled back into the soft leather armchair opposite Lily.

There was a comfortable silence as they sipped their whiskies in front of the roaring log fire. Soon the warm smokey haze from Archie's pipe and the warmth from the log fire, together with the effects of whisky, had them feeling drowsy.

"Shall we call it a night? It's been a long day and I'm rather tired."

"Yes, it has been a long but very interesting day, a bit like when we first met back in February," Lily smiled.

"We will have to see what tomorrow brings."

Lily rested her hand on Archie's arm, as they made their way upstairs.

"Good night, Lily." He kissed her on the cheek.

"Good night Archie, see you in the morning."

Eight

Tuesday 5th April

Six thirty and the familiar sound of Maisie scratching at Archie's door woke him. It must be half past six, he thought to himself.

"I'm coming old girl."

Washed and dressed, Archie made his way to the foyer, where Lily was waiting for him.

"Good morning Lily, did you sleep well?"

"Yes, I did, thank you. It looks like it's going to be another lovely day. Archie just look at that beautiful blue sky"

"Yes, and I believe it's going to get warmer. Perfect for a long walk before breakfast."

Putting the lead on Maisie, they headed for the main door. Tomasz, who was at the reception desk, called out. "Archie, the inspector is on the telephone for you."

"Thank you, Tomasz, I'm just coming."

Archie made his way past the reception desk and through to the back office.

"Good morning Noah, what can I do for you?"

"Good morning Archie, I'm sorry to call so early, but I'm afraid to say a body has been found. Arthur

Hewit, the newsagent, was delivering the morning papers. He was cutting through the copse by the river when something caught his attention on the river bank. He went to have a closer look and to his horror, it was a body."

"Goodness, how can we help?" an expectant Archie cut in, hoping he and Lily could get involved.

"Jones is away training for two weeks, if it is foul play, I'll be short-handed so could do with some help."

"We're on our way," Archie said, putting the telephone receiver down, he grabbed Lily's hand and Maisie's lead and set off for the copse, explaining what had happened as they went.

It had turned surprisingly warm as they approached the narrow bridge over the river. They saw that a small crowd had already gathered, and the tall figure of Sergeant Tom Hopkins with his imposing handlebar moustache was busy trying to keep them back.

Along the footpath, Noah was talking to Dr Stagg, the local doctor, who also doubled up as the police surgeon. Archie and Lily joined them.

"Is it the reverend," Archie called out, as he tried to look past Noah to the body lying on the bank.

"No, it's a woman, the doctor thinks she is in her mid-thirties."

"Not from round here," Hopkins shouted from down the path.

"Can I have a closer look?"

"Yes, of course, Archie."

Noah led Archie and Lily along the river by the bridge to where the body lay. She was face down with one foot, minus a shoe, in the water with her arms by her side. Archie instantly recognised the brown tweed suit and beige twin set. There was only one brogue shoe but he was certain who she was.

"It's Miss Hunt, she's staying at the hotel. Does the doctor know how she died, was it an accident?"

Noah pulled Archie and Lily to one side and spoke quietly.

"She has had her throat cut, just one wound, death would have been instantaneous, a pretty nasty way to go. Do you know what she was doing here?"

"Bird watching, that's all I know."

"Sergeant, move those children off the bridge and then take down Mr Hewit's statement," Noah shouted as a group of children on the way to school, whose natural curiosity was drawn to the events on the river bank.

"Yes, sir. Come on you lot, there's nothing to see," Tom said as he ushered them past the scene.

"Sorry Archie, what were you saying?"

"She's staying for a few days on a bird-watching holiday, I believe she's from London."

As they were talking the sound of the ambulance bell could be heard coming down River Street and was soon at the bridge.

"Can we move the body, doctor?"

"Yes, inspector, there's not much more I can do

here. I'll just finish off and give you my report later today."

Dr Stagg took some photographs, checked his measurements and jotted something down in his notebook. He then waved for the ambulance men to come and collect the body and take it to the morgue at Marlborough Hospital, where he would perform the autopsy.

As he passed Noah on the way to his car, he looked at Archie and Lily, smiled and mumbled, "Since you two came here, there's been nothing but murder and mayhem, life certainly is more interesting."

Slowly the crowd dispersed leaving the sergeant to secure the scene.

"I'll telephone Marlborough police station, and see if they will lend us a couple of constables. When they get here sergeant, I want the three of you to search the river bank, and see if you can find her other shoe or anything else that could be helpful."

Noah, Archie and Lily left the sergeant and made their way back to the hotel, being pulled along by Maisie.

In the foyer, Tomasz was writing in the guest book whilst several people were standing around waiting to be attended to. Among them almost hidden in one corner was John Allen, who, when he saw Noah come in, quietly slid out of the main door.

"I'm sorry to butt in Tomasz, but is Miss Hunt in her room?" Noah said, pushing his way past several people.

"Let me see, what room is she in," he mumbled to himself. Ah! room eight and her key is here, so she must be out." He handed Noah the key and confirmed she was in room eight.

At the bottom of the staircase, they bumped into Henry.

"Hello Archie, what's going on, not another murder," he joked.

"Hello Dad, sorry, but it looks like Miss Hunt from room eight has been murdered, we need to take a look in her room."

"I'm so sorry, I didn't realise, I was just joking. How was she killed? Do you need anything?"

"No, we're fine thank you, Henry, I can't disclose any information at the moment," Noah said as they proceeded up the stairs.

Outside room eight, Noah knocked on the door. "It's the police, is there anyone there?"

As expected there was no response, Noah placed the key in the lock and gently turned it. As the door opened, he called, "We're coming in."

The room was tidy, a paisley eiderdown was folded back, the bed looked like it hadn't been slept in. Her clothes, which were colour-coordinated, neatly hung in the wardrobe.

"That's funny," Lily peered into the wardrobe. "Not one tweed outfit or sensible pair of shoes. But there are some very jazzy dresses and shoes, there's also a couple of grey wigs. looked like there is more to Miss Hunt than meets the eye."

Archie noticed a suitcase partially hidden under the bed. He pulled it out, laid it on top of the bed and carefully opened it. On checking the contents, he found, tucked away in one corner among some jumpers a letter addressed to Mrs Isabella Valentino of Whitechapel London.

"Whitechapel, isn't that where Mr Allen in room seven is from?" Archie queried. "That's a bit of a coincidence."

"Inspector, Dr Stagg is on the telephone for you," Henry called up the stairs.

"Thank you, Henry, I'm just coming."

"Well, there's not a lot we can do here. I think we need to have a word with this Mr Allen," he frowned. "Shall we meet in the lounge for coffee after I've spoken to the doctor?" Noah suggested to the others.

"Good idea," replied Archie, "meanwhile I'll enquire at the desk if Mr Allen is in or not."

Nine

The air in the lounge was full of pipe and cigarette smoke, the warmth from the log fire roaring in the hearth gave the room a warm and welcoming atmosphere. It was a busy morning for the hotel, the room was full of people enjoying their morning coffee.

Archie and Lily had managed to find a table and were enjoying discussing the murder when Noah joined them.

"Coffee," Lily asked him as he approached the table.

"Thank you, that would be lovely."

"What did the doctor say," an eager Archie enquired.

"It's only a verbal report, he will put it in writing in the next few days. However, the general outline is firstly, she was a slim younger woman, early thirties with long wavy chestnut hair, olive skin, probably of Mediterranean descent. Her clothes were interesting, the tweed suit she was wearing was padded which gave the impression that she was overweight and she was also wearing a grey wig. She had a single wound to her neck inflicted by a sharp object. He thinks she was probably caught by surprise by a left-handed person. Death would have been approximately between five am and eight am this morning"

"How does he know it's a left-handed person?" Lily asked.

Archie interjected. "Apparently, when the head is pulled back and the knife is then drawn across the throat, the wound inflicted is deeper at the beginning and then tails off at the opposite side of the neck. From right to left by a left-handed assailant."

Lily and Noah looked at each other and smiled.

"On another subject, has the reverend turned up yet?" Lily asked.

"I don't know, I need to telephone the station and find out. Would it be alright if I used the hotel telephone, Archie? Oh, also did you find out whether Mr Allen was in or not?"

"He's out at the moment and yes, of course, use the telephone in the back office, it's more private."

"Thank you, our main priority is to find Ward, and Miss Hunt's killer," a concerned Noah said as he left the lounge.

On their own and with a sense of anticipation, Archie and Lily draw close to each other, so as not to be overheard.

"This is very exciting, well maybe not for Miss Hunt, but I do like a good mystery," Archie was pleased to be working with Lily and Noah again.

"Did you notice that Mr Allen quietly slid out of the hotel when we entered the foyer earlier?"

"No, I didn't."

"I thought at the time it looked suspicious, as though he didn't want to be recognised, and I think we may know why! What do we know about him?" Lily whispered.

Just then, Ruth appeared with a tray of coffee and biscuits, interrupting their conversation.

"Sorry to interrupt, but your father said you would probably need more coffee and something to eat."

"Thank you, Ruth, perfect timing, would you thank my father for me."

Just behind Ruth was Noah, he was pushing past people in the crowded room, eager to share his news.

"Mrs Ward telephoned, there's still no sign of the reverend. So I've arranged for a search party to meet at Manor Farm at two o'clock this afternoon. Can I count on the both of you joining us?"

"Yes, of course, anything we can do to help," Archie and Lily agreed.

Finishing his coffee, he put his cup down and got to his feet.

"Right, I should get back to the station and start organising things. See you both at two. We'll have to talk to Mr Allen tomorrow."

As Noah was leaving Archie called him back.

"Noah, just a thought, could you ask Dr Stagg if he could take a photograph of Miss Hunt and we can check to see if anybody knows her or has seen her."

"Good idea, I'll telephone him when I get back to the station and let you know."

After Noah left, Archie and Lily headed to the

dining room. They had decided it would be a good idea to have lunch before going to Manor Farm, it could be a long afternoon.

***

There was a slight mist in the air and the temperature had turned chilly as Archie and Lily, walking arm in arm, made their way to Manor Farm.

Entering the main gates of the imposing Victorian stone farmhouse they were greeted by around thirty volunteers who had gathered to help with the search.

They were standing around in small groups smoking and chatting with one another, while Sergeant Hopkins was desperately trying to attract their attention, to organise them into three groups.

"Come on you lot, we need to get a move on," he shouted. "Bob, can you take one group and search around the golf course and Wilcot Road area?"

Bob Vincent was The River Hotel handyman and gardener and along with his son Arthur was put in charge of one group.

"Flynn, I want you to take your group and search the areas around Southcott Road and Kepnal."

Flynn Watkins was the long-standing pub landlord at the Coopers Arms in Ball Road.

"Tomasz, can you take a group to the fields surrounding Manor Farm, Green Drove and up to Hill Farm?

"Right, off you go, make sure you check

everywhere, don't leave any stone unturned. We'll meet back at The River Hotel in about three hours before it gets dark."

"Archie, can you Lily and Hopkins take a look at any empty buildings in and around Pewsey," suggested Noah.

"Yes, of course, we will," they agreed and headed off towards Swan Meadow.

In no time at all, the farmyard was empty and as the groups disappeared into the distance it started to drizzle. On his own Noah stood by his car studying the map.

"Would you like a cup of tea, Inspector," the voice of John Strong came from behind him.

"That would be most welcome." With everybody gone, Noah was feeling rather at a loose end.

"Can I take a look around the farm buildings when we have finished our tea?"

"Yes, of course, inspector, I'll get the keys to the milking shed and outbuildings."

"Call me Noah, I don't like titles, it was alright in London but not here in Pewsey."

"Okay Noah, I'll just go and fetch the keys. How do you like your tea?"

"White with one sugar please."

John goes to his office to fetch the keys before making them both a cup of tea.

The two then started to search every barn and shed on the farm, it was hard work, as the sheds were full, and it took longer than Noah had anticipated.

However, there was nothing to find.

"Thanks for all your help John," he said, shaking the farmer's hand, "I'd better head back now in case there are any developments."

"Glad to be of help, I hope you find him soon, I'll make sure my lads keep an eye out for the reverend."

Pushing the heavy farm gate open John called out to Noah. "Noah, there are a couple of buildings over on the Everleigh Road on the other side of Hill Farm. They're pretty derelict, but I'll get someone to check."

Noah thanked John and left.

The drizzle had turned to heavy rain and a gale-force wind was blowing up a storm. The bedraggled and despondent volunteers began to gather in the car park at the rear of the River Hotel. It had been a disappointing and fruitless search. Every hedgerow, lane, ditch and empty building had been checked, but there was no sign of the reverend. It's as though he had just disappeared, vanished into thin air.

"I think we had better call it a day, it's starting to get dark and the weather's not improving. Thank you all for your help, I'll let you know if we need your assistance again," Noah called out, disheartened

The groups broke up, some started to drift home, while others went into the hotel for a warm toddy before heading home.

Archie and Lily were already in the lounge, they had settled in front of the roaring log fire. Archie searched his jacket pocket, took out his pearl-handled fruit knife, scraped it around the bowl of his pipe and then knocked it against the hearth to remove the loose ash, before pushing fresh tobacco into the bowl, he then lit it and took a long deep breath, drawing in the sweet taste of the smoky fumes.

They sipped their single malt whiskies in an attempt to get warm after their afternoon of searching for the vicar. As they sank into the deep leather chairs a sense of contentment came over them both.

"It really is good being back here with you Lily."

"Yes, I do feel at home, it's lovely being with you and your family again."

"I've reserved our table for seven-thirty if that's alright with you," said Archie.

"Perfect, I'll just finish my drink and then get changed and meet you in the dining room."

Staring into the fire, mesmerised by the flames, they finished their drinks in comfortable silence before going upstairs to change for dinner.

Before meeting Lily, Archie called into his parents' private lounge to see his mother, who was sitting by the fire with Maisie curled up at her feet.

"Hello darling, how are you and Lily? Is she settling in? Is her room comfortable? Did she sleep well? Have they found the reverend? What about-"

"One question at a time Mum," said Archie with a smile, as he leans over and kisses his mother. "We are both well thank you, and Lily loves her room. As to the reverend, there's still no news, the search didn't turn up anything."

"Maisie, down old thing," Maisie who had woken

up, saw Archie and was now leaping up to say hello. After chatting with his mother for a while and making a fuss of Maisie he confesses. "Sorry I have to leave you, Lily is waiting for me in the dining room. I'll let you know the moment we have any news. Have a restful evening."

"Bye darling, give Lily my love."

Ten

The dining room was bustling, hazy smoke from the log fire filled the air. Ruth and Dotty were busy running to and fro waiting on tables. Lily waved to Archie to get his attention as he entered the crowded room. Someone else had taken their special table and she was sitting at a table half hidden at the back of the room.

"Hello Lily, I thought I had reserved our table."

"Hello Archie, you had, but there was a mix-up. Ruth sends her apologies. I said it was fine and that you wouldn't mind."

"Thank you, yes quite right, at least we have a table."

After ordering their dinner Archie and Lily began to discuss the day's events.

"This brings back memories," said Lily.

"Yes, I was really hoping to spend some quiet time with you. But it appears that murder and intrigue follow us around. But we had such an interesting time in February working with Noah, the thought of getting involved in another case is really quite exciting. That's if there is a case to get involved in."

Lily leaned forward and took Archie's hand. "I must be honest, working together again is an exciting prospect. What do we know so far?"

"Well, firstly we have Miss Hunt, whose throat was cut and then there's the missing Reverend Ward, which happened the day before. The different clothes and wigs we found in Miss Hunt's room, and the letter addressed to Mrs Valentino. There is also the briefcase we found with the gun in it and a bank statement in the name of Mr Allen!" Archie listed.

"Do you think the missing reverend, Miss Hunt, Mrs Valentino and John Allen all are connected in some way? Of course, not to be forgotten is the reverend's ration card which was found next to the briefcase. It does all seem a bit of a coincidence and we…" Lily stopped.

"Don't believe in coincidences, do we," Archie cut in with a broad smile. "We need to speak to Noah and see if there have been any further developments and does he still need our help." Archie became more animated with every word.

Once they had finished eating they decided to retire to the bar for an after-dinner drink. The air in the bar was thick with tobacco smoke. The log fire raging in the hearth gave the room a cosy feel, with the constant noise of people talking and the clinking of glasses.

They found Bob, Dotty's husband, frantically trying to run the bar. Bob, noticing Archie had come in, called to him.

"I'm sorry Archie," he said with a sheepish grin, "is there any chance of you giving me a hand? I've never known it to be this busy."

"Yes, of course, I won't be a jiffy. I'm sorry Lily, but..."

"Not at all, would you like me to help?"

"That would be marvellous."

"I've not seen you working in the bar before, Bob."

"No, it's all very confusing, everyone is so busy and because they are short-handed, I volunteered to help."

"Not to worry we're here now."

At that Lily and Archie pushed through the crowd and were soon in their stride behind the bar pulling pints and serving people. With the continuous demand for drinks, the evening flew by and soon it was time to call last orders.

In no time at all the bar was empty, Archie, Lily and Bob slightly dazed after such a hectic evening, looked at each other and smiled, they had made it.

A somewhat relieved Bob sighed. "Thank you so much, I couldn't have managed on my own."

"Not at all old chap, it was great fun being back behind the bar, glad we could be of help. Would anyone like a nightcap in the lounge once we've tidied up here?"

Clutching several empty glasses Lily looked across to Archie, "That would be a perfect way to end the day."

"What about you Bob?"

"It does sound like a nice idea, however, Dotty is expecting me home, we have a busy day tomorrow.

But thank you for the offer."

Once they had cleaned up the bar and said goodnight to Bob, Archie and Lily went into the empty lounge and settled in front of the now-dying fire. Archie filled and lit his pipe breathing out a cloud of smoke with a contented sigh.

Lily snuggled down in the chair, holding her whisky in both hands, slightly lifting her shoulders. "Yes, there is nowhere and no one in the world I'd rather be, than right here with you."

Archie stared into the flames, smiled and felt a warm inner glow, life was good.

Eleven

Wednesday 6th April

The familiar sound of Maisie, his canine alarm, was scratching at Archie's door. "Just coming old girl."

In no time at all Archie and Lily were outside enjoying the unusually warm and dry weather as they walked Maisie across the fields behind Mill's Farm. Off the lead, Maisie was running around unsuccessfully trying her best to catch unsuspecting rabbits that were gathered by the hedgerows.

"Come on Maisie old thing, it's time to head home."

Soon the three were at the back door of the hotel where they were greeted by Emily.

"Good morning you two, have you had a good walk, hello Maisie have you been a good girl for Uncle Archie and Aunty Lily?"

"Hello Mum, yes we had a lovely walk, thank you, although it was a bit warm. What are you up to?"

"I have to go to Devizes later this morning, perhaps Lily would like to join me if you're not too busy?"

"That would be lovely Emily." Lily looked at

Archie, who nodded his approval, "I think they can manage a few hours without me. What time?"

"Ten thirty."

"Perfect, I'll wait for you in the foyer."

The three made their way into the hotel reception where Tomasz was busy answering the telephone.

Archie turned and hugged Lily, "I'll phone Noah and see whether he has any news. Shall we meet for breakfast in ten minutes?"

"Yes, that will give me time to freshen up."

Archie left Lily and went into the back office behind the reception desk. The office was always warm and airless but especially today with the sudden turn in the weather. The small coal fire was roaring in the corner and the smell of stale tobacco was overwhelming. He immediately opened the tiny window to the side of the desk in the hope of freshening the room before telephoning.

"Inspector Jackson, how can I help?"

"Hello Noah, it's Archie. I'm just checking to see if you've had any news."

"Morning Archie, well at the moment I've tried telephoning Mrs Ward but there's been no answer, so I've sent Hopkins around to talk to her. I'm still waiting for the autopsy from Dr Stagg, although I didn't really think he would be….. Just a minute, can you hang on?"

Archie could hear the sound of muffled voices coming down the receiver as he waited.

"Archie, are you still there?"

"Yes."

"Sergeant Hopkins has just returned from the rectory and there appears to be no one in. He checked around and the back door was unlocked, he went in and had a good look around but the place was deserted. The kettle was still warm on the hearth, the breakfast was set but hadn't been touched. It's all very strange, are you and Lily free to come and take a look around with me, later?"

"I'm free, but Lily is going to Devizes with my mother to do some shopping. Would you like me to meet you there?"

"Can you give me an hour to sort out some paperwork, and I'll see you at the rectory."

"Yes, of course, Noah. I'll see you around half past ten."

The dining room was fairly quiet, most of the hotel guests had eaten and set off for the day. Lily was waiting for Archie at their usual table.

An excited Archie hurried over to join Lily.

"Hello, did Noah have any news?"

"I'm sorry to interrupt, but would you like tea or coffee," Ruth had appeared ready to take their breakfast order.

"Good morning Ruth, coffee for me please. Lily?"

"Oh, the same, coffee thank you."

Ruth poured their drinks and left to collect their breakfasts, Archie pulled his chair closer to Lily. "Apparently Mrs Ward has also disappeared and Noah wants us to go to the rectory with him and check it out. I told him you had arranged to go to Devizes with my mother."

"That's okay, I'm looking forward to spending some time with her and you can tell me what happened when I get back."

***

Emily was waiting by the reception desk as Lily and Archie arrived.

"Can you drive Lily, my leg isn't quite up to it at the moment."

"Yes of course."

"Would you like to take my car," Archie said, holding out the keys to his 1936 MG 'NB' Magnette Sports Tourer, his pride and joy.

Lily, looking surprised, turned to Archie. "Are you sure?"

Archie realising he was perhaps a little hasty looked gingerly at Lily, "Yes, of course. Do be careful, though." There was a slight hesitancy in his voice.

Nevertheless, he had made the offer and was determined to stick to it. Waving to his mother and Lily as they drove away, Archie, still feeling somewhat unsure he had done the right thing, made his way along River Street to meet Noah at the rectory.

Twelve

Noah was already waiting outside the main gate to the rectory as Archie approached.

"Good morning, old chap."

"Good morning Archie. Well, we had better go and see what, if anything, has happened."

The two slowly walked along the main drive carefully looking around to see if anything was out of place. The front door was locked so they made their way around to the back of the house checking the garden as they went. The back door was slightly ajar, pushing the door a little wider Noah called out.

"This is the police, is anyone in?"

There was no reply, opening the door wider Noah called again, there was still no response. They cautiously made their way into the kitchen.

The table in the middle of the room had two places set for breakfast. A rack of cold toast was at one end of the table. Two cups of cold tea had formed a greasy skin and the Aga was churning out heat making the room quite uncomfortable. Several unseasonal flies were buzzing over the table, giving the whole place an unsettling atmosphere. Archie stared around the room taking everything in, then looked at Noah. "The Mary Celeste comes to mind."

"Yes, somethings not right, that's for sure, we need to have a good look around."

"Why two place settings? Does that mean the reverend came back or that someone else is staying here?" a pensive Archie asked.

"I'm not sure. I don't believe anyone is staying with them, although I'm not certain. I'll get Hopkins to check."

As they made their way into the sitting room the silence was broken by the rectory telephone ringing in the hallway.

They looked at each other, Noah picked up the receiver, " Hello, can I -?"

The call ended abruptly as the person on the other of the telephone hung up.

"Who was that?"

"I don't know, they put the receiver down when they heard my voice."

"Hm, that sounds a bit suspicious, we had better continue with our search"

The sitting room was neat and comfortable, one wall had several shelves full of books, and a stack of Bibles lay neatly on a small coffee table beside a large settee.

Archie sifted through the writing desk while Noah checked the bookcase and bibles.

"There doesn't appear to be anything of interest here," said Archie.

"No, you're right. I'll check the drawing room, you take a look at the dining room?"

In the drawing room, there were two beige armchairs with red velvet scatter cushions, once smart but now looking a little shabby. A round coffee table sat between the chairs with a stack of books piled high. It was a rather elegant room with oak panelling on three walls and a large bay window throwing the morning sunlight into the room.

Archie headed to the dining room, where he found a large dark oak dining table dominating the center of the room, with four oak chairs neatly placed on either side, and matching carvers placed one at each end.

A Welsh dresser full of blue and white china stood against one wall, there were several religious paintings hanging on the walls. He carefully searched through the drawers and cupboards, but nothing seemed to be out of place.

"Nothing in here," Archie called out.

"No, same here, I even checked behind the cushions and under the chairs! That just leaves the office, it's down here."

They both entered the office without much expectation, as, so far, there was such a lack of anything personal to be found in the house, only Bibles.

This room appeared to be no different. There was a desk and filing cupboard, plus a couple of tired-looking armchairs placed on either side of the fireplace, a captain's chair sat in front of an ancient desk on which, what appeared to be, the beginning of a sermon laying on top of the blotting-pad, there was also an inkwell, two pens and a desk lamp.

"Except for the sermon, you would think that nobody ever went into this room," Noah remarked.

Having checked every area of the office, they disappointedly returned to the hall.

Noah looked at Archie. "I suppose we had better check upstairs."

Each tread creaked as they climbed the wide staircase that led to the first floor. On the landing, Noah entered the first of the bedrooms at the front of the house, while Archie checked the back rooms.

In the front bedroom, the bed was unmade, clothes were scattered on a small chair beside a large oak wardrobe. The faint smell of tobacco was in the air and a picture of Jesus hung crookedly on the wall above the bed. Noah opened the wardrobe door and discovered there was no men's clothing, just a row of floral dresses. In fact, there was no trace of a man having occupied the room.

Meanwhile, Archie opened the door to one of the back rooms and looked in, a small single bed was pushed into the corner. A tallboy stood opposite the bed with several photographs of a family placed neatly on top. Placed precariously on the edge of a bedside table and still lit was a lamp. In a small single wardrobe hung several men's suits and shirts with dog collars attached. Two well-polished pairs of men's shoes lay hidden just out of sight under the bed.

Sticking his head around the bedroom door Archie

called out to Noah.

"Have you found anything helpful?"

"No, not really, the strange thing is there is no personal information lying around."

"Same here, however, there is a lamp still lit on the bedside table, which is rather odd, and what looked to be some family photographs on the tallboy. Also, rather curiously, there is only men's clothing in this room."

"There is only women's paraphernalia in this one. I'm not sure what is going on here, but I think we should take a deeper look into this pair, although I have to admit, it's not unheard of for married couples to sleep in different rooms."

As they were talking they heard a loud thump from downstairs.

"This is the police, who's there?" Noah shouted.

They heard the sound of a door slamming and then the crunch of footsteps running down the drive. Archie ran to the front bedroom window to see if he could see who it was, but only saw the front gate gently swinging.

They both headed downstairs in the hope of seeing what the intruder was looking for. In the drawing room, they found a drawer from the bureau had fallen or had been dropped on the floor, along with a few scattered papers.

Archie checked the sitting room and dining room while Noah, the kitchen and office, after a good look around, decided nothing else appeared to have been disturbed.

Noah lit another cigarette, drew on it and looked at Archie. "I'm not sure who it was or what they were looking for, but they're long gone."

"It looked like we may have to add a second person to our missing list. Somebody has obviously been staying here and has either left in a hurry or has been taken. As there's no sign of either of them, shall we head back to the hotel for a spot of lunch?" suggested Archie.

"Good idea. There's not a lot more we can do here and lunch sounds rather good. I didn't have time for breakfast this morning."

Thirteen

The dining room was unusually quiet with just a few people having lunch, which gave them the quiet they needed to discuss Mrs Ward's disappearance.

"That's a strange set-up at the rectory. What do you know about the Wards," Noah asked.

"Nothing really, would you like me to contact my old boss at the War Office and see what they can dig up?"

"If you wouldn't mind, the more we know about them the better chance of finding Ward and possibly Mrs Ward. That's if she is actually missing"

"Have you heard any more about Miss Hunt," Archie asked.

"No, there wasn't a passport or any other form of identification in her room or on her. Just that letter to Mrs Isabella Valentino. I've contacted the police at Leman Street Police Station in Whitechapel to see if they can throw any light on Miss Hunt or Mrs Valentino, but haven't heard back yet."

"Did you mention John Allen to the police, he is also staying at the hotel and he is from Whitechapel too."

"No, I didn't, I'll give them a ring again after lunch."

"Sounds like you have nothing solid to move forward on at the moment. Let's hope you have a breakthrough soon."

***

Lily, her arm linked through Emily's to help steady her, walked through the bustling Market Place of Devizes. As they chatted Lily noticed a familiar figure talking to a man outside the Regal Cinema.

"Isn't that reverend Ward's wife talking to that man over there?" she asked.

Emily looked discreetly at the couple.

"You're right, that is Mrs Ward, I wonder who it is she is talking to?"

The two pretended to be window shopping, casually moving closer to see if they could recognise the man. However, when they were only some ten yards away the man disappeared round the corner, leaving Mrs Ward walking off in the opposite direction.

"Did you recognise him?" Lily asked.

"No, I didn't really get a good look at him, what about you?"

"What I saw of him, which wasn't a lot, there was something familiar about him. I'm not sure, I just felt that I had met him before. But then I do see a lot of people in my line of work, however, the possibility of seeing anyone from London down here would be pretty unusual."

As Mrs Ward vanished into the crowd Lily wanted to follow her but felt she couldn't leave Emily on her own. Especially as she was finding it difficult to walk without the help of her walking stick.

Emily was starting to feel tired so they decided it was time to go home.

When they arrived at the hotel Emily thanked Lily for a lovely morning and retired to her apartment, whilst Lily joined Archie and Noah in the lounge.

"Hello Lily, how did your day go with my Mum?" Archie asked as he stood up to greet her.

"We had a nice time although I think your mother found it quite tiring. What about you?"

"We didn't really have a lot of luck, we went to the rectory to speak to Mrs Ward but the place was like the Mary Celeste. Someone had been there but disappeared when we arrived. It looked like Mrs Ward has either been abducted or for some reason done a-"

An excited Lily interrupted Archie's conversation. "I'm sorry to cut in Archie, but we saw her in Devizes, she was talking to a man, who I'm sure I have met before."

"I wonder what's going on," Noah said with a slightly puzzled look on his face. "I think I need to get back to the police station and see if we've heard from Whitechapel. Thank you Archie, for lunch and coffee. Come to think of it, would you two like to come with me, that is if you're not doing anything this afternoon?"

"I thought you'd never ask!" said Archie, giving Lily a sideward glance. "That is if you're free."

"Wild horses wouldn't stop me, but I need to freshen up first. Why don't you two go on ahead and I'll join you later."

Archie was caught in two minds, he felt he should wait for Lily but part of him was eager to go with Noah.

"I'll wait for you and we can go together." he hesitantly said.

"Oh Archie, that's lovely, I won't be a jiffy, I'll see you in the foyer in fifteen minutes if that's okay."

"Yes, of course, I'll wait for you there."

Fourteen

Walking to the police station, Archie was surprised at the amount of people who were out and about, enjoying the sudden unseasonal warmth. Maybe the thought that winter may eventually be over was bringing people out of their homes, there is nothing like a warm sunny day to give people a desire to be outside.

At the police station, behind the main desk, Sergeant Hopkins greeted Archie and Lily with a beaming smile.

"Hello you two, the inspector is expecting you. He's in his office, go on through."

"Thank you, Tom."

Archie knocked on Noah's door.

"Come in."

A cloud of cigarette smoke hit them as they opened the office door. Noah who was sitting behind his desk stood up and beckoned them in. On the wall behind him was Noah's, as yet, empty incident board.

He always wrote the names of the people who he thought were part of the ongoing case, on the board, a practice he brought with him from his days at Scotland Yard. This was something he relied on, mainly to make sense of any case he was working on.

"Come in, sit down," he quickly removed a stack of papers from one of the chairs.

"Would you like tea?"

"Not for me, what about you Lily?" Archie asked.

"No, I'm fine, thank you."

"Well, this feels like old times," Noah said, searching in one of his drawers for a piece of chalk, "ah, here we are, so what do we know so far?"

"Have you heard back from Whitechapel?" Archie enquired.

Noah leaned back in his chair, drew on his cigarette and sent a plume of smoke into the room.

"Yes, they called just before you arrived, very interesting. They've no record of a John Allen, certainly not from Parfett Street or Miss Hunt. But what is intriguing is Isabella Valentino is the wife of Leonardo Valentino the head of the Whitechapel mob. Apparently, they are a particularly vicious gang running protection rackets in Whitechapel and if there is a connection, we are to be very careful. They also offered to send down some officers to help, if we need it."

Noah pushed his chair back, stood up, turned, and wrote Isabella Valentino on one side of the incident board, along with John Allen and Miss Hunt. On the other side wrote the Reverend Ward and Mrs Ward.

Lily shuffled forward in her chair. "So, do we know anything about Miss Hunt or Mr Allen?"

"Not at the moment. I've asked Whitechapel if they can get a photograph of Mrs Valentino and send it to us. As to Hunt and Allen, we will have to do some digging. I checked with Tomasz to see if they have left their ration cards at the reception desk, they have and all seems to be in order. Have you heard back from Deans Yard and your old boss about the Wards?" Noah asked, looking across at Archie.

"No, I'm still waiting. If I haven't heard by first thing tomorrow I'll chase them up. So the only common thread that links them could be Whitechapel. And there's the Ward's. Are they connected to either of them in any way?"

There was a reflective silence as they stared at the names on the incident board, in the hope that something would come to mind.

The room was becoming heavy with smoke and the heat from the small coal fire that was still burning in the corner of the room, despite the warmth of the day outside, was making Lily feel slightly bilious. Archie turned and looked at Lily and noticed that she was not looking too comfortable.

"Shall we call that a day and meet tomorrow morning? Would you like us to come here or meet in the hotel?"

Noah reached across his desk and picked up his diary, thumbing through several pages. "The hotel would be good, say ten thirty?"

"That would be ideal, that gives us time to organise ourselves and take Maisie for her morning walk. See you in the morning."

With much relief they left the office, Archie knew

Lily felt uncomfortable with the amount of smoke that Noah generated while chain smoking.

"I look forward to it. Have a good evening."

"You too Noah."

Tom was still at the desk as they left the police station.

"Goodbye Archie, Miss Lily, have a nice evening."

"Thank you Tom and you."

It was a balmy evening as Lily snuggled into Archie as they walked back to the hotel.

"Thank you, I was finding it very uncomfortable in Noah's office. I'm pleased we are meeting in the hotel tomorrow," Lily said as she squeezes Archie's arm.

"Not at all, I could see you were looking a little green and thought it was time to leave."

As it was such a lovely evening they decided to take the long walk back to the hotel, along the High Street to Ball Road and then back through the copse and eventually home.

The moment they walked through the foyer Ruth called out to them. "Hello Archie, we are very busy tonight, so I've already reserved your special table for you in the dining room, I hope that's okay?"

"Hello Ruth, yes that's perfect, thank you."

Archie and Lily made their way up the wide-panelled staircase to the first floor.

"I'll just pop to my room and freshen up, shall I meet you in the dining room in half an hour?" asked Lily.

"Yes, that gives me time to get changed too, and to

call in to see how Mum is, especially after her tiring morning."

In their private lounge, having a drink, Emily was talking to Dotty while Maisie was fully stretched out on the settee. As soon as Archie walked in Maisie jumped down and ran across to him.

"Down old girl."

"Good evening Archie, would you like a drink?" Emily gestured to him to join them.

"Hello Mum, Dotty. No thank you, I'm meeting Lily for dinner at seven o'clock, so I haven't really got time. I just called in to see how you are feeling after your busy day?"

"Surprisingly well, thank you darling. It was wonderful spending time with Lily, she's such a lovely girl, so considerate. May I start looking for a hat yet?" she asked, giving him a sideways glance with a wry smile.

Archie's mother, who always managed to embarrass him, grabbed his hand and squeezed it.

"It's alright, I'm only teasing, the two of you are so good together and any mother would be proud to have Lily as her daughter-in-law."

An even more embarrassed Archie manoeuvred his way to the door and left Emily and Dotty to their evening.

After their meal, Archie and Lily retired to the lounge. They sat drinking their whiskies, Archie smoking his pipe. They talked late into the evening, comfortable in each other's company, till it was time to retire.

"Will you be joining me in the morning for Maisie's walk?"

"Of course I will, it's the best part of the day."

"Shall we meet at quarter to seven in the foyer?"

"Yes, I'll look forward to it."

"Good night Lily, sleep well," he kissed her gently on top of her head.

"Good night Archie, thank you for a lovely evening. See you in the morning."

Fifteen

Thursday 7th April

Archie was already up, dressed and waiting for Maisie. "Come on, old girl, it's nearly quarter to seven, where are you?" he said quietly under his breath feeling a little impatient. Eventually, he went down to the foyer, where he found Lily waiting with Maisie.

"Maisie, what are you doing down here, I've been waiting for you."

"Good morning Archie, she scratched on my door and woke me up at quarter past six."

"Sorry Lily, and good morning. It seems she has a new favourite, and I've lost my alarm," Archie smiled, feeling just a little jealous.

They set off through the copse to Kings Corner and then to the open fields beyond. Maisie enjoyed running freely across the open countryside, chasing rabbits and deer. The silence was only broken by the sound of birds singing and a blast from the train's horn as the eight-o-five left Pewsey station.

"It's so beautiful here, so peaceful, and the air so clean and fresh after London," Lily said, breathing deeply.

"Yes, where else would you rather live? After all the uncertainty of the last few years this is heaven."

A contented Lily snuggled closer into Archie's side as they made their way back to the hotel. At the reception desk, several people were booking out, hoping to make an early start to their day. Tomasz was busy scribbling in the registration book whilst juggling answering the telephone.

"I think we had better leave Tomasz to it and have breakfast," Archie said, taking the lead off Maisie, who immediately dashes upstairs.

Just before they went into the dining room, Tomasz called out to them. "Archie, Lily, before you go for breakfast Major Osborne is waiting to speak to you in the office."

"Thank you, Tomasz."

In civilian clothing, with shoulders back, chin pushed forward and hands behind his back the Major stood staring out of the office window.

Major Osborne, based at Parkhill Garrison, had worked with Archie and Lily before Easter, breaking up a spy ring working out of the garrison. The ring was led by Colonel De Villiers-Blyth and Staff Sergeant Doherty an I.R.A. sympathiser and Soviet spy, along with several others who were apprehended.

"Ah, Freestone, Miss Forester, I heard you were both back, how are you, good to see you both?"

"We are both very well, thank you Major. Good to see you too. What brings you here?" Archie asked while pumping the Major's hand in greeting.

"We need both of your expertise. I heard that you had resigned your commission at the War Office, but because of your connection to the Frolov case, I thought you would like to know, as you are in the area, that De Villiers-Blyth has gone AWOL."

Colonel De Villiers-Blyth had avoided prosecution by agreeing to work with MI6 as a double agent passing false information to East Germany. To date he had been kept under armed guard at the garrison. Doherty, along with three others had been hanged at Newgate Gaol for their part in the spy ring.

"We have been keeping a close eye on De Villiers-Blyth and so far he has been quite useful. However, a week ago he went into Amesbury with an armed guard, but managed to give them the slip and hasn't been seen since."

"How does this concern us major?" Archie's interest piqued.

"A reliable source has led us to believe that a Soviet agent has come to or is coming to operate in the area. Intelligence leads us to believe they have or will set up a command centre somewhere in Pewsey. We are also of the opinion there may be a connection with De Villiers-Blyth going missing."

"I'm still not sure what this has to do with us," Lily interjected.

"Because of the seriousness of the situation, if you agree, I have been authorised to ask you both for your assistance."

"I'm not sure how we can help, as much as we

would feel it's our duty to assist you, we don't have the authority," Archie said.

"You have my full authority to act as you feel necessary. My department appreciates that you are both better placed to gather information, under the radar, so to speak. Because of your history and contacts in the county, you are probably in the perfect position to see people coming and going and you have the skills to assess situations. Plus you have a history with this particular spy network."

"In that case, Major, yes, of course, anything we can do to help. One thing however, can we share this information with Inspector Jackson and Tomasz Kazimierz, their help on the Frolov case was invaluable."

"I can understand the inspector, but this Polish chappie, why him?"

"Tomasz's assistance was extremely useful when Baptiste was shot. He's discreet, loyal and a good man to have your back and I would trust him with my life. Plus he is better placed to keep an eye on people coming and going."

"I understand, but I shall have to clear it with the appropriate authorities. Thank you, Freestone, Miss Forester. Before I go, I think you may need these."

Osborne reached into his briefcase, took out two Enfield revolvers and a small box of ammunition and handed them to Archie.

Looking slightly surprised Archie took the pistols and ammunition and put them discreetly into his jacket pocket.

"Thank you, major. Let's hope we won't need them."

"I will contact you regarding Jackson and Kazimierz as soon as I hear, in between time here is a dossier with all the information we have so far."

Archie took the dossier. They shook hands with Major Osborne, deep in thought. As he was leaving the room Osborne turned and looked back at them.

"Don't forget this is highly secret, not a word to anyone."

Archie frowned. "Yes, we understand."

Archie and Lily made their way to the dining room hoping that breakfast was still available. Ruth was humming quietly to herself whilst busily clearing tables, the breakfast service was now over and the room was empty.

"Are we too late for breakfast? Archie asked.

"Hello Archie, Miss Lily, no I'm sure Sam can rustle something up for you."

"Sorry Ruth, good morning. We will have whatever Sam can conjure up, thank you."

Archie leaned across the table to draw close to Lily. "I think under the circumstances it may be better if we met at Noah's office."

"Yes, of course, I understand." Disappointed, Lily agreed.

Before they had breakfast Archie telephoned Noah to say they would be late for their appointment and suggested they meet at his office.

With an air of excitement, Archie and Lily settled down to await their breakfast and discuss the twists and turns of the morning's revelations.

"Does this put a different emphasis on what's been happening in Pewsey over the last couple of days?" A reflective Lily asked.

Archie pulled his chair closer to the table and looked from side to side, whispering. "I'm not sure, we need to read the dossier and see if it has any bearing on what's going on here."

Whilst they were talking Ruth approached the table. "Would you like coffee or tea?"

"Coffee for me thank you."

"Same for me, thank you Ruth," said Lily.

Looking at Lily, Archie said under his breath. "I think we ought not to discuss this here but wait until Noah gets the all-clear."

"Agreed, walls have ears."

Once they had finished their breakfast the pair went upstairs to change. Archie had rearranged to meet Noah at eleven thirty at the police station. In the foyer, Archie was waiting for Lily when Tomasz called over to him. "Major Osborne is on the telephone for you in the back office."

"Thank you, Tomasz."

Sixteen

Archie opened the office door and was greeted by a burst of heat from the small coal fire burning in the hearth. We must stop lighting the fire. He thought to himself as he picked up the receiver.

"Hello, major, what news?"

"Ah, Freestone, you can take Jackson and Kazimierz into your confidence. My department has given the all clear."

"That's good news, thank you Major."

"Before you go, I think it would be safer if we contact each other via the police station from now on. We're not sure what we are dealing with at the moment."

"I agree, that's probably for the best."

"Thank you Freestone, we'll speak later."

"Goodbye, Major."

Leaving the office Archie saw Lily coming down the main staircase. She was wearing a floral green summer dress and a beige jacket. He was still taken aback by her beauty and couldn't help feeling how blessed he was to have her in his life.

"You look lovely."

"Thank you, Archie."

Taking Lily to one side and looking around to

make sure no one was within hearing distance, Archie quietly spoke under his breath.

"Noah and Tomasz have been given the all-clear."

"That's good news, we should speak to Tomasz before we see Noah."

At that moment Henry came into reception.

"Good morning Dad, have you seen Tomasz?"

"Good morning, I've just relieved him, he's running an errand for your mother in Marlborough, not sure how long he will be."

"Not to worry, we'll catch him later. We are just off to see Noah, not sure what time we will be back."

"Okay, I'll let Tomasz know you want to speak to him, see you both later."

Outside Lily tucked her arm into Archies as they headed off to the police station. Spring was in the air and Pewsey was bustling, the sudden heat had brought people away from their fireplaces to enjoy the unexpected warmth.

Behind the main police station desk and twiddling his grand handlebar moustache was the rather full figure of Sergeant Hopkins. As they entered he greeted Archie and Lily.

"Good morning, what a wonderful day."

"Good morning Tom, yes it is rather lovely," said Lily.

"Go on through, the inspector is expecting you."

The familiar smell of thick cigarette smoke hit them as they knocked and entered the office.

Archie waved the smoke from his face. "Hello old

chap, before we start, can we open a window? It's a bit foggy in here."

"Yes of course, sorry I hadn't noticed. Please take a seat."

Noah pushed his chair back, opened the small window and started furiously waving his hands in an attempt to clear the smoke. Lily gave Archie a grateful look.

"Thank you, Noah, I do appreciate it, smoke and I just don't get on," admitted Lily

"Yes, thank you, Noah."

"Coffee," Noah suggested.

"No, I'm fine thank you, we've not long had breakfast and we have a lot of news to share."

"Lily?" Noah asked.

"No, I'm fine as well, thank you."

Soon the smoke had all but cleared and Noah sat back behind his desk, with a quizzical look he stared across at Archie.

"What news?"

Archie proceeded to explain about De Villiers-Blyth and the possible spy ring operating in the area, and that the Major would be contacting them only through the police station.

"Good grief, this brings back memories. How can I help?"

Archie stood up and with an air of excitement said. "Firstly, we have to ascertain whether there is any connection to events here in Pewsey over the last few days and De Villiers-Blyth going AWOL. Secondly, have we heard from Mrs Ward?"

"Ah, yes, Hopkins called into the rectory on his way to work, she was back home. He asked her to come to the police station today. Her husband is still missing and I haven't received the photograph of Mrs Valentino from Whitechapel police yet. Have you had a chance to check with Deans Yard regarding Ward?"

"No, not at the moment, if I can use the front desk I'll call them now."

"Yes, by all means, help yourself."

Archie grabbed a pen and notepad from Noah and headed to the front desk.

An enthusiastic Noah looked at Lily.

"I think we need to add De Villiers-Blyth to the incident board, the whole thing is becoming quite intriguing, a case of deja vu, perhaps?"

"There was no seminar at Deans Yard this weekend," an excited Archie said, bursting into the room.

Noah stopped writing and turned around.

"Well, this case is becoming more curious by the minute."

Just at that moment, Sergeant Hopkins knocked on the door.

"Sorry to disturb you, but Mrs Ward is here to see you."

"Thank you, sergeant, can you take her to the interview room? We'll be along in a minute."

Seventeen

Noah, Lily and Archie made their way along the narrow corridor that led to the interview room, where Mrs Ward was patiently waiting. She was sitting on one side of the small metal table that stood in the middle of the room. The air was stuffy and hot with a single light handing over the table.

"Good afternoon Mrs Ward, thank you for coming in. We need to check a few things with you. Have you heard from your husband yet?" Noah asked as he sat down.

"No, not a word, I'm quite concerned. It's not like him to go missing."

Lily leaned forward in her chair. "Can I ask, who were you speaking to in Devizes yesterday?"

"Devizes? No one, why?"

"I saw you talking to a man outside the Regal Cinema in the Market Place."

"No, I don't think- oh, yes, a man was asking for directions."

"Where too?"

Florence Ward hesitated. "I can't remember, although, yes to Castle Road, that's right Castle Road."

"Did you know there was no seminar at Deans

Yard over the weekend? Do you know what he was doing in London?" Archie joined in the questioning.

An indignant Mrs Ward leaned back in her chair. "No, my husband doesn't tell me everything. What are you accusing him of?"

The atmosphere was becoming tense and there was an aggressive tone to Mrs Ward's voice.

"We are not accusing your husband of anything. We're just trying to find his whereabouts and we need to know as much about him and his movements as we can. I'm sure you understand," Archie said, calming the situation.

"Yes, of course, I understand, I'm just finding the whole thing hard to comprehend."

At that, Noah decided to end the interview and called Sergeant Hopkins into the room.

"Thank you for coming in Mrs Ward. If we hear anything we'll let you know. Sergeant, can you show Mrs Ward out, oh, before you go, is there anyone else staying with you at the rectory?"

"Not exactly, an old university friend, Miss Belmont, stayed over on her way to Penzance. But she had to leave early yesterday morning to catch the six-thirty train to Bristol. Why do you ask?"

"No reason, just asking. Sergeant, please show Mrs Ward out."

"Yes, sir."

Noah, Lily and Archie went back to Noah's office. With one hand in his pocket and an unlit pipe in the other, Archie stood facing the incident board. He studied it for several minutes, Lily stood beside him both staring at the board.

"A penny for them, Archie," Noah breaks the silence.

"Well for starters I'm not sure if I totally believe Mrs Ward. It appears they may have had an unconventional marriage, but she must know something about her husband's activities."

Lily stood back and turned to Noah.

"When I saw her in Devizes, I had the impression she knew the man she was talking to. Also, if you're giving someone directions wouldn't you make some sort of gesture, like, looking around or pointing and she didn't."

"But I can't see any reason for her to lie, for all we know someone did stay and she was just shopping and someone did ask for directions."

"Yes, you are quite right, that is a possibility Noah," Archie agreed.

Noah sat down, took out another cigarette and lit it, swivelling around in his chair, studying the incident board.

"I think our priority should be to talk to Mr Allen while we are waiting for our inquiries to be answered. I'm going to grab something to eat, shall we meet at the hotel, say, three-thirty."

"Good idea, Noah. We'll see you there."

Archie and Lily walked arm-in-arm back to the hotel.

"I don't know about you Archie, but I'm starving."

"Yes, I could manage something, even if it is afternoon tea and cake."

"That sounds just the ticket, cake it is then."

Tomasz was working at the reception desk as Archie and Lily entered through the main hotel door.

"Ah, Tomasz, we need to speak to you privately."

Ushering Tomasz into the back office, Archie explained all that had happened that morning and suggested he was in the best place to see the coming and going of people at the hotel. Tomasz was happy to help and would report anything he thought was unusual.

"Archie, whilst I think of it, I thought it odd that the couple of gentlemen who signed in for a golfing holiday didn't have any golfing equipment with them. Also, I think they may be foreign, but I can't be sure," Tomasz pondered.

"Thank you, Tomasz, that is interesting, yes, very interesting."

***

While they were eating, Dotty came in.

"Sorry to disturb you Archie, but Colonel Gibson from your old office is on the telephone for you."

Colonel Gibson was Archie's old boss at the War Office, over the years they had developed a close working relationship.

"Thank you Dotty, I'm just coming."

"Hello Colonel, how are you? What news?"

"Hello Archie, I'm very well thank you. Why don't you call me Bernard as I'm not your boss anymore? Right, as to your inquiry regarding the Wards. I haven't found out very much, they both studied theology at Cambridge and met at a debating club. He's aged 41, they have been married sixteen years with no children. Nothing has come up on our radar, so there is not a lot more I can tell you. I hope that helps."

"Thank you, Bernard, that is most helpful. We must meet for a drink sometime."

"Yes, I'll look forward to that, don't leave it too long."

Archie said his goodbyes and returned to the dining room where he found Noah had already arrived and was having a coffee with Lily. He shared the new information from his old boss, and then asked,

"Do you have any news?"

"I've contacted Penzance police to see if they can locate Miss Belmont. Other than that…

Lily interrupted Noah. "Isn't that Mr Allen at the reception desk?"

"Yes, you're right, let's go and speak to him," said Noah.

Eighteen

In amongst a small group of people, half hidden from view, Lily had noticed John Allen. When he saw them coming he turned his back on them and tried to leave the foyer. Lily, being somewhat impulsive, managed to block his way and stop him.

"Mr Allen, can we have a word?" Noah called out to him.

Allen turned around looking a little uncomfortable. "Who are you?"

"I'm Inspector Jackson, these are my colleagues, Mr Freestone and Miss Forester."

"How can I help you, inspector?"

"Just a quick word in private, can we use the back office, Archie?"

"Yes, of course, come this way, Mr Allen."

Archie led John Allen past the reception desk to the small back office, closely followed by Noah and Lily.

The four squeezed into the small room, Allen sitting on one side of the office desk. Lily sat opposite him while Noah and Archie stood beside her.

"Can you give me your full name and address, please, Mr Allen?" Noah asked, looking down at him, "And do you have your passport with you?"

"Why, why do you want to know, have I done something wrong?"

"Just answer the question," Lily insisted, leaning forward, staring at Mr Allen.

Allen, staring back at Lily, shuffled nervously in his chair.

"I want to know why you need my address." He said after in awkward silence. It seemed as though he'd been giving himself time to think.

"Mr Allen, there have been a series of events in and around Pewsey recently, and during our investigations, your name has cropped up several times. Now, answer the question, your full name and address, please," Archie demanded.

With some reluctance, Allen answered, "John Anthony Allen of 67 Parfett Street, Whitechapel, London."

"Let's just confirm, you said, 67 Parfett Street, Whitechapel. This is a little strange because according to Leman Street Police Station in Whitechapel, they've never heard of you nor does anyone of that name live at that address. Can you explain?"

"They must have it wrong, I've lived there for the past six years," Allen became rather uncomfortable, his face turning red, a bead of sweat forming on his forehead.

"Can you also explain why you had an Enfield No. 2 Mk I . 38/200 caliber revolver hidden in the bottom of your briefcase," Archie continued.

"Who said I have one, I don't own a briefcase,"

Allen became more indigent.

An increasingly tense atmosphere was broken when Tomasz brought two more chairs into the room. Archie and Noah sat on either side of Lily.

"I'm sorry Mr Allen but we saw you on the train with one, it's no good denying it."

"You must be mistaken. Are you charging me with anything? If not, I'm leaving."

"No, we are not mistaken."

Allen leaned forward and with a smirk. "Oh, yes that one. I lost it, I'd forgotten. I shall make myself clear, there was no secret compartment and I don't own a revolver. Now, if that's all, I'm leaving"

Noah leaned forward across the table. "It doesn't work like that here. When we are satisfied with your answers, then you can go."

Noah persisted. "Where did you lose it?"

Allen sat silently looking around the room.

"Right, you leave us no choice. Until you answer all the questions you will be taken to the police station and held overnight."

Allen suddenly jumped to his feet and banged his fist on the table. "You can't do that."

"Sit down Mr Allen, this isn't helping," Noah insisted.

"What do you know about Wage-Labour and Capital by Karl Marx?" Lily pushes Allen.

Allen sat back down, leaned back in his chair and folded his arms in a sign of defiance and remained silent.

"Do you know the Reverend Ward?"

"Who?"

"You heard me."

The silence was palpable.

"What is your business in Pewsey?"

Allen lowered his head and picked under his fingernails.

Noah looked at Archie. "There's no point wasting our time. Can you help escort Mr Allen to the police station?"

"Yes of course."

"Lily, can you telephone Sergeant Hopkins and warn him we are bringing a suspect to the station. Also, can you take a photograph of Mr Allen, we will send it up to the Whitechapel police? I'll call in a favour at the chemist and see if we can get it developed this afternoon, hopefully we can get it off by dispatch first thing in the morning."

An anxious John Allen stood up shouting profanities, kicking his chair into the corner of the room, he made a dash for the door, aggressively waving his fist at Noah. Archie pushed the table out of the way, knocking into the back of Allen's legs. Allen stumbled, giving Lily just enough time to grab one of his arms and expertly twist it up behind his back causing him to yell in pain. Tomasz, on hearing the commotion, burst into the office.

"Do you need a hand?"

"Thank you, Tomasz, but I think we'll be alright," Noah said, turning to him.

"You will regret this, you don't know who I am," he shouted with uncontrollable anger, spitting with every word that came out of his mouth as he was led from the office.

Before all the commotion Lily had managed to take a photograph of Allen. She now telephoned Tom to advise him that Noah was on his way to the station with Mr Allen.

With his arms secured behind his back, Archie and Noah ushered Allen along the busy River Street, past King Alfred statue and then on to the police station. They were causing quite a spectacle with Allen ranting obscenities at the top of his voice.

Seeing the immense figure of Tom waiting outside the main station door gave Noah and Archie a sense of relief.

"What have we here," he bellowed in an attempt to drown Allen's aggressive and voluble voice.

"Take Mr Allen straight to a cell and empty his pockets, sergeant. Let's see if that quietens him down."

The sergeant grabbed Allen's arm. "Right Mr Allen, this way." He marched him into the station cell, "now, empty your pockets."

In the turmoil, Allen managed to yank his arm free from Tom's grip and tried to force his way out of the cell. But he was no match for the immense figure of the sergeant, who grabbed Allen's hair and forced him to the ground. With his knee in Allen's back, he shouted.

"I won't ask again. Empty your pockets. NOW." Tom's voice echoed around the room and reluctantly Allen complied.

"Thank you, Mr Allen. That wasn't so painful, was it?"

He then dragged Allen by his arm back into the cell, threw him in and slammed the door.

"You will regret this, do you hear? I'm warning you, you will regret this," Allen's booming voice carried from inside the cell to the front desk.

Archie glanced toward Noah. "I think I need a pipe. What do you make of all that? Who is he?"

Back in the office Archie filled his pipe and lit it, drew on it and pondered on what had happened. While Noah reached into his jacket for his packet of cigarettes. The room soon became full of smoke. Noah turned to Archie.

"Let's look at what he had in his pockets."

Archie picked up the small box containing Allen's possessions.

"Not much here, just a packet of cigarettes, matches and a dirty handkerchief. It's not telling us anything, perhaps we will find out more once we've sent his photograph to Leman Street nick."

"Yes, you're probably right. Before we call it a day, have you got time to come and search his room, and see if we can find anything?"

"Absolutely, I've nothing planned and I'm sure Lily would love to join us," said an enthusiastic Archie.

They said good night to Tom and wished him all the best with Mr Allen. "Telephone me if you have any trouble with him."

Nineteen

Outside the early evening was unusually warm and pleasant as Archie and Noah left the police station. They could still hear Allen ranting from his cell.

"You will regret this, I'm telling you. You don't know who you're dealing with. I know people, you country plods are out of your depth."

"Who on earth is he!" Noah said, giving Archie a puzzled look.

"I don't know, he sounds very important or he thinks he is, he's certainly making a spectacle of himself," smiled Archie.

Before going on to the hotel Noah decided he needed cigarettes from the newsagents and they both headed off down the High Street.

Although he closed the shop at five thirty Arthur Hewit, owner of the newsagents, who had a cigarette permanently stuck to his lip and ash tumbling down his grey cardigan, saw Noah coming and opened up, especially for them.

"What can I get you, Noah, your usual?"

Without a word, he turned around and took two packets of Woodbine filter tips from the shelf.

"There you go, that will be seven bob."

"By the way Arthur, you don't happen to have seen

the Reverend Ward in the last few days, have you?" asked Archie.

"No I haven't, sorry, I heard he was missing. If I see him I'll let you know."

Noah thanked Arthur and then he and Archie set off for the hotel.

The High Street was quiet with just a few people around, mostly dog walkers, enjoying the early spring weather. Soon they arrived at the hotel and found Henry working behind the reception desk.

"Good evening, Henry."

"Hello, Noah, Archie, have you had a productive day?"

"Not totally, we need to take a look at Mr Allen's room. Can we possibly have his room key, please?"

"Yes of course." Henry turned and removed the key from the rack behind the desk and handed it to Noah.

"Oh Archie, before you go Lily is in the lounge waiting for you."

"Thank you, Dad."

Archie peered around the door of the lounge and saw Lily quietly reading. She was some distance away from the fire, which was slowly dying down, but still managing to give out a considerable amount of heat.

Going over to her, he explained what had taken place at the police station and asked if she would like to join them in searching Allen's room.

"Try stopping me," she replied, leaping up from her chair.

They met Noah in the reception and all three made their way upstairs. Noah knocked on the door of Allen's room to make sure the room was empty.

"This is the police, open the door."

After waiting a while, with no reply Noah unlocked the door and cautiously went in.

"All clear," he whispered.

The room was neatly organised with a pair of pyjamas folded on the bed, an opened, empty suitcase, was placed on a bedroom chair next to the set of drawers. Archie unlocked the wardrobe door and found several smart tailored suits hanging on the chrome rail, along with a double-breasted Carlington overcoat, two Homburgs were placed on the top shelf. Archie searched quickly through the suit pockets but found nothing.

Meanwhile, Lily pulled open the top drawer of the chest, socks were neatly placed in colour order along with matching ties next to them. The two lower drawers were empty except for his underwear.

"Nothing here," Lily said, turning around as she studied the room.

Noah stood with hands on hips looking around and then ruffled his hair.

"Same here, not even a passport or any other form of identification, all we have is his ration card. Look, it's getting late and there's not a lot we can do. So shall we meet tomorrow at the station and see what we have?"

"Good idea, I am feeling a little peckish. What

about you, Lily?" Archie said without thinking, knowing that she was always ravenous.

"I could manage a horse, if there's one about," she said, smiling at Archie.

"What time would you like us tomorrow, Noah?"

"Shall we make it ten o'clock?" He suggested while locking the bedroom door behind them.

They agreed to meet at ten, Noah thanked them for their help and left the hotel. Archie and Lily made their way to the restaurant, which only had a few people still eating. Huddled in one corner were the middle-aged man with wavy red hair and the younger man, who were in Pewsey on a golfing holiday. They leaned in toward each other as if having an intense, almost secretive conversation.

On their way to their table, Lily moved close to them in the hope she could hear what they were talking about so intensely. But as she got close both fell silent and pretended to be discussing the hotel menu.

As they passed Lily looked down at them.

"Good evening," she remarked.

Only to receive a half-hearted grunt from the older man.

"Indeed."

Archie and Lily settled down at their table and in no time Ruth was by their side ready to take their order. Having chosen their meal they settled down to discuss the day's events.

Looking across the room at the two men, Lily

turned to Archie.

"Do we know anything about those two, they seem such an odd couple and not at all friendly. I'm not sure but I think one had a hint of an ascent?"

"Dad said they are on a golfing holiday, but apart from that, nothing."

Archie always considered people with an air of suspicion if they looked slightly out of place and to him these two certainly fit the bill.

"Perhaps we will get Noah to check them out tomorrow."

"Yes, good idea."

Having finished their meal Archie and Lily withdrew to the lounge for a nightcap before retiring to bed.

Twenty

Friday 8th April

Six thirty a.m. and Archie was woken by Maisie scratching impatiently at his door. Lily was already up and about having been woken by her earlier.

"Okay old girl, I'm just coming."

Soon Archie was washed and dressed and making his way down the main stairs.

"Good morning Archie." Lily's voice came from behind him.

"Good morning, did she wake you up too?"

"I think Maisie wants me to join you on her morning walks."

"What a clever girl she is," said Archie, taking Lily by the hand, "I'm glad of your company. Come on Maisie, let's go for that walk."

It was still pleasantly warm and the balmy weather had once again brought the people out to enjoy the early taste of spring. From nowhere blossom had filled the trees and spring flowers were in full bloom. Archie and Lily walked hand in hand through the country lanes, with a very contented Maisie walking between them.

"Good morning Archie, Miss Lily, a grand

morning," the voice of Sergeant Hopkins resounded from behind them.

"Good morning Tom, what are you up to this time of the morning?"

"I've been to visit Mrs Ward to see if she has heard from her husband. But still no sign of him. I'm beginning to think he's just gone AWOL for some reason. Who knows what is in a person's head or life."

"Yes, you're right, he'll probably turn up some time and have a plausible reason why he appears to be missing."

At that, a very patient Maisie, who had been quietly sitting decided it was time to move on and started barking and pulling on her lead.

"Okay old thing, you've been a very good girl, it's time to head home."

"See you later, Tom," Archie said as they headed off back to the hotel.

The foyer was quite crowded, suitcases were stacked up by the main door and several people were booking out. Dotty was sorting out Ration cards and handing them back to the guests. Archie took Maisie's lead off. She immediately raced upstairs to Emily and Henry's private lounge.

"Breakfast?" Lily looked at Archie.

"Good idea, I'm starving."

The hotel, being in the countryside and despite rationing, had all the local connections to offer a full English breakfast, which Archie and Lily enjoyed most mornings. After a satisfying breakfast, they went to their rooms to freshen up before going to meet Noah.

Before leaving for the station, Archie went to the hotel desk to check the names of the two men they saw in the restaurant the evening before. He made a note of their names then rejoined Lily and set off for the police station.

"Hello again," Tom greeted Archie and Lily with a broad smile. In the background, they could hear John Allen still ranting from his cell. Banging and kicking the door. "Let me out, you plods don't know what you're doing. Heads will roll."

"Has he been going on like that all night?" Archie asked, looking past Tom at the cell door shaking as Allen kicked it.

"I think we have someone very special staying with us," the voice of Noah reverberated down the corridor.

"I think you're right, shall I roll out the red carpet," Archie shouted to be heard over Allen's uncontrollable outbursts.

Before they arrived Noah had opened the windows in his office to clear the air of smoke, much to Lily's relief.

"Come on in, would you like coffee before we start?"

"Yes please." they replied in unison.

"I received the photo of Miss Hunt from Dr Stagg and sent it off with the other one." Noah informed them. He had arranged for a police dispatch rider to take the photographs of Miss Hunt and Mr Allen to Leman Street police station overnight, in the hope of hearing something by mid morning.

"Noah, there's a couple of names I would like you to check out, two chaps are staying at the hotel who look a little out of place. Elijah Braithwaite and Leonard Coombes registered at two addresses in London. Braithwaite is 47 Pekin Street, Tower Hamlet and Coombes 23 Bartlett Close, also Tower Hamlet. Perhaps it would be a good idea to send them to your people at Scotland Yard and Leman Street, they may be able to throw some light on them."

Noah took out his little black book and wrote down their names and addresses.

"Okay, I'll give them a call."

Just then Tom carrying a tray of coffee and biscuits back into the office.

"There you go." He placed the tray on Noah's desk and looked at the incident board.

"That all looked very intriguing," he remarked, "what do you want me to do with Allen? He's still kicking up a fuss?"

Noah spun around in his chair and thought for a while.

"I don't suppose we can hold him any longer, unfortunately, we will have to let him go. I would still like to know who he thinks he is though. Let him go, Tom, but keep an eye on him."

"You've marked your card, Jackson, this isn't the end." The voice echoed down the corridor as Tom released Allen from his cell.

They chose to ignore the rant coming from him as he passed the office.

"Have we heard from Leman Street yet," Archie asked as he lit his pipe and sat back in his chair.

"Yes, just before you got here. They received the photographs of Hunt and Allen but don't recognise either of them. A bit of a dead end there. I'll phone the Yard and check on those names and addresses".

"Also there's still no sign of the Reverend Ward, I can't help thinking the two cases are connected somehow. Both Miss Hunt, the reverend and Mr Allen were on the same train at the same time and all of them got off at Pewsey. Is this Allen chappie part of the story? It's all too much of a coincidence and…"

"We don't believe in coincidences," looking at each other, Noah and Lily spoke simultaneously, breaking Archie's train of thought.

Archie looked at them with a rye smile, "You took the words right out of my mouth. Let's hope the Yard can give us something to go on."

"I'll call them now," Noah said, removing the receiver and dialling the operator. "Operator, can you get me Whitehall 1212, Thank you."

"Whitehall 1212, hold the line please, connecting you now."

Twenty-One

Archie and Lily, feeling hungry, decide to return to the hotel for a bite to eat and leave Noah to make his telephone call. Archie got up and gestured to Noah that he and Lily were leaving.

Noah put his hand over the telephone mouthpiece and whispered, "I'll see you at the hotel after lunch if that's alright?"

Archie gave Noah the thumbs up as he pushed his chair under the desk and tilted his head slightly to one side, whispering, "Three o'clock?"

"Hello, this is Inspector Jackson in Pewsey, Wiltshire. Can I speak to Superintendent Brentwood please?"

Superintendent Brentwood had been Noah's boss at Scotland Yard and had become a trusted colleague since leaving London.

"Hold on, sir, I'll see whether he's available," came the response.

"Brentwood here, Good morning Jackson, how can I help you?"

"Good morning sir, can I impose on you, we are having trouble receiving information about certain people that are here in Pewsey? Firstly Elijah Braithwaite and secondly Leonard Coombes registered at two addresses in London. Braithwaite 47 Pekin Street, Tower Hamlet and Coombes 23 Bartlett Close, also of Tower Hamlet. Also, I'm having trouble receiving information from Leman Street police station in Whitechapel in regards to a couple of other names Miss Hunt and Mr Allen of Whitechapel, they-"

"Stop there Jackson, I can't discuss this on the telephone. We need to meet as soon as possible, are you free this Sunday? If so, can you find a pub or something where we can meet discreetly? Can I leave that with you, just let me know where and when?"

Hearing the conversation Archie's interest peaked, he didn't want to leave, but realised that Lily's appetite was far more important, and after all, they would be seeing Noah later that afternoon.

As Archie and Lily went through the office door Noah looked up and returned the thumbs up with a smile.

"Yes sir, leave that with me."

There were very few people out and about despite the warm weather as Archie and Lily made their way back to the hotel.

"It seems quiet for a Friday afternoon," Lily remarked.

Archie looked up and down the High Street. "It does, doesn't it? I wonder why."

On the other hand, the foyer of the hotel was a different story. Tomasz and Henry were struggling to cope with the sudden influx of people who were coming and going. Some, mostly travelling salesmen were booking out, eager to avoid the busy Friday traffic on the roads and get back to their families. Others were booking in for a weekend break, golf seeming to be the main attraction.

Archie, being aware that a Russian operative could either be already in the area or planning to come, intently observed everyone Tomasz was booking in, studying their behaviour, what they were wearing and what they were carrying, to see if anyone looked out of place. Several people appeared to fit the category.

There was a rather stout elderly gentleman who was accompanied by a slightly younger pretty woman, with just one suitcase between them, hovering nervously at the back of the queue.

Looking slightly out of place were a few town folk, dressed in country attire, with heavy tweed jackets and bow ties, plus-fours and newsboy caps, carrying golf clubs. They were making a bit of a din in the hopes of being noticed by the other guests. The air was filled with smoke as people jostled to get to the front of the queue. The atmosphere was charged with a sense of expectation of the weekend's pleasures ahead.

A latecomer, a tall well-dressed man in a tailored dark blue three-piece suit, wearing a dark grey homburg with a copy of The Times tucked under his arm was last in the queue. A black attache case and a small brown leather suitcase sat on the floor by his feet.

"This could be interesting," Archie whispered to Lily.

They waited for the foyer to clear before approaching Tomasz.

"Did anyone appear suspicious to you?" Archies asked as he leaned discreetly into Tomasz.

"There was a gentleman who was last to sign in, what was his name?" Tomasz said whilst thumbing through the registration book.

"Ah, here we are. Mr Issac Isenberg from Palmers Road, Bethnal Green, apparently here on business, a bit of a cold customer if you ask me."

"What do you mean?"

"Well, he didn't seem very communicative, just the odd word, almost a grunt, he could be foreign of course."

"Perhaps you can keep an eye on him. Anyone else?"

"Not really, just the normal weekenders playing at being country folk. Although the elderly gentleman with the young lady was a bit odd, perhaps a naughty weekend away"

"Can you get their names and addresses? It is always worth checking. Thank you, Tomasz."

"They gave their names as Mr and Mrs Delfonty from fifty-nine Friar Street, Reading."

Archie took his notebook from his inside pocket and wrote Isenberg's and Delfont's names and addresses to pass on to Noah when they saw him later that afternoon.

Before going to the dining room, Archie suggested that Tomasz collect all the ration books from the people who signed in earlier and give them to him.

Blocking the door of the dining room was John Allen. He gave Archie and Lily a long cold stare as they attempted to enter. In response, Archie took a hard look into Allen's eyes, neither backing down.

"Excuse me." Dotty, realising there was tension between them, pushed past, carrying a tray of food. Allen moved to one side letting her through, then continued to the foyer turning around still staring at Archie.

"That man certainly has a problem," Archie remarked as they entered the dining room.

Sitting in the corner were Braithwaite and Coombes huddled in deep conversation. On seeing Archie and Lily they suddenly fell silent.

"I've managed to keep you a table." Dotty directed them to a table opposite Braithwaite and Coombes.

"Thank you, Dotty."

After ordering their meal, Lily stared at the two men and wondered why they were so secretive. Archie took her hand.

"A penny for them?"

"It's those two, there is something not quite right about them, but I can't put my finger on it."

"Perhaps Noah has some information from the Yard."

"Yes you're right, let's just enjoy our meal, I'm starving."

When they had finished, Archie and Lily retired to the lounge, leaving Braithwaite and Coombes still huddled in the corner.

"It's quarter past three, Noah's late," said Lily finishing her coffee.

"That's unusual for him, he's always-"

Just at that moment, Noah, somewhat flushed, came into the lounge.

"What is it Noah, what's happened?" Archie said, standing up to greet Noah.

Twenty-Two

Catching his breath and still flushed, an excited Noah joined Archie and Lily.

"I can't say too much. But I've spoken to my old boss at the Yard and I've arranged to meet him on Sunday afternoon."

"Do you know why?" Archie interrupted.

"I have a vague idea, but he didn't really say too much on the telephone. So we've arranged to meet in Hungerford at The Barley Mow Inn on Bridge Street. I've told him about you two and he's pleased to have you on board. Are you both free to join us?"

"Of course, old chap, we wouldn't miss it. I'm sorry Lily, am I being presumptuous? Have you got plans?"

"Not at all, count me in."

"What news on the Reverend Ward, have you heard anything?" Archie asked changing the subject. He leaned forward and reached for the box of matches that were lying on the coffee table.

"No, it's been five days now and there's not been a sign of him anywhere. Things didn't seem particularly normal when we searched his home. It appears he and his wife live separate lives. Perhaps he's had enough and done a runner and started somewhere new. We have widened our search and will keep looking, but I don't hold out much hope."

"Well, for a vicar, he never seemed a jolly sort of chap. If that is the case, let's hope he has found somewhere he can start afresh," Lily said.

Lighting another cigarette, Noah leaned forward.

"Until we meet Brentwood on Sunday there's not much we can do, other than keep a close eye on Allen and those two other chappies you were telling me about."

"Hello you three," Emily, came up behind them leaning heavily on her walking stick.

"Have you found the vicar yet?"

"Hello mum, we were just discussing him. No, no joy yet, he appears to have vanished."

"Oh dear, it's Palm Sunday this week, I imagine church will be cancelled. I hope they find Reverend Ward or a curate or another vicar by Easter. Perhaps I'll speak to Florence and see if she knows anything"

"Yes, I suppose so," said a distracted Archie, whose mind was on the whereabouts of Ward.

"Will you and Lily pop in and have a drink after dinner this evening."

"We would love to, Emily," Lily said, noticing Archie's attention was elsewhere.

"See you around seven o'clock then."

Lily taps Archie on the foot in an attempt to attract his attention.

"Look forward to it mum." Archie had no idea what he had agreed to, but he appeared to have said the right thing.

Emily hobbled out of the lounge, leaving Archie, Lily and Noah to ponder the week's events.

"Good to have you both back, it's been a bit of a week. What with our missing vicar, the murder of Miss Hunt and some very dubious characters around at the moment, I need all the help I can get. But for now, I'll head back to the police station and leave you to enjoy the rest of your day. I'll let you know if anything crops up."

"Don't forget De Villiers-Blyth going A.W.O.L.," Archie interjected.

"Yes, I'd forgotten about him, gosh, a lot is going on, can it get any worse."

There was a moment of silence as they were all in deep thought only to be broken by Noah.

"Would one-thirty on Sunday be okay with you two? Oh, Lily, have you still got a photograph of John Allen?"

"Yes."

"Could you bring it with you on Sunday please, I will bring Miss Hunts?"

"Yes, of course."

"See you Sunday," Noah said as he headed out of the lounge.

"Look forward to it. Have a nice weekend and give our regards to Anne and the children," said Archie.

"I think I will freshen up before dinner," said Lily, "shall we meet in the dining room at five-thirty?"

"Yes, five-thirty is fine, I'll see you there," Archie

pulls Lily's chair back for her as she gets up.

He watched Lily disappear up the stairs before heading off to the office to find Tomasz.

"Tomasz, have you got a moment? I need to update you about what has been happening."

"Of course, Archie, I'll be with you in just a minute."

Archie explained all that had gone on during the week and asked him if he had noticed anything strange about the guests.

"Not really, just those two chaps on a golfing holiday, who just keep themselves to themselves. But I will watch them and let you know if anything crops up."

Archie thanked Tomasz and went to his room to change for dinner before meeting Lily.

After they had eaten Archie and Lily called in to see Emily, she was reclining on the settee with one foot carefully placed on a small pouffe. As usual, Maisie lept from her armchair and ran towards them, barking with excitement before they had one foot in the room.

"Okay old girl, calm down, yes, you're very beautiful."

At that, Maisie rolled onto her back waiting for her tummy to be tickled, to which Archie happily obliged.

"What news, what have you both been up to, have you managed to get any time together, have you settled into your rooms, and do help yourself to whatever you would like to drink."

Archie gave Lily a sideward glance, finding the situation slightly amusing, as it was Emily's disposition to fire questions before receiving any answers.

"There is no news I'm sorry to say, just helping Noah, the rooms are perfect and yes we have had some quiet time together. Seriously, it really is good being back home with you and Dad," he said as walked over to the sideboard to pour them all a drink.

At that, Maisie sat up and barked.

"And of course you old girl, it's good to see you again."

Emily, holding Lily's hand and giving it a squeeze asked, "What about you Lily?"

"You've all made me feel so welcome it feels like home to me, it's lovely being back." She confessed as she sipped her whisky.

With a hint of a tear in Emily's eye, she suggested they both spend the evening together once they finished their drinks.

Twenty-Three

Saturday 9th April

From under Archie's bedroom door, the sound of snuffling woke him. Archie looked at his clock. Six-thirty.

"On my way old girl."

Archie flung the sheets off the bed, jumped out and opened the curtains allowing the early sunrise to light up the room. He had arranged to meet Lily in the foyer at seven o'clock. Going down the main staircase he found her talking to Henry, Archie's father, with a very patient Maisie sitting by her side.

"Good morning you two, lovely morning,"

"Hello Archie, yes, it is a beautiful morning. Perfect for our walk," Lily agreed, giving Archie a peck on the cheek.

"What are you both up to today?" Henry asked.

"I thought we could pop into Marlborough for a spot of lunch if that's alright with you Lily?"

Nodding her approval, Lily squeezed his hand, "That would be lovely."

The morning was strangely warm with a light mist as Archie and Lily walked arm in arm along Green Drove just south of Pewsey.

John Strong, the farmer, had just finished milking his cows and was now herding them back to the open field surrounding his farm.

Archie and Lily squeezed themselves to the side of the lane to allow the cows to pass by, Lily was unsure whether they were friendly or not, so tucked herself in behind Archie.

"Good morning. How are things, any news on the vicar?"

"Good morning John. No, there's been no sighting of him since last Monday."

"A queer turn of events, let's hope he turns up soon."

"Indeed," Archie replied.

"Don't worry Lily, cows don't bite, they're a friendly bunch and they won't hurt you. Especially with Archie blocking their way," John said with a sideward glance, he smiled at Archie.

"Can you let us know if you find anything else around the farm that shouldn't be there?"

"I'll keep an eye out, Archie."

He and Lily watch John tapping the stragglers with his thumbstick as they disappear down the lane.

"I think we had better get back, I need to reserve a table before it gets too late," Archie said, pulling Maisie out of the hedgerow where she had been hiding.

"Come on old girl, let's get going."

For a Saturday morning, the hotel was relatively quiet. Dotty was flicking a duster over the reception desk, while Tomasz tidied the back office.

"I think we'll leave them to it and have some breakfast. I imagine you are quite hungry," Archie said, not really expecting an answer.

"Ravenous," without drawing breath the word came out of Lily's mouth, even before she had moved her lips.

***

Driving down the hill that led into Marlborough, they could see the town was packed with people, the normal parking in the center of the High Street was full. But after driving up and down several times, Archie managed to find a space at the far end of the town.

By now they were running late, Archie had reserved a table at the Borough Arms Hotel on The Parade, for twelve-thirty. With his hand on Lily's back, he gently guided her through the hotel's main door and into the dining room.

Although the hotel appeared to be relatively small from the outside, the dining room was deceptively spacious with comfortable, soft padded chairs placed around each of the tables. Two wood burners were filled with wood ready to light on cold evenings. Although the room was busy the atmosphere was relaxed and welcoming, with the hum of conversation filling the air.

"I've put you in the corner by the window, Mr

Freestone. I hope that will be alright," the eager young waiter directed them to their table.

"Perfect, thank you."

"This is rather smart."

"Only the best for you."

"Why thank you, Archie."

He passed the menu to Lily.

"What would you like to eat?"

Having studied the menu at length, they eventually ordered their meal.

After an hour or so when they had finished eating, they sat back in their chairs, fully replete.

"That was a lovely meal, thank you, Archie."

Much to Lily's surprise, Archie suddenly sprung to his feet and went around the table. Reaching into his inside jacket pocket, took out a small red box. Kneeling on one knee next to Lily and looking up at her he took a deep breath.

"I know we haven't known each other very long. But it feels like I've known you all my life and have fallen head over heels in love with you. You are beautiful, intelligent, kind and sensitive and I can't imagine what life would be without you. Would you do me the honour of becoming my wife?"

The room fell silent in anticipation, all eyes fixed on Archie and Lily.

"Oh Archie, yes, yes!" For once Lily was lost for words.

Spontaneous applause broke out from around the dining room as people stood up to congratulate them.

The waiter, who was waiting out of sight suddenly appeared with a bottle of champagne.

Carefully putting a diamond ring on Lily's finger, he turned around.

"Champagne for everyone," he shouted, hardly able to contain his joy, as he hugged her.

"Archie, you've made me so happy, I've been dreaming about this moment for a long time."

Smiling like two Cheshire cats who had got the cream, they eventually left the restaurant. Stepping out into the bright sunshine. Archie took a deep breath and sighed with contentment.

"This is the best day of my life."

He suddenly stopped.

"Lily, isn't that De Villiers-Blyth over there outside Hurds the ironmongers?"

Lily squinted as she strained to get a good look at the man on the far side of the wide street.

"I think you're right. We need to cross over and see what he has to say for himself."

Huddled in among the afternoon shoppers was the distinguished-looking figure of Colonel De Villiers-Blyth, a former Provost Marshal at Parkhill Garrison. He appeared to be in deep conversation with a short well-dressed woman wearing a blue spotted shirtwaister dress.

Archie and Lily struggled to cross the busy road and for a moment lost sight of them.

"Over there," Archie shouted.

De Villiers-Blyth had turned away and was now

fifty yards or so ahead of them, disappearing amongst the crowd.

"Drat, I think we've lost him." Archie groaned.

Lily, frowning, remarked, "I can't swear to it, but as De Villiers-Blyth was almost out of sight I realised he looked a lot like the chap who was talking to Mrs Ward in Devizes."

"If you're right, we need to speak to Mrs Ward again, something isn't adding up."

"Archie, did you recognise the woman he was talking to?"

"I didn't really get a good look at her but no one sprung to mind."

Checking up and down the High Street they were unable to find De Villiers-Blyth or the woman. Abandoning their search, Archie and Lily headed back to the hotel to share the news of their engagement.

Twenty-Four

The journey back to the hotel seemed to take hours, Archie had never seen so many tractors or cyclists on the road making their progress painfully slow. They were excited to share the news of their engagement with family and friends and were already making plans for the future as they drove along.

"We will have to pop down to Hastings and speak to your parents. Mum has been on about buying a new hat from the moment she first saw you, she'll be overjoyed."

Eventually, they arrived back at the River Hotel. Henry was at the reception desk and saw them coming in, and noticed their excitement.

"You two look very pleased with yourselves. Solved another case?"

"Something like that. Dad, can you get Ruth to take over from you and come up to your lounge?"

"Yes, of course, it sounds very serious. I'll be up in a minute."

In the lounge Emily was reclining in her armchair with her foot on the pouffe, Maisie was cuddled up contentedly beside her on the floor.

"Hello you two, you're back early, did you have a nice time, did you manage to do any shopping, how was lunch?"

Archie let her ramble on whilst they waited for his Dad to come up. Maisie lifted her head, flopped it back down and gave a deep sigh.

"What have you done with Maisie, she looks exhausted?" Lily asked.

"Oh, she's been out with Dotty across the fields. What sort of day have you had?" Emily persisted.

Henry appeared at the door with something discreetly hidden behind his back.

"We have some news for you, Lily has agreed to become Mrs Freestone and we ….."

Unable to contain her joy Emily jumped up and burst into tears.

"Oh, how marvellous, I'm so happy for you both, and you have a ring, do let me see, it's beautiful, do you-"

"Just what I thought," said Henry interrupting his wife, while producing a bottle of champagne from behind his back.

"I knew something was going on, Archie, get the glasses."

"Have you set a date yet, do your parents know, will you be getting married in Pewsey, can I-?"

"Slow down, Mum. We haven't discussed anything other than popping down to Hastings to tell Lily's family. Rest assured whatever is going on, you will be the first to know. Oh and yes you can start looking for that new hat"

There was a loud knock at the door. Tomasz had

collected some knitting wool from Nichols the department store in Pewsey for Emily.

"Come in Tomasz, help us celebrate. Archie and Lily have just got engaged."

"That is marvellous, congratulations I'm so happy for you both." Tomasz, taking a glass from Henry, raised it towards Archie and Lily with a broad smile.

The rest of the afternoon and early evening passed quickly. After several glasses of champagne, and many congratulations from all the members of staff, Lily started to feel a little squiffy, so she and Archie decided to go down to the dining room and have something to eat.

For a Saturday evening, the room was unusually quiet, only a few people were dining. After they had finished their meal, still discussing when they would be able to get to Hastings, they retired to the lounge for a nightcap. Sinking back into a comfortable settee, whisky in hand, happily relaxed and content with life, they both agreed that it was a perfect end to a perfect day.

Twenty-Five

Sunday 10th April

Archie was up and about waiting for Lily in the hotel foyer. A confused Maisie came bounding enthusiastically down the main staircase and jumped up and down in front of him.

"Down, old thing, we'll be going for walkies in a minute."

There was a spring in Archie's step as he and Lily walked the lanes around Pewsey. An early morning mist floated just above the ground along the Vale of Pewsey. The valley had become an enchanting and magical place as the couple, with linked arms, contentedly wandered home.

The morning passed quietly as Archie and Lily planned their future in the comfort of the hotel lounge.

Tomasz popped his head around the lounge door, disturbing the moment.

"Archie, Noah is waiting for you in the foyer."

"Good grief, it's one-thirty already," Archie jumped up, looking at his watch.

They were so engrossed in conversation they had forgotten the time and unusually, Lily had not eaten but was only just starting to feel hungry.

"We can get something to eat in Hungerford," Archie tried to take her mind off food.

"Sorry Noah, time just slipped away from us. We have a lot to talk about."

"I know, congratulations to you both, it's very exciting."

"Who told you?" Lily asked.

"Pewsey is a small place and news travels very quickly, you're the talk of the village. We love a good wedding, that is, if you are getting married here."

"We haven't planned anything yet, it's still early days," Archie said following Noah out of the main door. Twenty minutes later they arrived in Hungerford, despite the unusually hot weather the town was quiet. Most people had made their way to Hungerford common, which was always a little cooler with an afternoon breeze.

The tall, smartly dressed figure of Superintendent Brentwood, was impatiently pacing up and down outside The Barley Mow Inn, carrying his brown leather briefcase.

"Are we late?" Noah, feeling a little embarrassed, asked.

"Not at all, old chap, in fact, you're early, but we have a lot to discuss."

"These are my colleagues who I spoke to you about, Archie Freestone and Lily Forester. They come with top clearance from the War Office."

"Good to meet you, Freestone and Miss Forester, shall we go in?"

The Barley Mow was an old-fashioned coaching house, it was open seven days a week hoping to catch passing trade. Brentwood ushered them into the lounge to a small private table in the corner of the room. Opening his briefcase he looked discreetly around to ensure no one was listening.

"What I'm going to tell you is highly confidential, it can not be shared with anyone beyond the four of us."

Interrupting Brentwood, Noah leans across the table, asked Lily for the photograph of Allen, and passes it to the Superintendent together with the one of Miss Hunt.

"I'm sorry Sir, but before you start, can you take a look at these photographs taken of the two people we are investigating? They gave their names as Miss Hunt, who was murdered last week and the other is John Allen from Whitechapel. We have contacted Leman Street nick but…?"

"Can I stop you there for a moment?"

Brentwood stretched over the table and took the photographs from Noah. As he studied them the colour drained from his face, shaking his head and leaning back in his chair he sighed. He bent down, took a large folder from his briefcase and put it on the table.

There was a long silence, Noah lit a cigarette and Archie puffed on his pipe.

"This is worse than I thought. Firstly John Allen's real name is Leonardo Valentino from Parfett Street,

Whitechapel. We know that his father is Italian, and his mother is Russian. He heads the Valentino mob in Whitechapel and has over a hundred gang members who are known for their vicious razor attacks. We also know that he has in the past imported Sicilian gunmen. Valentino has extensive police and political connections including judges, politicians and police officials.

"It is most unusual that he has stepped outside his territory, in fact, we have never known it happen before now.

"Now, this information stays with the four of us. I head up a team investigating corruption in the force, which includes Leman Street police station. We believe Valentino has several officers on his payroll. He is a very powerful and dangerous man and what is worse, Mrs Hunt is his wife, Isabella Valentino, he will be baying for blood."

There was a stunned silence as they tried to take the information in, Noah drew on another cigarette sending up clouds of smoke.

"There is one thing you need to know, Valentino was a cruel and violent man toward his wife and it is worth considering that she was trying to get away from him. Why Pewsey? I don't know, did she know anybody there, you will need to do some digging."

"Can I get you gentlemen and lady a drink or something to eat?" The overweight landlord with his apron tucked into his trousers was standing over them.

"Yes, thank you," Archie said. They study the

menu and give their orders.

Once the landlord had gone, Lily was eager to hear more.

"What about the other two chaps, do you know anything about them?"

"Can you describe them?" Brentwood asked.

"One of them is a youngish man, slim, clean-shaven, dark brown hair heavily Brylcreemed and brushed straight back, looked like it is beginning to recede. The other chap is middle-aged, has wavy reddish hair, a very neat beard and is rather overweight, both men were smartly dressed," Archie said as he puffs intensely on his pipe. Brentwood pondered for a moment. "Is there any chance of getting a photograph of them?"

"I'll see what I can do, it won't be easy," Lily said.

"Thank you Miss Forester, I know you will do your best. There's not much more I can tell you right now. Would you like a couple of extra chaps to help out?"

"Thank you for the offer, sir, but we'll see how we get on first. I have a good and experienced team working with me."

Still waiting for their meal Lily was feeling ravenous. Seeing her starting to look pale, Archie was just about to get up to chase their order when the landlord appeared balancing all four dinner plates in his hands and on his arms.

"There you go, sorry it took so long but we've had a bit of a rush of bookings this afternoon. Is there anything else I can get you?"

"No, we're fine thank you," said Archie looking up at him.

Over dinner they discussed all the relevant people who happened to be in Pewsey simultaneously and what could possibly connect them, Miss Hunt's murder, and the Reverend Ward's disappearance. When they finished eating they all agreed that there was not much more to discuss and that Brentwood would wait for the photographs to arrive before he could do more.

"Here's my private home telephone number and address, only contact me on this number and send any correspondence to my home. I'll keep you up to date from my end, any help you need just ask," Brentwood said, handing a small piece of paper to Noah.

"Thank you sir, likewise, if there are any developments this end we will keep you in the picture. Have a safe journey back to London and we will speak soon," Noah said, standing up and shaking Brentwood's hand.

Twenty-Six

The drive back to Pewsey was charged with speculation, there were so many unanswered questions. Has any of this got anything to do with Ward being missing? Were the two strangers involved in some way, what was Valentino's wife doing here in disguise and why would Valentino leave the safety of his patch?

"We need to get Valentino back in for questioning first thing tomorrow," Noah said, his driving was getting faster and faster.

Archie, still puffing excitedly on his pipe, leans forward.

"Slow down old chap."

"I'm sorry, I didn't notice," he took his foot off the accelerator and slowed down. "I just find the whole thing quite exhilarating. Who would have thought a small village in Wiltshire would have so much intrigue."

"Yes, I moved back to Pewsey for a quiet life helping Mum and Dad in the hotel. But this is just the ticket to keep the grey matter activated."

"Normal service resumed," Lily smiled as she sank back in her seat.

In no time they were back in Pewsey, Noah pulled

up outside the hotel.

"Can I suggest we meet at the police station at, say nine-thirty in the morning? I'll brief Tom and then we can go and pick Valentino up for questioning."

"That's going to be interesting, I'll look forward to it," Archie smiled as he and Lily got out of the car.

"See you tomorrow," Noah shouted as he drove off.

Tomasz was in reception finishing some paperwork, when he saw Archie and Lily he called them over, taking them to one side so as not to be overheard he tells them.

"I had the opportunity to search Braithwaite's room, he had a telephone call arranging to meet someone in Marlborough, so I knew that I had plenty of time to have a good look around."

"How did you know he had to go to Marlborough?" Archie interrupted Tomasz.

"I was on the switchboard and connected the call to his room and somehow managed to listen in," he said, looking over his glasses and giving them a sideward grin.

"The room was quite neat, with everything in its place, nothing unusual, until I moved his suitcase from under the bed which was rather heavy considering it was empty. Hidden in a secret compartment were two loaded revolvers along with shoulder holsters. I put everything back as I found it, so he wouldn't become suspicious."

There was silence as they took in this latest

information. Archie looked at Lily.

"This is becoming more and more intriguing. Thank you Tomasz, good work, if you have a moment, I'll update you on what we know so far."

Archie explained in part, all they had learned earlier that afternoon from Superintendent Brentwood and that discretion must be maintained.

After speaking to Tomasz, Archie and Lily went to the bar for pre-dinner drinks. Although Archie was still full up from lunch he knew Lily would still be hungry and would want to eat. The room was relatively quiet, Henry was there cleaning glasses to while away the time.

"Hello you two, have you had a nice day?"

"Yes, thank you, Dad, we've had a very interesting day, very interesting indeed. The bar's quiet this evening," Archie remarked.

"A little quiet, but sometimes it makes a welcome change as it's been a bit frantic lately."

When they had finished their drinks Archie and Lily went upstairs to freshen up and spend some time with Emily who was always eager to see them.

Emily cross-questioned them for around half an hour, until Archie decided it was time to take Lily down for something to eat and have a nightcap before retiring for the night.

Twenty-Seven

Monday 11th April

Archie and Lily were already up and about in the foyer while Masie was waiting patiently by the main door for her morning walk. Outside was a warm day, the sun was shining brightly, while white fluffy clouds drifted across the clear, blue sky. With an extra spring in their step walked arm in arm along the deserted lanes.

"This is my idea of heaven. Beautiful day, beautiful countryside and with the man I will share my life with."

Archie squeezed Lily's arm, pulling her closer to him and gently kissed the top of her head.

Back at the hotel, Noah was pacing up and down, while waiting for Archie and Lily to return from their walk.

"Hello you two, I'm glad you're back. There has been a report of an incident on the north perimeter of RAF Avon, as it could be outside the camp they've asked us to look into it. I'm just on my way to check it out. Are you free to join me?"

"As there's such a lot going on at the moment," he continued, "I've had to recall Jack from Mill Meece, he should be on his way now, pretty pleased to be called back I should imagine, hopefully, he will arrive later this afternoon."

(Jack Jones was reluctant to go to Mill Meece's training course after he found out Archie and Lily would be working with Noah on another murder case).

"Yes of course, what sort of incident?" Archie asked.

"Jump in and I'll explain on the way."

As they would be missing breakfast, Archie quickly popped into the hotel, dropped off Maisie and grabbed some toast for Lily, then climbed into the car as they drove off.

"Well, what's it all about Noah?" Archie asked as he handed a grateful Lily the toast

"It would appear that a couple of shots were heard on the north boundary of the camp, the RAF Police have investigated but so far found nothing. We are to meet Group Captain Huntington-Lewis who will give us the necessary permission to carry out our investigations on the camp."

In no time at all they arrived at the guard house that was situated next to the camp entrance. They were greeted by the very authoritative figure of duty officer Flight Sergeant Sparky Miller, with his swagger stick tightly tucked under his arm he directed Noah to an empty parking space beside the guardhouse.

"Good morning, my name is Flight Sergeant

Miller. Inspector Jackson?" he enquired as Noah lowered his window.

"Good morning Flight Sergeant, yes I am Inspector Jackson, these are my colleagues Mr Freestone and Miss Forester."

"Follow me please, Group Captain Huntington-Lewis is expecting you?"

Sparky Miller, with one hand on his swagger stick and the other swinging vigorously, marched them across the main parade ground to the Group captain's office.

The flight sergeant knocked with a certain amount of determination on the office door.

"Who is it?"

"Miller, sir, I have Inspector Jackson and his colleagues waiting to see you."

"Just a moment, Miller," came the quietly spoken voice of the Group Captain, followed a moment later by, "Come."

The tall, slim, distinguished figure of the Group Captain, wearing tortoiseshell glasses, sat behind a rather old battered desk.

The man, who looked like he had seen his fair share of action, stood as they entered his office, leaning heavily on a stick, he held out his hand to Noah, Archie and Lily. After shaking hands, he sank back into his soft leather chair. "Do take a seat," and offered them a cigarette.

Noah accepted the offer. "Thank you. I'm Inspector Jackson, these are my colleagues, Miss Lily

Forester and Mr Archie Freestone.

They have full authority from the War Office."

"Good to have you three on board."

Three chairs were placed opposite the group captain, Lily sat in the middle while Archie and Noah either side of her. Noah lit his cigarette while Archie filled and lit his pipe. Aware that Lily was uncomfortable if there was too much smoke in the room he asked the group captain if it was possible to open a window.

"Yes of course, can I ask you to open it, old chap? The old leg is giving me a bit of jip today."

Archie thanked him. While opening the window Huntington-Lewis began to explain the morning's events.

"This is a bit of a strange case and we're not sure whether it involves the military or it's a civilian matter. Two of my airmen were patrolling the fence on the northern perimeter earlier this morning when they distinctly heard several pistol shots. They are experienced airmen and know what a round of small arms fire sounds like. They weren't sure where the shots came from and after thoroughly searching the area, found nothing out of place, so contacted Flight Sergeant Miller, who in turn got in touch with me."

Archie pushed more tobacco into his pipe, relit it and thought for a moment.

"Do you know if any army manoeuvres were going on at the time? And can we take a look around the area?"

"I checked with local military establishments but all their activities are in the north of Salisbury Plain and not around here. And yes, of course, I'll get Miller to show you around and perhaps you would like to join me for a spot of lunch in the officer's mess when you've finished."

"Thank you, that sounds lovely," Lily's enthusiasm was plain for all to see.

"This way," the short, neatly dressed figure of Miller marched them across the busy parade ground and onto the northern perimeter.

"Where did they hear the shots," Lily asked.

"Just over here, Miss."

Miller points to some open ground behind one of the camp's hangers that leads to a small copse. Archie and Lily wandered toward the hanger and the high barbed wire fence that surrounded the camp.

"Is there any chance of us going round to the other side of the fence?"

"Yes. Follow me, Mr Freestone."

Miller led the three back past the guardhouse and out to the wild overgrown countryside.

Noah stood with his hands on his hips, then scratched his head. "I know this is asking a lot, but is there any chance of any of your chaps clearing this area for us?"

"I'll have to clear it with the Group Captain, but I'm sure it will be alright."

As Miller disappeared behind the guardhouse, the three started to scuff the grass around the area with their shoes to see whether anything obvious could be seen. After a short time, Miller returned.

"I've ordered a group of volunteers to carefully clear this land for you. They have been told to take their orders from you."

From behind Miller six reluctant and what looked like unwilling airmen carrying shovels and scythes approached.

Looking somewhat disinterested, the men leaned on their shovels and those with scythes swung them back and forth as if cutting grass.

Noah worked out a grid system and allotted one man to each grid.

"Right, let's get going, the sooner we get started the sooner you can get back to camp. Mr Freestone, Miss Forester, and I will be working with you. Take care and keep your eyes open for anything unusual."

Carefully cutting away the overgrown undergrowth they made their way through Noah's grid system until they reached a small group of trees about hundred yards from the fence.

"Over here, sir," one of the airmen shouted to Noah.

"What is it?"

Noah, Archie, Lily and the other airmen huddled around, to see what had been found.

"This gets more intriguing by the hour," a surprised Noah said as the group studied the ground.

Twenty-Eight

Noah bent down and poked the ground with a small stick.

"Lily, have you brought your camera?"

"As always."

"Can you take some photographs around this area," Noah asked, pointing to a small space under some bushes. Lying almost hidden were two bullet casings. After Lily had taken several photographs Archie bent down and carefully lifted the casings with a small twig, put them in his handkerchief, being careful not to spoil any fingerprints, handed them to Noah.

"Right, let's get these back to ballistics. I don't think there's a lot more we can do here, so we can call it a day. Thank you gentlemen for all your help."

The small party made their way back into the camp where Sparky Miller was waiting for them. He dismissed the airmen and took Archie, Lily and Noah to the officer's mess where the group captain was waiting for them.

The mess was bustling with the sound of cutlery on china and the constant hum from chatter, the room was filled with smoke, much to Lily's disappointment.

"This way," the group captain beckoned them to a

table tucked away in the corner of the mess.

"I hear you had some success outside the camp?"

"Yes, I think we can call this a civilian matter."

Standing over the table and interrupting Noah was the mess sergeant.

"I'm sorry to interrupt, sir, but there's a telephone call for Inspector Jackson."

"Thank you, can you show the inspector where to take the call?"

"Sir."

The sergeant led Noah through the mess to a small office behind the bar.

"Jackson here."

"It's Tom, sorry to trouble you but what do you want me to do about Allen? Tomasz has telephoned to say he is acting a little strange."

"What do you mean?"

"He's been hanging around all morning staring at everyone who comes into the foyer."

"Is Jack there yet?"

 "Yes, he arrived about half an hour ago."

"Right, can you and Jack pick him up and hold him till we get back? Be careful, he's a dangerous man."

"Yes sir, it will be a pleasure."

Noah rejoined the others in the mess hall to discuss the morning's events. Once they had finished eating Noah, Archie and Lily thanked the Group Captain and headed back to Pewsey.

***

Tomasz was behind the reception desk when Tom and Jack arrived.

"Hello Tomasz, where is he?"

"He's just popped into the bar."

For a Monday the place was quiet, at the far end was Allen propping up the bar unaware of what was about to happen. Henry was sitting behind the bar reading the Daily Sketch oblivious to Tom and Jack entering the room.

"Mr John Allen?" Tom said assertively, grabbing Allen's arm.

"Don't touch me, get your filthy hands off me."

Allen pulled his arm free, and completely out of the blue turned and threw a punch at Jack hitting him firmly on the chin, sending him flying into Tom. Allen ran toward the door and put his hand inside his jacket pocket.

"He's got a gun," Tom shouted out.

Hearing the commotion Tomasz burst into the room, seeing what was going on he threw himself at Allen trying to tackle him to the floor. The sound of breaking glass resounded around the room as they wrestled, sending tables and chairs flying.

The noise of Allen's gun being randomly discharged echoed around the hotel, sending people in the foyer diving for cover.

Grappling with him and trying to force him to the ground, Tomasz managed to wrap his arms around the now furious Allen and wrestle him to the floor. With one knee in his back Tomasz, with the help of Henry who had climbed over the bar, managed to remove the pistol from Allen's hand.

By now Tom was up and taking his handcuffs from his pocket and between the three of them, they were able to restrain him.

"You will all pay for this, you plods, I know where you live." The rantings spewed violently from Allen's mouth.

With one foot on his back, the calming figure of Tom stood over Allen.

"Oh dear, I think we have a bit of a problem, sir," Tom said, sarcastically.

With Allen's hands secured behind his back, Tom reached down and hauled him off the floor causing a great deal of discomfort.

Looking Allen straight in the face, Tom cautioned him.

"I'm arresting you for the possession of a firearm and discharging it in a public space. You do not have to say anything but anything you do say will be taken down and may be given in evidence, do you understand?"

Valentino was silent.

"Tomasz, if I watch him could you search him, as Jack is a little indisposed at the moment?"

"It would be a pleasure, Tom."

While Tom pinned Valentino against the wall Tomasz searched him, he removed a flick knife which was tucked into his sock, a knuckle duster and a second Enfield revolver from inside his jacket pocket.

"This man is a walking arsenal," Tomasz remarked.

Tom turns to Tomasz and Henry. "What you did was very brave and very stupid, all the same, I'm happy you were here, who knows what might have happened if you hadn't been."

Holding his jaw and looking dazed Jack was just starting to come too.

"What did I miss?" he asked looking around at the bullet holes, the ceiling plaster on the floor and all the damage caused by Tomasz's struggle with Allen.

Tom gave a sideward glance at Tomasz and Henry with a rye smile.

"It's all under control, we only just about managed without you. How is your jaw?"

"A bit painful but I'll live."

"You need to pop along to Doctor Stagg."

"I'll be alright, thank you sarge."

"That's not a request, it's an order. Now go."

A reluctant Jack headed out through the main door just as Noah was dropping Archie and Lily off before going on to the police station.

"Hello Jack, you look a bit rough, what have you been up to?" Noah asked through the open car door.

"Hello sir, there's been a bit of an incident in the hotel bar involving Mr Allen or Mr Valentino, whatever he calls himself."

"What sort of an incident?" Archie enquired, looking through the main door into the foyer.

"There's been a shooting and Allen has been arrested."

"Was anyone hurt?" Lily asked, climbing out of the car.

"Only Mr Allen's pride," Jack said with a broad smile.

Jack filled Noah and the others in on the afternoon's events and reluctantly left to see the doctor. Then the three entered the hotel to see what damage had been done, they could hear Allen's rantings as they entered the foyer.

Twenty-Nine

Archie, Noah and Lily made their way to the bar, which looked like a bomb had gone off, and were greeted by Tom gripping Allen's jacket collar and forcing him against the wall.

"Good afternoon Inspector, you've missed all the fun. I have charged this man on two accounts, one of possession of a firearm and the other of discharging a weapon in a public place. How long do you think he will get, sir?" The reassuring and calming figure of Sergeant Hopkins pushed Allen even more forcibly into the wall.

"Hello Tom, these are pretty serious charges. That sort of offence will be at least twenty-five years minimum. Tomasz would you mind helping Tom to escort Mr Allen to the police station? "

"It would be my pleasure, Noah."

"I won't serve a day, Jackson it's the end for you. Now let me go before you regret it. If you don't you're dead and I know where you and your family live, you're all dead."

Incensed at Allen's arrogant rant Archie grabbed him by the throat and pushed him back against the wall.

"Touch one hair on the inspector's head or his

family and you will have me to answer to and believe me you won't like that, you think you know people, the difference is, I do."

"It's okay Archie, I've met his sort before and most of it is hot air. Now take him away before I let Tom have five minutes alone with him."

Grabbing an arm each from behind Allen's back, Tom and Tomasz, almost lifting Allen off his feet, dragged him, still uncontrollably ranting, along River Street to the police station.

Hearing all the commotion Braithwaite and Coombes stood quietly just outside the bar, they appeared to be observing all that was happening. When Lily turned around and looked at them however, they quickly looked the other way and shuffled out of the foyer.

"Sorry about the mess, Henry, the police will compensate you for the damage."

"That's okay, Noah, I'm glad we were of some help. The hotel has plenty of spare tables and chairs in the outbuildings, so no need to worry."

"That's very good of you, thank you. I'll get Jack to remove the bullets from the ceiling and arrange for someone to repair the damage."

"Thank you, Noah."

Archie started to clear the broken glass from the floor while Henry collected the shattered wooden tables and chairs. Ruth appeared with a dustpan and brush and was busy sweeping up cigarette buts and any other rubbish scattered in the brawl.

"Noah, before we go to the police station I must telephone Major Osborne and keep him up to date on what's been happening here over the last few days."

As Archie made his way to the hotel office, Noah thanked Henry for all his help in apprehending Allen. Without him and Tomasz, it would have been a different kettle of fish, their actions were greatly appreciated by him.

Speaking to Osborne, Archie quickly briefed him.

"Good afternoon Major, I just want to keep you up to date. You've probably heard we have a missing vicar and a murdered woman, a Miss Hunt. At the moment we don't think they are connected to De Villiers-Blyth. But we do have two possible sightings of him. Firstly in Devizes by Miss Forester and the other in Marlborough by myself and Miss Forester. We both felt it could have been him, although we couldn't really substantiate it. If it was him he was talking to two women, one was Mrs Ward the vicar's wife and the other we didn't recognise."

"Can you describe the other women?"

"Yes, she was short, well-dressed, wearing a blue spotted shirtwaister dress, I remember she had a wide-brimmed hat which hid her face. Does she sound familiar, I know it's not much to go on?"

Major Osborne thought for a moment.

"No, but I'll give it some thought, the vicar's wife is very interesting, especially with her husband missing."

"We have spoken to her, but she denies knowing

him and suggested we made a mistake, but we will keep looking into it. Also, I'm not sure if this has any connection to De Villiers-Blyth but there was an incident north of RAF Avon. Shots were fired in a small copse just north of the camp. As I said, whether this has anything to do with De Villiers-Blyth, we are not sure. We are having two bullet casings analysed, I will let you know if there are any further developments. Do you have any leads?"

"Not at the moment, if I do you'll be the first to know. Thank you, Freestone, Keep me posted."

"Of course Major."

Noah and Lily were waiting in the foyer when Archie came out of the office.

"Well, let's see what Allen has to say for himself, are you both ready?" Noah asked., eagerly.

"Oh yes, I'm looking forward to this," Lily said, grabbing Archie's arm.

The three got back in the car and drove to the police station. Before they even got inside the door they could hear Allen's offensive angry outburst.

"Inspector, before you see Allen there's a telephone call for you. It's Chief Inspector Booker from Leman Street police station."

"Thank you, Tom."

"Jackson here, how can I help, sir?"

Thirty

"Jackson, you're holding John Allen, he is an important source of information to us in our enquiries here in Whitechapel. I would appreciate it if you would release him and-"

"I'm sorry to interrupt sir, but you must know he is Leonardo Valentino and that his wife Isabella was murdered here in Pewsey. That makes him a person of interest in our case and I need to question him."

"It wasn't a request, Jackson, it's an order. Now release him. I have a couple of chaps down there who will escort him back to London."

"Chaps? Who are they."

"They're good men, trustworthy." Booker avoided answering Noah's question.

"I would like to talk to him before we release him."

"Do you value your career, Jackson, have I not made myself clear or do I have to go over your head? Now release him."

Archie could see the atmosphere was becoming tense and moved closer to hear what was being said.

"You leave me no choice, sir."

"Good man, Jackson. My men will call into the police station and pick him up."

Replacing the telephone handset, Noah looked at

Archie and Lily and explained what had happened.

"Tom, can you get me Cunningham 4597 and transfer it to my office?"

"Yes sir."

Cunningham 4597 was Superintendent Brentwood's private telephone number in Maida Vale.

The atmosphere was uneasy in Noah's office. Archie lit his pipe sending a plume of smoke into the ceiling while Noah, staring out of the window leaned back in his chair and lit yet another cigarette. The heat and smoke were intensifying the tension. Lily gave a pretend cough and proceeded to open the office window.

"How did Leman Street know we had arrested Valentino so quickly?" Lily asked as she takes a deep breath of fresh air coming through the open window.

"It must be the two fellows at the hotel, Coombes and Braithwaite."

"You could be right Archie, they were acting a bit suspicious outside the bar back at the hotel."

The telephone rang breaking into their conversation, Noah picked up the handset.

"Brentwood."

"Jackson here sir, I'm sorry to trouble you so late and at home but we have a situation here in Pewsey."

Noah explained everything that had taken place that afternoon.

"Is that Valentino ranting in the background?

"Yes, he hasn't stopped since we arrested him."

Right, this is what will happen: hold him

overnight, question him and I'll send a couple of my men tomorrow who I do trust. I'll tell them to take their orders from you and your colleagues. My men will be armed, in-between time I suggest you arm yourselves. Valentino is a dangerous man, don't trust anyone."

"How will we know who your men are?"

There was a moment of silence and Brentwood continued.

"They will give the opening passage from John Steinbeck's The Grapes of Wrath. You will quote the first part and they will complete it. It's a bit cloak and dagger but under the circumstances, I think it's the best way to go."

"What about Chief Inspector Booker, sir?"

"Leave him to me. I'll be in touch."

"Thank you, sir," a satisfied smile played on his lips as he replaced the handset and turned to face Archie and Lily.

"Tom, can you and Jack come in here for a minute?"

Noah relaid all the information and suggested that if they didn't want to get involved, it would be alright with him, it wouldn't affect their careers. Tom looked at Noah.

"You can count me in, I never did like Allen or whatever he calls himself."

Jack thought for a moment and a grin came across his face.

"It's why I joined the police, count me in."

Noah thanked them and told Tom to get three revolvers from the safe locker. Archie and Lily had previously been given pistols by Major Osborne. Archie puffing vigorously on his pipe was deep in thought.

"Penny for them?" Noah interrupts Archie's thoughts.

"We need to get him out of here before Booker's goons get here. Noah, if it's okay with you, can Tom bring the car around to the front and wait outside? Jack, you and the Inspector get Valentino, handcuff him and take him to the back door. Lily, can you discreetly go back to the hotel and get my Dad's car and bring it around to the side? Can you see if Tomasz can join us?"

Noah, Lily, Tom and Jack looked at each other and after a short silence simultaneously agreed.

Not to arouse suspicion Lily strolled casually back to the hotel, while Tom collected the car and drove it around to the front of the police station.

At the hotel, Lily found Tomasz and filled him in on Archie's plan; he was more than eager to get involved.

Opening the cell door, Valentino made a lunge at Noah catching him on the shoulder, Jack was quick to react and managed to wrestle him to the floor.

"Get your filthy hands off me, you're dead Jackson."

Still lying on the floor, Valentino's hands handcuffed behind his back and his ranting echoed even louder around the police station.

Just at that moment Lily and Tomasz arrived at the side door, leaving the car running in the side alley.

"Tomasz, glad you're on board. Lily, did you see Coombes and Braithwaite at the hotel?"

"No, it was all very quiet."

"Jack, can you get Valentino's jacket from the front desk and bring it here? Tomasz, you are about the same build as Valentino." Handing him Valentiono's jacket.

"Can you put it on and then you and Noah meet Tom out front? I've got to make a telephone call."

Archie returned from Noah's office to be greeted by Valentino.

"You think you're clever, if you think my boys will be fooled by your stupid trick, think again," a red-faced Valentino spat out.

Ignoring the rantings Archie ordered.

"Tom, when Tomasz is in the car, can you drive around for about half an hour, then drop him off around the back of the hotel and then return here. Meanwhile, we will take Valentino to a secret location."

"It's a trick, don't be fooled," Valentino bellowed out at the top of his voice.

"Gag him," Archie quietly said.

At that Noah took off his tie, got a handkerchief from his trouser pocket and stuffed it into Valentino's mouth and tied the tie around the back of his head, silencing him.

"That's better, I can hear myself think now," Archie smiled, making the best of a difficult situation.

"We all know what we are doing? The fewer people who know where we are taking Valentino, the better. We'll see you back at the hotel later. Good luck."

Noah led Tomasz by the arm to the waiting police car, pushed him into the back seat, sat beside him and drove off in the direction of Pewsey Station. Archie and Lily dragged a struggling Valentino out through the backdoor to their waiting car. Opening the boot and grabbing him by his shirt bundled him in. The two smiled at each other as they got into the car, and disappeared into the night. Leaving Jack to lock up before going on to the hotel to meet the others.

Turning the key in the station's front door, Jack felt the presence of someone behind him—pushing him against the door, two men waved some sort of warrant cards in front of his face.

"Don't turn round, where is he?" a deep menacing voice rang out.

Feeling what felt like the barrel of a gun being pressed into his back, the colour drained from Jack's face.

Thirty-One

Arriving back at the hotel Archie parked his father's car, he and Lily had been so engrossed in all the excitement that they had forgotten to eat and now they were starving.

Going through the foyer into the lounge they noticed Issac Isenberg talking on the reception desk telephone and writing in a small blue notebook, who, upon seeing Archie and Lily, turned his back on them, bowed his head and started to talk quietly under his breath.

"Have we heard anything more about him?" Lily discreetly asked as they enter the lounge.

"At the moment, only that he lives in Bethnal Green and has no criminal record, other than that nothing else has appeared on the radar."

The lounge was hot and smoke-filled. Several people were reading, some were chatting, while the Delfontys were holding hands, staring into each other's eyes and behaving secretly in the corner.

Waiting eagerly around the unlit fire were Noah, Tom and Tomasz, who had already organised food, knowing it was late and Lily would be ravenous.

"Archie, how did it go?" Noah jumps up to greet them.

"He's safely locked away, although my ears are still humming from the constant barrage about who he knows and what will happen to us. How did things go this end?"

"Oh, by the way, we've already ordered food," Noah said, looking at Lily.

"Thank you so much, I'm starving."

"You're welcome, we thought you would be hungry. There is nothing to report, it all went very smoothly, other than Jack's confrontation. But I'll let him explain when he gets here."

"Where is he?" Archie's interest was aroused.

"He won't be long, he's just popped in to see his mother on his way here."

The plump rosy-cheeked figure of Ruth appeared at the lounge door.

"Your table is ready."

"Thank you, Ruth," Lily was the first to jump up and head for the door.

As they entered the dining room Coombes and Braithwaite were just finishing their meal deep in conversation. As the group passed them they fell silent.

Lily, remembering Superintendent Brentwood had asked for a photograph of them, thought this would be a good opportunity to discreetly use her little camera. Seeing Lily take the camera from her handbag, Archie realised what she was about to do, so decided to cause a distraction to get their attention. Fortunately, at that moment, Jack appeared in the dining room doorway, so Archie jumped up and headed toward him calling out.

"Jack it's so good to see you, how's your mother?"

Archie took Jack to one side so they wouldn't be overheard, while Lily took the opportunity to take the photographs of Braithwaite and Coombes, who, keenly watching Archie and Jack didn't notice what Lily was doing. After a few minutes, they quietly slid out of the dining room hoping not to be noticed.

Jack, joining them at the table looking confused, explained what had happened.

"I was just locking up when these chaps came up behind me and demanded to know where Allen was. They flashed warrant cards in my face, I couldn't say if the cards were real or not, they could have been false."

"Did you get a good look at them?"

"No, they pushed me against the door and told me not to turn around."

"Then what happened?" Lily asked.

"I thought one of them had a gun, it was pretty scary. I told them I was only the trainee officer and wasn't privy to what was going on. One of them pushed my face hard against the door and insisted I knew more than I was letting on. So I told them, all I knew was that Allen had asked to be taken to the railway station where he would meet two men. They muttered something to each other and no sooner had they appeared than they disappeared. I looked around, but they were gone, so I've no idea what they looked like."

"Good man Jack, you kept a cool head and sent them on a wild goose chase," Noah said.

It was late by the time they had finished eating, so Noah, Tom, Jack and Tomasz decided to call it a day and headed home.

"Would you like a nightcap before retiring?" Archie asked Lily.

"That would be lovely, it's been a long day."

Thirty-Two

Tuesday 12th April

The hot weather continued as Lily and Archie walked Maisie along the narrow lanes that surround Pewsey. They were in deep conservation when they met Jacob, the local milkman busy on his round.

"Good morning, Jacob, how are you?"

"Good morning, very well thank you. How's the case going?"

"There's not a lot to go on at the moment, you hear most things that go on around here, is there any talk regarding that woman that was killed last week?"

"I'm glad I bumped into you, I was going to call into the police station, but being so busy I forgot. I was speaking to Amos yesterday, you know the sheep farmer from Milton Lilbourne. I suggested he call in to see the Inspector but said he was too busy and didn't have time. Anyway, he was making an early start last Tuesday on his way to the market and was driving along River Street, when he saw two men and a woman walking toward River Street away from the bridge by the river. He didn't think much of it at the time and forgot all about it."

Archie remembered Amos from when he

mistakenly identified him as the train conductor involved in the Frolov case last February.

"Thank you, Jacob, that is very helpful. We may need to speak to you again."

"Any time, but I must hurry, I'm running late."

Jacob carried on with his milk round, while Archie and Lily headed back to the hotel eager to telephone Noah.

Emily was sitting at the reception desk writing in the registration book.

"Hello Mum, do you know if the office is free?"

"Good morning darling, as far as I know, it's not being used. Before you telephone, a man called Brentwood called and left a message, did you have a nice walk, where did you go, did you meet anyone"

"Thank you, Mum, what did the message say?"

"Oh, yes, where is it, ah, here it is. He said he has spoken to Noah who suggested he speak to you. The two gentlemen you are expecting have been held up and will call down tomorrow. Can you meet them at eight forty-three? He said you would understand."

"Thank you, Mum, when we have a moment we'll pop up and see you for a chat."

It had been a week since Miss Hunt had been murdered and so far they had made little progress, so Archie was eager to tell Noah about Amos.

Telephoning Noah, Archie asked him why Brentwood had contacted him direct.

"We think the police station is being watched and agreed it would be a good idea if you picked his men up from the station, as we don't think you are being watched. Can you take them back to the hotel and I'll call in to see them later."

"Yes of course I will." Archie then told him about bumping into Jacob, and what Amos had said. They agreed that this could be the breakthrough they needed in the case. Noah arranged to pick Archie and Lily up after breakfast.

After they had finished eating, Lily went to her room to change while Archie went to see his mother, who was still at the reception desk. He told her about their morning walk and bumping into Jacob and that they would call in later to see her.

"Are you ready?" Lily appeared behind Archie.

"Yes, we had better go, see you later Mum."

"Be careful you two."

Outside the hotel, Lily and Archie paced up and down the pavement in anticipation of Noah's arrival, there was an air of excitement as they drove off towards Milton Lilbourne. Pulling into Upper Farm they could see Amos coming out of one of his outbuildings.

"Mr Spredbury, can we have a word?" Noah's voice echoed around the farmyard.

With his head pushed forward the short, portly figure of Amos Spredbury meandered slowly toward them.

"What do you want? Ah, young Freestone, where did you see me this time? It wasn't me," he said with a smile.

"I'm sorry about that, Mr Spredbury I….."

"Not at all, I was only joking with you and I think we know each other well enough now, do call me Amos."

"Thank you Amos, call me Archie," a somewhat relieved Archie said.

"Mr Spredbury, perhaps you can help us. Were you driving through Pewsey early last Tuesday morning?" Noah asked.

"Last Tuesday, yes on my way to market. Oh, it's about those people I saw heading to River Street. I meant to come in and speak to you."

"Can you describe them?"

"I wasn't really paying attention, they looked fairly average, nothing springs to mind. If I remember correctly I thought she looked tall, the two men were fairly unassuming and nothing stood out."

"Did you see which way they were headed?" Lily asked.

Amos thought for a moment, scratched his head and pushed his cap back.

"No, I'm sorry, that's all I remember."

"Thank you, Amos, you've been very helpful," Archie said, shaking Amos's hand.

A slightly disappointed Archie climbed back into the car, he had hoped Amos would have had more information for them. As the car started to pull away from the farmyard, Noah saw Amos waving to them in his rearview mirror. Stopping, Noah got out of the car, quickly followed by Archie and Lily.

"What is it, Mr Spredbury?"

"This may not be important, but I remember having the impression that they weren't together."

"What do you mean?" Archie asked.

Amos reflected and after a short silence commented. "The two men were quite a few yards behind the woman and didn't seem to be with her."

"Would you recognise them if you saw them again?"

"I don't know, I might remember the woman and maybe one of the men."

"Thank you, Mr Spredbury, that is extremely helpful. We may need to speak to you again," Noah said.

"You know where I am," said Amos as he pulled an old cigarette from behind his ear.

As they were getting back into the car Amos turned around, taking a long pull on his cigarette.

"Now come to think of it, I think one of the men had red hair, but I couldn't swear to it."

"Thank you, Amos. If you think of anything else, could you let us know?" a relieved Archie said, now they had something more concrete to go on.

Lily wound her window down as the car started to fill with smoke. Without thinking, Noah would chain smoke when he was excited.

"I'm sorry Noah, but could you open your window, it's getting a little stuffy in here."

"I'm sorry Lily I wasn't thinking, of course."

The drive back to Pewsey was full of anticipation,

at last, they had the breakthrough that they needed.

"Lets get Coombes and Braithwaite in for questioning as soon as we get back."

As his excitement increased so did the speed he was driving, Noah continued smoking and was unaware how fast they were travelling.

"Slow down old chap, lady on board."

"Sorry, Archie, I hadn't noticed. We need to get back before either of them decides to leave the village."

"You're right, of course, but we'll soon be back."

In no time at all, and much to Lily's relief, they pulled up outside the hotel. Noah dropped Archie and Lily off at the main door and then parked the car at the rear. Dotty was working on the reception desk talking to Mr and Mrs Defonty as Archie and Lily came into the foyer, they were soon joined by Noah.

The three hovered, waiting for the Defontys to finish their conversation, which seemed to be taking ages, but eventually, they left.

"Hello Dotty, do you know if Mr Coombes and Mr Braithwaite are in?" Archie asked.

Dotty checked the registration book to see which rooms they were in.

"Ah, here we are, rooms twelve and ten, let's see, no they must be out, their keys are here."

"Thank you, Dotty."

Archie pondered on what to do next, his thought process was broken by Lily.

"Shall we take the opportunity to have some

lunch?"

"Good idea, Lily, I'm feeling a little peckish myself."

"Can I use your office telephone, I need to inform Tom as to the morning's events, and ask him to keep an eye out for Coombes and Braithwaite, I'll also get him to send Jack along to the railway station to make sure they don't slip away."

"Yes, of course, you know where it is."

The dining room was quite crowded, the villagers tended to use the restaurant as well as the hotel guests. After his early start, Jacob always ate lunch at the hotel and was in deep conservation with Author Hewit the newsagent.

Ruth, who was running to and fro, managed to find them a table in the corner, where fortunately they had a clear view of the reception desk.

"Did you manage to speak to Amos?" Jacob's voice broke through the noise of the room.

"Yes, thank you Jacob he was-."

"Archie, sorry to break in, but Braithwaite is at the reception desk."

A middle-aged, overweight figure, with wavy red hair, was collecting his room key. Dotty was frantically waving her hand discreetly behind his back trying to get their attention. Just at that moment, Noah came out of the office and as he passed.

"Thank you, Mr Braithwaite, did you have a good morning?" Dotty asked loudly in an attempt to attract Noah's attention.

Noah stopped in his tracks and turned to face Braithwaite who at the same time turned and faced Noah. There was an awkward silence, and then Braithwaite started to move away.

"Mr Braithwaite, Can I have a word with you?

Thirty-Three

"What-a you want-a? Who-a you?" Braithwaite unsuccessfully tried to disguise an Italian accent.

"I'm Inspector Jackson, and you may be able to help us with our inquiries. Firstly, do you know where Mr Coombes is?" Noah asked.

"He-a is-a my-a friend but I'm-a not his-a keeper." a defensive Braithwaite retorted.

By now Archie and Lily had joined Noah and had boxed Braithwaite into a corner.

"Just answer the question."

"I dunno where-a he is-a, okay."

Remembering that Tomasz had found firearms in their bedrooms, Archie was taking no chance and took Braithwaite's arm, restricting his movements just in case he had a gun on him. Braithwaite struggled, unsuccessfully trying to break free from Archie's grip.

"I think you need to come with us," Noah grabbed his other arm.

"Ah, you-a cannot do this-a, I've done-a nothing wrong. I'm-a here on-a holiday with-a my friend!"

A small inquisitive group had started to gather in the foyer, among them was Tomasz, who was pushing his way through to the front.

"Can I help?"

"Thank you Tomasz, we may need you, perhaps you could hang around?"

"Yes, of course."

"Dotty could you telephone ahead to Tom at the police station and inform him we are bringing Mr Braithwaite in for questioning?"

"Straight away," Dotty answered, enthusiastically.

Archie couldn't help but notice that Braithwaite had an empty shoulder holster under his right arm and deduced he was left-handed.

An inquisitive crowd had now formed in the foyer and the atmosphere was growing tense, as they jostled one another to get a better view of what was happening.

"Can you all move back, there's nothing to see," Noah shouted in vain.

In all the confusion Braithwaite managed to break free from their grip. Pushing through the crowd, Tomasz lunged at him only to be greeted by Braithwaits left fist to his face. A blood-covered Tomasz holding his nose fell to the floor.

"Grab him," Noah yelled out in vain as Braithwaite escapes through the front door being chased by Archie and Lily.

Struggling to get through the crowd, they eventually got outside, but found the street was busy, somehow Braithwaite had managed to vanish in the crowd.

A despondent Archie and Lily wandered through the streets looking in every doorway and down every alley, eventually, they were joined by Noah and Tom. After an hour or so of fruitless searching, they returned to the hotel.

On their return they found Emily tending Tomasz's face which was a bit worse for wear, his nose was bright red and his right eye was starting to close up.

"Tomasz, you do look a bit of a mess. How are you feeling?" Archie inquired.

"My nose is a bit sore, I can still see you and I have a headache, other than that I'm okay, thank you. I'm just sorry I couldn't catch him."

"That's okay, it's not your fault, you did your best. He's a bit of a slippery customer, we'll soon have him under lock and key," Noah continued. "I got Tom to put out an all-points bulletin on Braithwaite and Coombes. They won't get far."

Turning to Dotty, Archie asked. "Can we have the keys for rooms twelve and ten, please?"

Dotty handed Archie the keys. Then he and Noah made their way upstairs. However, before going into either room Archie thought it would be a good idea to fetch his pistol from his room.

Standing outside Coombes's bedroom, Noah thumped on the door.

"This is the police, open the door."

There was no reply, so he tried again and still no reply.

"Mr Coombes we are coming in."

Archie turned the key and cautiously pushed the door open with his foot. Armed, they slowly entered the room, Archie proceeded to search for Coombes's guns, while Noah checked the wardrobe to see if he could find any information about him. Two Italian-tailored suits hung side by side on the top rail and a homberg hung on a hook behind the bedroom door. Several cigarette ends were stubbed out in an ashtray on the bedside table and an empty packet of Alfa lay crushed in the bottom of the waste bin.

Noah turned to Archie. "Have you come across this brand of Alfa cigarettes before?"

"They are Italian low-grade cigarettes, you can only buy them in Italy."

"Hmm, there is certainly an Italian connection here, what with his suits handmade in Italy and the cigarettes."

"But there is a bit of a contradiction, expensive hand-made suits and cheap cigarettes, it's all very strange," Archie commented as he continued to search through Coombes's suitcase and a chest of drawers that stood in the corner of the room but couldn't find the guns anywhere.

"No nothing here, I'm just going to pop down and ask Tomasz where he saw them."

"Okay, I'll carry on," Noah said

Downstairs Tomasz was nursing his wounds in the back office, Henry had poured him a welcoming glass of Glenlivet, one of his special malts, which Tomasz was cradling in both hands.

"Tomasz, I'm sorry to trouble you, but where did you say you saw Coombes's guns?"

"It was in his suitcase under the bed Hidden in a secret compartment there were two loaded revolvers." Archie thanked Tomasz and made his way back up to Noah, who was standing in the middle of the room with both hands on his hips looking around. He had completely turned the room over and had not found the guns or a passport, in fact, there was nothing to give them any clue who Coombes was.

Archie heaved Coombes's suitcase from under the bed again and searched the secret compartment but drew a blank.

"No guns here."

"We can only draw one conclusion, Coombes has the guns with him. As we are not sure what we are dealing with, I think my old boss is right, it would be a good idea to arm ourselves from now on. I'll warn Lily and Tomasz to be prepared." Noah said, scratching his head.

He looked back into the room, pondered for a while, closed the bedroom door and locked it.

"A penny for them?" Archie asked.

"I don't know, I just get a really bad feeling about this. Are they Italian hitmen, the only thing I am sure about is they are not here on a golfing holiday."

"I agree, nothing is as it appears. We need to get those photographs of Braithwaite and Coombes off to Superintendent Brentwood. Lily has already dropped the film into the chemists."

"I thank God that you and Lily are here to support us, and to add your expertise on these cases," Noah said as they went downstairs to find Lily.

"We wouldn't have it any other way, old chap, glad to be of assistance."

In the foyer, Henry sat behind the reception desk, reading.

"What are you reading, Dad?"

"Oh, hello, it's Christie's new book *'The Crooked House'* it makes a good read. Have you ever thought about writing a book? Especially with all the escapades you both get up to."

"I wouldn't know where to start, Dad."

Archie smiled as he and Noah crossed the empty foyer and headed toward the lounge. They found Lily and Emily having afternoon tea in deep conversation.

"What are you two up to?" Archie asked.

"Oh, just planning your big day, darling."

"We haven't had time to fix a date, but when we do, you will be the first to know, Mum."

Archie carried on talking to his mother while Noah took Lily to one side and explained what they had discovered and suggested Lily get her pistol and carry it on her at all times from now on.

"We need to be vigilant and-"

"Archie, Jacob is on the telephone for you," Henry called from the reception desk.

"Coming, Dad."

Thirty-Four

Archie made his way to the back office where he found Tomasz still nursing his wounds and on his fourth glass of Henry's whisky.

Nearly falling out of his chair, Tomasz looked up."Am I in your way, Archie, old chap?" He slurred his words and spoke with a certain confidence that only alcohol can give.

"Not at all, old chap," a broad smile came across Archie's face as he picked up the telephone.

"Hello, Jacob, how can I help you?"

"Archie, I don't know if this is important, but Mrs Ward has just telephoned and ordered an extra pint of milk to start tomorrow. I thought, what with the vicar missing? Maybe he's back home?"

"Thank you, Jacob, yes that is very interesting, thank you for letting me know." Archie raised his voice to be heard over Tomasz's rendition of Oj chmielu, a popular Polish folk song.

Tomasz eventually slumped back in the office armchair and fell asleep.

With a spring in his step, he left the office, excited to share this new information with Lily and Noah. Yes, that is very interesting, he thought to himself.

Lily and Noah had left the lounge and were waiting

in the foyer when Archie returned.

"That was Jacob, apparently Mrs Ward has ordered extra milk! Somewhat intriguing, does this mean the Reverend Ward is back?" Archie's enthusiasm was hard to hide.

"Strange, if he is back I thought Mrs Ward would have informed us," Lily remarked thoughtfully.

"You're right, I'll send Jack around to check."

"If it's okay with you Noah, after we've eaten, I would like to go with Lily and check for myself."

"That would be really helpful Archie, we have a lot on our plate right now, what with Valentino, the murder of his wife, and Ward missing, plus Tom just telephoned to say Mr Strong has contacted us, apparently someone suspicious was wandering around his fields."

"Things are becoming more curious by the hour. I wonder what that's all about," Archie mused.

"I don't know, I'll find out more when I get back to the station. He did have the impression it was a man. I'll get Jack to pop over and chat to him later and I'll let you know what happens. Right, I'll get off now, see you later."

As Noah was going through the main door, Lily called out.

"Noah, could you do me a favour? I dropped the film of Coombes and Braithwaite at Walkers in the High Street earlier. Mr Walker said he would rush the order, and it would be ready to pick up later this afternoon."

"Yes, of course, the sooner we get them off to Superintendent Brentwood the better."

Noah returned to the police station while Archie and Lily went to the dining room, being late they hoped there was still something to eat. Ruth was tidying up after the lunchtime rush.

"Are we too late to eat?"

"No, I'm sure Sam can rustle something up for you, I'll pop into the kitchen and check."

Archie and Lily sat at their special table that was quietly tucked away in the corner of the dining room. Around fifteen minutes or so later, Ruth brought them a plate of roast chicken and vegetables, which they devoured with great delight. A semi-satisfied Lily, who was always starving, thanked Ruth and asked if there was any pudding, unfortunately, there was none, so she went upstairs to freshen up before leaving to speak to Mrs Ward.

***

Jack had arrived at Manor Farm to speak to John Strong.

Ringing the large bell that hung beside the front door of the grand farmhouse, Jack stood back and waited.

"Good afternoon Mr Strong, PC Jones, it's about your stranger."

"I don't think he's my stranger, PC Jones," John Strong said with a rye smile.

"I didn't mean he ………"

"I was only joking. It's about the man I've seen a couple of times, who just seems to be wandering around the place."

"Yes, can you describe him?"

"I was walking my daughter's dog Tiffin when I noticed he was in the field by Hurley Lane over Kepnal earlier this morning. By the time I managed to get there, he had vanished. I had the impression he was quite tall, oh, he wore a dark suit and hat and was carrying a briefcase. I'm sorry but that's all I can tell you, he just seemed to be out of place."

"Thank you, Mr Strong, I will personally look into it."

John Strong thanked Jack and watched him cycle off in the direction of Green Drove toward Kepnal.

***

Archie looked up at the long drive that led to the rectory. Lily squeezed her arm through his as they made their way determinedly up to the house. They hoped to discover why an extra pint of milk was required by Mrs Ward.

Archie pulled the handle of the bell on the impressive front door and waited, but there was no reply, after some time he tried again, but still no reply.

"Shall we take a look around the back, she may be in the garden," Lily suggested.

"Good idea."

Opening the small side gate they entered the imposing large landscaped rear garden.

"Mrs Ward, it's Archie Freestone. Can we have a word?"

There was no reply.

"Did you hear that?" Lily whispered.

The sound of glass breaking followed by a woman's scream of pain came from a small potting shed to the side of the house. Archie ran to where the sound was coming from, closely followed by Lily.

Thirty-Five

Carefully pushing the door open, Archie found Mrs Ward slumped in the corner on the ground with broken pots and dirt surrounding her.

"Are you alright Mrs Ward?"

Florence Ward lifted her head, smiled and held her hand out to Archie to help her up. With a deep sigh, she brushed the dirt from her dress as with Archie's help she pulled herself up.

While Archie was assisting Florence, Lily noticed the back door was gently swinging closed as though someone had just left the shed and didn't want to be seen.

"Oh, just a silly accident. I slipped and tried to grab the worktop but missed and brought a couple of pots down on top of myself, but I'm alright thank you. How can I help you, have you found my husband?"

"No, I'm sorry we haven't. Have you heard from him?"

"Oh dear, I'm beginning to think that something has happened to him or he has left me. It's been over a week, and I've not heard a word from him." A distressed look came over her features as she thought about what could have happened to her husband.

"Do you have anybody staying with you at the

moment?" Lily asked, always getting straight to the point.

"No, what makes you ask?"

"Oh, no reason, we have to ask, it's normal in cases of missing persons. Sometimes a family member comes to help. Are you alright on your own, Florence?" Archie sounded sympathetic and tried not to give anything away.

"Yes, I'm fine, thank you Archie." she replied with a wan smile.

"If we can help in any way, please let us know," Lily said.

Archie thanked Mrs Ward and he and Lily headed out of the sidegate to the front of the house.

Outside Lily looked discreetly over her shoulder at the house, hoping to catch a curtain being twitched or a figure being reflected in one of the windows.

"Did you see the back door swinging closed? I had the distinct impression someone else was there before we went in?"

"You're right she definitely has someone staying with her. I can tell when an individual is lying to me and she was. We need to keep an eye on the place. I'll ask Noah to get Jack to do a spot of surveillance, he'll enjoy that."

For the time of year, the spring evening was quite balmy as Archie and Lily strolled arm in arm back towards the hotel.

"As it's such a lovely evening, would you like a walk before going home?"

"That would be lovely," Lily replied as she snuggles closer into Archie's side.

The couple wandered along the High Street. When they reached Ball Road, they bumped into Issac Isenberg walking toward them.

"Good evening, Mr Isenberg."

"Mr Freestone," he said as he hurried past them.

"Tomasz was right, he's not at all communicative. I wonder what he's doing here this time of the day?" Archie stopped and turned around to take a good look at Isenberg.

"I don't know, shall we follow him and see where he's going?" Lily said with an air of excitement in her voice.

Keeping their distance, they followed him along the High Street. Outside the newsagents, Isenberg stopped and studied the notice board for several minutes before continuing to River Street and back to the hotel.

Archie followed Isenberg leaving Lily to study the notice board, to see if there was anything that looked out of place. When she arrived back at the hotel she found Archie at the bar watching Isenberg who was sitting on his own, reading through a bundle of papers he had taken from his briefcase.

"Did you see anything on the notice board?"

"No, there was nothing obvious, just the normal adverts, rooms to let, help wanted and things for sale."

"I would really like to talk to him, but at the moment I don't have any reason. I've got you a drink, shall we sit down?"

There was a free table next to Isenberg, as they made their way to the table, Lily discreetly tried to see what he was reading. But as they got close he quickly shuffled the papers together and stuffed them back into his suitcase, stood up and left the bar.

Archie and Lily settled down and watched him leave.

"He really is unsociable and secretive and with so much going on it's easy to lose focus and think he has something to do with the events happening here. He's probably here on a short holiday, let's put him to one side, we have bigger problems to think about. The trouble is too many people in one place simultaneously and they all look guilty of something," Archie remarked, thoughtfully.

"We mustn't forget the possibility of a Russian agent operating in the area, or what has happened to De Villiers-Blyth. Does anyone, besides everyone, strike you as acting suspiciously?" Lily asked with a smile.

"Yes, they certainly look a guilty lot and where did Coombes disappear to, there is plenty to think about, but we won't go into that this evening. We are seeing Noah at ten-thirty tomorrow, we can put our heads together and see if we can't make sense of things. Oh, I've told Dad to expect two guests tomorrow morning and to get Dotty to make two rooms ready in the annexe away from the main hotel."

Archie leaned across the table, took Lily's hand

and gently kissed it. "Shall we grab something to eat," he suggested, to which Lily's normal enthusiasm for food was plain to see.

Having finished eating they thought it was about time they went to see Emily and Henry. Things had been so busy they had rather neglected Archie's parents, sharing a glass of whiskey in their comfortable lounge would be a welcoming end to a busy day.

Thirty-Six

Wednesday 13th April

Six-thirty a.m. Archie is woken by Maisie scratching at his door.

"Hang on, old thing, I'll be there in a jiffy."

"I hope you're not referring to me, Mr Freestone" came Lily's voice from the other side of Archie's door.

"Not at all, I was talking to Maisie," Archie said feeling a little embarrassed.

"I know, I'll see you downstairs when you're ready."

In the foyer, Lily was talking to Henry when Archie came running down the stairs.

"I'm sorry I'm late."

"You're not, it's only quarter to seven," said Lily as she slipped the lead around Maisie's neck who, as usual, was sitting patiently waiting for her walk.

In no time at all they were walking along Southcott Road toward Green Drove.

"Phew, it's very hot for the time of the year, I think I'm a little overdressed," Archie said as he removes his jacket.

"Good morning, what a beautiful day," came the

voice of Jacob from one of the cottages that dotted the lane.

"Good morning Jacob, yes it is, perfect for an early morning walk, or in your case delivering milk."

"Any news on the vicar?"

"No, he's still missing, but thank you for the information regarding the rectory, it was most helpful, if you hear anything else let us know."

"I will. Have a nice day."

"And you, Jacob."

Arriving back at the hotel Archie and Lily went to their rooms to change before breakfast. Archie was the first to get downstairs where he found Tomasz, who was supporting two black eyes and a very sore head, working at the reception desk.

"Good morning Tomasz, how are you feeling today? You don't look too bright?"

"I am fine thank you, Archie. Noah has telephoned, to say he has some very interesting information and can you and Lily go straight to the police station after you have picked up your guests from the station and dropped them at the hotel?"

"Thank you, Tomasz, are you free to come with us?"

"Your father is taking over from me in half an hour, so I would love to join you when you get back."

"Good, that will give us enough time to have breakfast and get back from the station. I'll clear it with Noah and give you a shout when we are leaving."

Lily joined Archie, who was waiting in the dining room. He explained about Noah's telephone call and that Tomasz was going to join them. After breakfast, Archie and Lily left for the railway station to pick up the two men.

The train ground to a halt, and people started to disembark. Archie scanned the platform to see whether he could see Brentwood's officers. Walking toward them were two men who looked like characters from The Maltese Falcon. Both of them were tall with dark wavy hair, one had a small pencil moustache, and the other was clean-shaven, the pair stood upright and wore dark suits and dark brown hombergs. They could have been twins.

"Inspector Jackson?" one said, with a distinct cockney lilt.

"*To the red country and part of the grey country of Oklahoma,*" Archie quoted from The Grapes of Wrath.

"*The last rains came gently, and they did not cut the scarred earth.*" One replied, completing the sentence.

"Good to have you chaps on board, I'm Archie Freestone, Inspector Jackson has been held up," Archie said with a smile. "This is my associate Miss Forester."

The two men introduced themselves.

"I'm Sergeant George Dixon and this is my colleague PC Benjamin Martin. We have been told to take our orders only from you and Inspector Jackson and that we are working undercover."

Archie explained the situation as they drove back to the hotel.

Henry was waiting at the back of the hotel ready to greet them and show them to their rooms. They thanked Archie and arranged to see him and the others later at the police station.

Archie had explained to Henry a little about the men and asked him to be discreet about them staying at the hotel, then called for Tomasz before making their way to the police station.

Jack was manning the front desk while Tom was talking to Noah in the back office.

"Good morning, Jack, is the inspector in?"

"Yes, he said to go straight through. They're waiting for you. That's a bit of a shiner you have there, Tomazs."

Tomazs grinned at Jack as he followed the others to the office.

As Archie opened the office door, a cloud of smoke filled the corridor. Waving his hand in front of his face to clear the air, they entered.

"Glad you're here, I've got some very interesting news. By the way, how are you feeling Tomasz, you look awful."

"I'm fine thank you, it looks worse than it is."

Before they sat down, Lily went over and opened the office window.

"Can we keep the smoke down, chaps?" Archie said before Lily started to cough.

"Yes of course, sorry Lily. Right, my old boss Brentwood has telephoned. Firstly, did his men arrive safely?" Archie nodded, " Good, he has received the photographs of Coombes and Braithwaite early this morning. He has been in contact with the Special Branch at Scotland Yard who have identified them as two gunmen imported from Sicily. They were spotted going through Tilbury Docks two weeks ago. Elijah Braithwaite, real name is Salvatore Buccafusca and Leonard Coombes, whose real name is Alfio Rizzuto, were followed to two addresses in London. Buccafusca at forty-seven Pekin Street Tower Hamlet and Rizzuto at twenty-three Bartlett Close also Tower Hamlet.

"They believe Valentino has employed them as bodyguards and are considered extremely dangerous."

The silence was quite tangible, only to be broken by Jack who had been listening outside the office door and nearly fell into the room.

"I'm sorry but would anybody like a drink?" He asked, feeling somewhat embarrassed and thinking of why he should be hovering outside the office.

"Not at the moment Jack, thank you, but stay around, this concerns all of us."

"To answer your earlier question, the two men have arrived safely, we are seeing them later this afternoon, here, if that is alright with you Noah?"

"Yes that's fine, shall we say three o'clock?"

"Perfect," Archie replied.

Noah turned around, faced the incident board, lit

another cigarette, and gently hummed.

"We need to make some sense of all this, let's get these names up there."

Noah proceeded to draw three columns, in the first he wrote the Reverend Ward and Mrs Ward.

"Before you move on Noah, can you add a question mark in that column? We believe someone else is staying there, we don't know who, but we're pretty sure there is. Can I suggest you get Jack to keep an eye on the place," Archie said, interrupting Noah's flow.

"Jones, did you hear that? Can you pop around and keep an eye on the place."

"Yes, I'll go straight away, sir."

"Thank you, Jones."

The room was starting to fill with smoke, which was making Lily feel bilious. Archie noticed and opened the office door, suggesting she sit by the open window, to which Lily eagerly agreed.

Noah continued to write in the second column Mrs Valentino, Leonardo Valentino, Salvatore Buccafusca and Alfio Rizzuto. In the third column the missing De Villiers-Blyth.

"What about this Isenberg character, he seems a bit shifty, but that doesn't mean he's connected to any of them, perhaps I'll try and speak to him later" Archie said.

"Good idea, I think we can add him to the board, but until we hear from Scotland Yard we'll keep an open mind."

"Let's presume the two chaps that threatened Jack were Valentino's men, who have disappeared. But if they are his men they will leave without him. Tom, can you do some door-to-door around the village to see if anyone has seen anyone acting suspicious? They have to be here somewhere. Do they know anybody? Who could be hiding them?" Noah asked.

"What about this woman Amos saw coming from the river the morning Mrs Valentino was murdered?" Lily asked.

"Tom went door-to-door around Market Place and River Street but there was nothing to report. We've drawn a blank."

"Until we have more information we might as well leave it for now and meet later," Noah said, still staring at the incident board.

***

Archie, Lily and Tomasz made their way back to the hotel and arranged to meet later. An excited Maisie greeted Archie and Lily as they entered Emily's lounge.

"Down, old girl," Archie said, in an attempt, unsuccessfully, to calm her down.

"Down," Lily's voice resounded, causing Maisie to quietly lay in front of her.

"Very impressive, how did you do that?" Archie asked, feeling slightly inadequate.

"Oh, it's easy really, you just have to show her

who's boss. It's quite simple."

Archie smiled. After half an hour of chatting about anything and everything with his mother, he realised that he and Lily had better get a bite to eat before meeting Noah. He kissed Emily on her cheek and said they would catch up again soon.

There was a bustling atmosphere in the dining room with Dotty and Ruth being rushed off their feet.

"I'm sorry Archie, I'm not sure what is going on, but we don't have any tables free for at least an hour."

"That's okay, we'll grab a sandwich from the kitchen."

Tomasz was standing at the back of the hotel as Archie and Lily came out of the back door. Brentwood's two men were waiting just out of sight to the side of the building. Archie suggested that the three of them go on ahead. Archie and Lily would give them a five-minute start. He thought five people walking down River Street would attract attention, while three and then two wouldn't be as noticeable. Tomasz and Brentwood's men set off for the police station.

"We'll give them a few minutes and then we'll go," Archie said, checking to see if anybody was following the others.

"All clear, let's go."

When they arrived at the police station Tom who was minding the desk, ushered them through to Noah's office. Somehow they all managed to squeeze into the room. Archie introduced Noah to Sergeant

Dixon and PC Martin and all seven settled down to discuss all three cases. The heat and smoke were almost unbearable for everyone, especially Lily. After several minutes Noah swung around in his chair.

"This isn't working, we need to find somewhere large and private enough to take all of us. I suggest we leave it for today, sleep on it, and see what we have come up with in the morning."

As he walked home, Archie racked his brain as to where they could meet that was private.

"I suppose the hotel would be the best place, although I'm not sure where."

"I have an idea," Lily continued, "what about your mother's private lounge? I'm sure she wouldn't mind. I think she would find it quite exciting."

"That is a good idea. It's private, there's plenty of room, I think you're right, she would find it exciting. I'll speak to her when we get back."

Emily was curled up on the settee with a glass of sherry. She was reading 'The Crooked House' on Henry's recommendation, while Maisie lay at her feet.

"Hello darlings, would you like a drink? Have you any news about the vicar? I'm not sure what will happen this weekend, Easter has always been special in Pewsey."

"Hello Mum, a sherry would be nice thank you. Shall I top you up?" he crossed the room and poured them all a sherry. "There's still no news on the Reverend Ward. I'm sure Salisbury will sort something out. Mum, we have an extremely important favour to ask of you."

"Oh dear, that sounds ominous."

"Not at all, can Noah use your lounge for a meeting tomorrow? We need somewhere private and discreet and where better than here in the hotel."

"It all sounds very intriguing. Yes, of course, I'll make sure you have coffee and biscuits and no one will know."

"Thank you Mum, you're a brick. It's been a long day, thank you for the sherry, I think we are going to have dinner then call it a day. Speak to you in the morning, thank you again."

"Not at all, it's a pleasure being able to help."

Thirty-Seven

Thursday 14th April
(Maundy Thursday)

There was a gentle knock on Archie's door. He leaned over to look at his clock, it was two a.m.

"Archie, are you awake?" Henry's voice interrupted Archie's sleep.

"Archie, Noah is here with Tom, are you awake?"

Archie rolled over, blinked, rubbed his eyes and got out of bed.

"Yes, I'm just coming."

"I'm just going to wake Lily." Henry's voice faded as he went down the corridor to Lily's room.

Noah was striding up and down in the foyer as Tom sat patiently waiting. Soon Archie, still doing up his shirt came running down the stairs.

"What's up, Noah?"

"Flynn from the Coopers Arms has telephoned. He was woken by someone banging on his door. There were two men, they said they had discovered a body in a field over Kepnal."

"What two men in the middle of the night?"

"He couldn't say. He said they were probably poachers and they didn't want to be known."

"What's going on?" Lily's voice came from behind them.

"Grab your coats and I'll explain as we drive along."

"Do we need Tomasz or Brentwood's men?" Archie asked.

"I don't think there's any danger, it could be someone who's had an accident. But I think it is wise to be armed and to include you both."

Both Archie and Lily ran back upstairs to finish dressing, grabbed their coats and pistols and dashed down stairs to join Noah.

Soon they arrived at The Coopers Arms, where Flynn was waiting outside.

"This way," Joining them in the Land Rover, Flynn pointed to a small track that led to the fields.

It was a clear night as they made their way along the small dirt track. Flynn told them that one of the men had lit a small fire to direct the police to the body.

"Over there," Lily said, pointing to an orange glow in the darkness.

Cautiously they pulled into the field, stopped and with their torches on, got out of the Land Rover.

"Right, I suggest Tom go that way, Lily over there and …"

"Here, over here," Archie's voice penetrated the night silence.

The four joined him, they stood looking down at the body slumped face down on the ground.

"Can you see who it is?" asked Noah.

Archie bent down to get a better look. "I'll just roll him over." he suddenly jumped up and stood back, shock and surprise written on his face. He recognized the dark hair that was greying at the temples, the distinguished-looking figure lying in front of him.

"It's De Villiers-Blyth."

The four stood in silence staring at the body.

"Can you see how he died?" Lily asked.

"Hang on, let's have a closer look."

Archie examined the body and rolled it back over.

"Yes, he's been shot in the back of the head, twice by the look of it."

Noah leaned forward, "That looked like a professional hit, he's been executed."

The silence was tangible as they stood staring at the body.

Noah looked at Flynn. "Not a word to anyone, this is highly sensitive. But I will need to speak to those men. Tell them I'm not interested in their night activities, we just need to talk to them."

"Yes, of course, I will keep this to myself. If I see them again, I will ask them to contact you."

"Thank you, Flynn, and thank you for your help."

"Tom, can you get Dr Stagg out here, this is no ordinary killing. We need to know the time of death. I'll get Jack to secure the area. Tom, can you wake him and bring him? Take the Land Rover and we will do a preliminary search of the area. Oh, and can you arrange an ambulance to pick the body up?"

As the light of dawn broke the darkness, there was a faint mist lying across the ground. The three searched the area around the body, but there was nothing to be found. In the distance, they could hear the sound of the Land Rover's engine purring.

They all stood watching Tom driving towards them, silhouetted in the early dawn.

"What have we here?" Doctor Stagg said as he climbed out, looking somewhat dishevelled.

"It looks like he's been shot in the back of the head. Can you give us any idea how long he's been dead?" Noah enquired.

"It's difficult to say, the fact the body has been outside and the temperature has been chilly doesn't help."

"Just a rough idea would help," Noah pushed for an answer.

"This is only a guess, but as the grass hasn't wilted and there are no insects present under the body. He was probably dumped here sometime after being shot. Rigor mortis has started to subside, this typically occurs around twelve to eighteen hours after death. His body is becoming more relaxed. I would suggest death occurred over twelve hours ago and probably more like eighteen. I'll know more when I get him back to the morgue."

"Thank you, doctor. I will arrange to have the body moved, once we have photographed the scene."

In the distance, the sound of ambulance bells ringing out could be heard. Noah had sent Jack back to Ball Road to wait for them and show them the way to the body.

"Why here, what was De Villiers-Blyth doing in a field, during the night in the middle of nowhere? We need to speak to those poachers, they must have seen something." Archie said, looking around with one hand rubbing the back of his neck.

The early morning sun was just breaking through the trees as the medics removed De Villiers-Blyth's body, placing it in the ambulance ready to take it to the morgue in Marlborough.

They watched as the ambulance, with Dr Stagg sitting in the back, slowly disappeared down the narrow dirt track and out of sight.

"This a queer business. Who would want to kill him, unless the Russians have found out he is a double agent? It begs the question, are the Russian agents already here and if so, who are they?" Archie pondered, frowning deep in thought.

"I think we ought to make our way back and all meet up after breakfast, though I'm not sure where at the moment."

"I have a suggestion, we could all meet at the hotel in my mother's private lounge. It's big enough and very private and she's more than happy for us to use it," Archie said looking at Noah.

"If she's happy, then that's perfect. Thank her for me," Noah said.

"Jack, can you give the place a thorough search, and when you've finished, make your way back to the hotel for some breakfast? Lily, have you got enough photographs of the scene or do you need more?" Noah continued.

"No, there's not much to look at really."

Archie, Lily, Tom and Noah climbed back into the Land Rover and were just about to leave when Jack shouted out.

"Over here," he said, pointing to the ground.

"What is it?" Archie asked as he climbed back out.

"Two sets of tyre tracks going in and possibly out of the field, although they look the same tread."

"Well spotted, Jack. I'll get Tom to pick up some plaster of paris and pop back and take some impressions. Can you wait and give him a hand? I'll make sure the hotel keeps a breakfast back for you."

They left Jack guarding the scene and headed back to the hotel.

Thirty-Eight

At seven-thirty a.m. Noah pulled up at the back of the hotel. He was greeted by Tomasz, who was taking breakfast to Brentwood's men in the annexe.

"Ah, Tomasz, I was hoping to catch you. Can you bring Dixon and Martin to Mrs Freestone's private lounge at nine-thirty, and will you be available to join us?"

"Yes I'll bring them over, however, I don't know if I will be able to get away."

"Don't worry I'll sort that out with my Dad, we need all the help we can get," Archie said as he climbed out of the Land Rover.

"Oh, Tomasz, do you know if Maisie had her walk yet?" Lily said being concerned that she had been forgotten.

"Yes, Dotty took her earlier, Maisie is upstairs sleeping."

"Thank you, Tomasz."

"Don't forget the plaster of paris and to pick Jack up." Noah turned to Tom as he left.

"No sir, I'll just grab something to eat and go to Walkers when he opens at nine to get the plaster."

On their way through the foyer to the dining room, Archie noticed his father in the back office. Leaving

Lily and Tom, he went over to speak to him.

"Dad, are you busy? Can I have a word?"

Archie explained the situation regarding Tomasz and that they needed all the help they could get.

"Of course, consider him working for you, whenever you need him. It's far more important he helps you, we will manage, don't worry."

"Thank you, Dad, I appreciate it. I need to make a telephone call to Major Osborne"

Henry left Archie to call the major and report on the night's events.

"Thank you for letting me know, Freestone. I'll come straight over, would you like me to bring a couple of men to help out?"

"Yes, that would be very helpful, we have a lot going on at the moment. Can I suggest you go straight to the morgue in Marlborough, we need someone to officially identify the body, then can you meet us at the police station in Pewsey. Also, it would be advantageous if you all came armed and in plain clothes."

"Yes, of course, we will go to Marlborough straight away."

"Thank you major, I look forward to seeing you later."

Tom and Lily were waiting for Archie as he entered the dining room. The three settled down to a very welcome breakfast, it had been a long night.

"Tom, have you heard of any strangers hanging around Pewsey at the moment?"

"No, not really Archie. All the newcomers are booked into your hotel. Nothing has turned up going door-to-door, I have been keeping an eye out for any strangers, Pewsey is a small place, so it would be hard to conceal someone without anybody knowing."

"More coffee?" Ruth interrupted their conversation.

"Not for me, thank you, Ruth," Lily said.

"Nor me, thank you."

"That would be most welcome, thank you," Tom said, holding his cup up for her.

When they had finished Tom left to pick up Jack and the plaster of paris, while Lily and Archie went to their rooms to change. In his room, Archie looked at the clock. A quarter to nine, I've still plenty of time to see Mum before meeting the others, he thought to himself and made his way to her lounge.

Emily was relaxing with one leg resting on the small pouffe, Maisie was curled up beside her and didn't even move when Archie entered the room.

"What has Dotty done to her, she looked exhausted."

"Hello darling, Dotty has a habit of striding out. I'm not sure if Maisie actually appreciates it. What happened last night? I hope your meeting goes well today."

Archie explained a little of the night's events and told her not to worry, they had everything under control. There was a knock on the door.

"It's only me," Lily's voice came from outside the

room.

"Come in dear," Emily called.

"I'm sorry, but Noah is here along with Brentwood's men, can-"

"I'm just leaving, come on Maisie it's time we were going. These gentlemen need the room."

"Thank you, Mum. I will let you know when we have finished."

"I'll get Ruth to bring you tea, coffee and biscuits later."

"That would be lovely, thank you."

"Can you keep the smoke down, please it's not good for Maisie."

"Yes, I will tell them."

"Have you seen Tomasz?" Archie enquired, looking at Lily.

"Yes, he's just on his way. He is waiting for Dotty to take over from him," Lily replied, settling herself just under the open window.

Soon all six were sitting waiting for Noah to start. Archie lit his pipe, while Noah had another cigarette. Fortunately for Lily, neither Dixon nor Martin smoked, so for a change the room wasn't being choked with smoke.

"Sergeant Hopkins will be joining us when he's finished at the crime scene and Jack will take charge of the police station when he has finished his breakfast. I know I don't have to say this, but what is said in this room stays in the room."

Noah relayed what had occurred during the night,

then briefed Brentwood's men on the murder of Valentino's wife, Reverend Ward missing and Valentino being safely locked away.

There was a loud knock on the door.

"That must be Tom. Come in," Archie shouted.

The large reassuring presence of Tom Hopkins stood filling the doorway, quietly followed by Ruth, carrying a large tray of drinks and biscuits.

"Where would you like these?" Ruth looked around for somewhere to put it down.

"I'll take that, Benjamin Martin stood up," He took the tray from Ruth, who looked a little flustered.

Martin was a dashing young man with neatly Brylcreemed dark hair wearing a tailored suit. Lily noticed there was an attraction between them.

"What news, Tom?" Archie puffed gently on his pipe.

"I've taken casts of the tyre tracks, Jack will send them off to London for analysis. Oh yes, before I forget, Jack said he stayed quite late outside Mrs Ward's house, and someone else is staying there."

"How does he know?" Lily leaned forward in her chair.

"Apparently Mrs Ward went out, quite late and after she had gone Jack hung around for a while, he was just leaving and a light came on in one of the rooms. He stayed a bit longer and then another light came on in a different room, he couldn't make out who they were."

"Right, Martin, I'll get the sergeant to show you

where Mrs Ward lives, can you keep an eye on the place and I'll get Jack to relieve you later this afternoon?"

"Do you think this has anything to do with Valentino, sir?"

"We can't rule anything out at the moment. Keep me posted if you see anything."

"Do we have any idea where Valentino's men are?" Dixon enquired.

"We can't be sure that they are Valentino's men and they seemed to have vanished. I'll give you a description of Mrs Ward and the two Italians before you go."

Noah described Coombes, Braithwaite, and Florence Ward to Martin.

Tom then took him to a small wooded area opposite the rectory, where he could see the rectory clearly, but would be well hidden, before heading back.

***

"There are a couple of things we need to look at," Archie said.

"There is Isenberg, who we saw coming from Ball Road at around the same time as De Villires was possibly shot and we need to talk to Mrs Ward, who appears to be hiding something."

"Can I leave that to you and Lily? I need to find Coombes and Braithwaite. Do you need any help?"

"No, we'll be fine, if we need any help we know where you are."

Noah and Dixon thanked Emily for kindness before leaving the hotel. They went back to the police Station, leaving Archie and Lily to speak to Mrs Ward and Isenberg after lunch.

Thirty-Nine

As they passed the small wooden copse opposite the rectory. Archie discreetly nodded to Ben Martin, who was hidden among the bushes. They stood at the end of the drive, studying the house to see if there was anything unusual going on. At the front door, Archie pulled on the large bell and waited. The door creaked partially open and Florence Ward peered through the small opening.

"Hello, Archie, what can I do for you, is it about my husband?"

"Can we come in?"

"I was just about to go out, is it important?" Florence said in an attempt to avoid talking to them.

"It won't take long and we do need to talk to you."

"Very well, come in." She reluctantly invited them in.

"Go through to the sitting room, I'll be with you in a minute."

In the sitting room, Archie carefully scanned the room to see if anything had changed. The stack of Bibles was still neatly stacked on the small coffee table, nothing appeared to have changed. Lily sank into the large settee while Archie studied the books that ladened the shelves.

"Would you like anything to drink?" Florence broke Archie's concentration.

"No thank you, we've just had lunch."

"Are you still on your own or has someone come to stay with you?" Lily, a little impatient, asked.

"Yes and no, yes I am still on my own and no there's no one else staying here. Why do you keep asking?"

"You were seen leaving the rectory yesterday evening and several lights were switched on and off whilst you were out. Can you explain?" Lily pushed Florence.

"Yesterday evening," a thoughtful Mrs Ward said.

"I'm not sure what you've been told, but I didn't leave the rectory at all yesterday."

Archie leaned forward in his chair.

"We have a very reliable witness that said otherwise."

Mrs Ward shuffled uncomfortably in her chair.

"Ah yes, I did have a visitor, Mrs Fishwick, who wanted to know what was happening at the church during Easter. I would suggest that whoever thinks they saw me has mistaken me for her. Instead of questioning me about what appears to be nothing, your time would be better spent searching for my husband. Now I have to go out. Do you need anything else?"

"One thing, do you know where Mrs Fishwick lives?" Archie enquired.

"Not really, I believe she lives with her husband

somewhere near the hospital. Perhaps Wilcot Road. That is all I know, I really have to go," Florence said, becoming more agitated.

"Thank you, we may need to speak to you again."

Mrs Ward ushered Archie and Lily out of the front door and watched them disappear down the drive. At the bottom of the drive, Archie turned around with his head slightly tilted and gave a final look back at the rectory, then arm in arm he and Lily walked slowly back to the hotel, deep in thought.

"There's something not quite right, I can't imagine Jack would have mistaken Mrs Ward for someone else. Still, Tom will know where the Fishwick's live, we'll pop into the station and check."

When they reached the hotel entrance the Delfonty's rushed out and brushed past them, almost knocking Lily over.

"Are you alright? What's their hurry?" Archie said as he steadied Lily.

"I'm fine, thank you. It looked like they've had a bit of a lover's tiff and she stormed off."

Archie watches them as Mr Delfonty waves his arms frantically pleading with her to come back.

She squeezed Archie's hand. "That will never be us, we will always talk any problems through,"

"Yes, it is important to be honest with each other. I can't ever imagine arguing with you."

They watched the Delfontys, still arguing past the statue of King Alfred onto North Street and then out of sight.

"I'll just pop in and see if there are any messages," Archie said.

In the hotel, Tomasz was sitting at the reception desk reading.

"Hello Tomasz, it seems very quiet. Have any messages been left for me?"

"Yes, it has been very quiet other than the din the Delfonty's were creating. No, no messages. But, when I was walking earlier there were two men I didn't recognise walking down Marlborough Road from the station."

"That's interesting, what did they look like?"

"I can't be sure but I had the feeling they were policemen. It was more of an instinct, there was something about them. But I could be wrong, so I followed them, and they went to the Greyhound."

"Can you describe them?" Archie's interest was piqued.

"They were quite tall, I should think." Tomasz pondered for a moment.

"Yes, about six foot and slim. They both wore dark double-breasted, pin-stripe three-piece suits and long raincoats that were unbuttoned and wore trilbys, which I thought strange as the weather was so warm. Oh, and one had one of those thin pencil moustaches."

"Thank you Tomasz, that is very interesting, we'll check it out."

Having finished his lunch at the hotel, Jacob was outside talking to Lily, who was waiting for Archie.

"Hello Jacob, any news?" Jacob was always a great

source of information about the goings on in Pewsey.

"Hello Archie, no nothing new. When there is, I'll let you know."

They chatted for a while and said goodbye to Jacob and made their way to the police station.

Archie was eager to check out The Greyhound.

"Would you like a drink before we meet with Noah?"

"Yes, why not."

"Shall we try The Greyhound? There's something I want to look into." Archie explains what Tomasz had told him.

Lily, always inquisitive, agreed, "I think we ought to."

When they arrived at the Greyhound, they made their way through the hotel, to the lounge bar. Inside, a thick smoky atmosphere dominated the crowded room. Archie scanned carefully around the room, trying to see if anybody matched Tomasz's description. In the corner were two men who fitted the bill, sitting back in their chairs and observing everyone in the room.

"That's them, over there," Archie whispered.

"I see what Tomasz means, they do look like policemen," Lily observed.

"We need to keep an eye on them and inform Noah. I'm not sure what they are doing here. Of course, we could be wrong about them."

They decided to leave the Greyhound, and straight to the police station. At the reception desk, a very enthusiastic Jack greeted them.

"The inspector is expecting you and said to go straight through and, Archie, he has three official-looking men with him."

Archie thanked Jack, and he and Lily went to Noah's office. Upon entering the crowded room, the normal thick cloud of smoke greeted them.

Noah beckoned to them. "Come in, we've been expecting you."

Opposite Noah sat Major Reggie Osborne who immediately stood up and shook both Archie and Lily by the hand.

"Good to see you, old chap. I'm sorry but I can't stay, I'm needed back at the garrison. But these are two of my most trusted men: Sergeant Les Whiting and Private George Keeling." They both promptly stood to attention.

Osborne continued, "Stand easy men. You can trust these gentlemen implicitly. I've agreed with the inspector to leave them at your disposal."

"Thank you, Major. I have a feeling we will need them. Did you see the body?"

Osborne, leaving the office, looked back. "Yes, it was De Villiers-Blyth, keep me up to date on developments. We will speak soon."

Overwhelmed by the smoke and heat, Archie heads straight for the window and opens it. Lily quietly thanked him. Sitting with his back to the incident board and smoking another cigarette Noah acknowledged Archie and Lily's arrival.

"Find yourselves a seat and we can go through what we know so far."

Lily sat under the open window while Archie sat beside her and looked at Noah.

"Before we start there have been some inconsistent statements up at the rectory." Archie proceeded to explain what had taken place when they visited Mrs Ward earlier that morning.

"Can we still use one of Brentwood's men to keep an eye on the place?" Archie enquired.

Noah reflected for a moment. "Yes, Dixon, can you take over from Martin, Sergeant Hopkins will show you where Martin and the rectory is located."

Deep in thought Archie sucked on his pipe, sending rings of smoke into the room.

"We may have another problem. We are not sure but it appears that two out-of-town policemen are in the village. They are in The Greyhound at the moment, can I suggest you put one of the major's men on them? Archie gave Noah a description of the two men.

"Sergeant Whiting can you-?"

There was a loud thump on the door.

An eager Jack pops his head around the corner. "I'm sorry to trouble you, sir, but there are two officers from Whitechapel in reception for you."

"Did they say what they want?"

"They will only speak to you, sir."

Standing in the doorway, Noah looked back. "This should be interesting."

Forty

On such a hot day, Noah's attention was drawn by the long dark raincoats worn by the two men hovering by the reception desk.

"Can I help you, gentlemen?"

One of them moved menacingly in front of Noah. "I think you know why we're here."

"I'm sorry, who are you?"

"Detective Sergeant Brooks and this is Detective Constable Haynes attached to Leman Street nick. We have a warrant for the arrest of Leonardo Valentino and orders to take him back to Whitechapel."

"Who's orders?"

"Chief Superintendent Booker."

Noah considered the situation. "What is he charged with?"

Brooks thought for a while. "It's classified and none of your business."

"Well, three things, firstly you have no jurisdiction here, secondly he's a suspect in the murder of his wife and thirdly he's not here."

At that, Brooks thumped his fist on the counter, reached over and grabbed Noah by the collar.

"Am I not making myself clear, we don't deal in jurisdictions nor your trivial village murder case.

Don't make me ask again, where is he?"

There was an uneasy atmosphere and tempers were starting to rise.

"Is there a problem Inspector?" The reassuring figure of Sergeant Tom Hopkins filled the station doorway, returning from having shown Dixon where the rectory was.

"No sergeant, these gentlemen are just leaving."

An indigent Brooks turned to face Tom and reached into his jacket.

Archie appeared from the back office holding his pistol, with an air of authority he quietly spoke into the situation. "I wouldn't do that if I were you. Tom, can you take their guns?"

Taken by surprise, Brooks and Haynes looked at Archie and held their arms out to their sides, allowing Tom to remove them. As he moved in to take Hayne's however, Haynes lunged at Tom, missing him, he fell awkwardly to the floor. In the confusion, Brooks managed to grab Noah around the throat and almost dragged him over the counter.

With all the commotion that was going on, Brooks hadn't noticed Osborne's men who had silently appeared from Noah's office. He soon felt their full force, as they dragged him off Noah and forced him onto the floor.

Noah, slightly shaken, straightened his jacket and glowered at Brooks and Haynes. "Throw them into the cells and charge them before I lose my patience."

"You can't charge us, we're police officers and

you'll answer to Chief Superintendent Booker."

Noah leaned on the counter and stared at them. "Charge them with assault and battery on a police officer and resisting arrest. Sergeant, read them their rights and lock them up."

"With pleasure." growled Tom.

Sergeant Whiting lifts Brooks off the floor. "You won't get away with this Jackson. I have to telephone the chief at seven o'clock, if I don't he will be straight down here and your head will roll."

Noah casts a wry smile at Brooks. "Well, we will see about that. Now take them away."

Tom and Whiting led them to the cells, while the others returned to Noah's office.

A tense atmosphere permeated the air. Noah leaned back in his chair and lit yet another cigarette. "I need to telephone my old boss, he needs to be kept in the picture."

Archie agreed and turned to Tom who had just re-entered the room. "Tom, have you heard of the Fishwicks?"

"Joshua Fishwick, yes, why do you ask?"

"Apparently his wife visited Mrs Ward yesterday evening. Do you know where they live?"

"Well, he lives at eighty-three Wilcot Road and Mrs Fishwick is buried in St John's cemetery. So unless that was her ghost, it certainly wasn't her."

Archie and Lily looked at each other. "We need to get a search warrant for the rectory and see what is going on." Archie continued. "Noah, can you arrange that?"

"As soon as I have telephoned Superintendent Brentwood, consider it done."

Archie filled his pipe and turned to Tom again. "How did the door-to-door go, did you find anything out?"

"No, nothing to report back. There's no sign of the two Italians anywhere."

A tense silence hung in the air as everyone contemplated the twists and turns of the day's events.

Archie stood up. "Before we go, can I make a suggestion?"

Noah leans back and puts his hands behind his neck. "Anything at the moment."

"I'm not sure if you think this a good idea, I would like to take a few men and organise a dawn raid on the rectory. There is definitely something going on up there."

"What time did you have in mind?"

"Five o'clock."

"Count me in," Lily said,always up for a challenge.

"Me too," Tom and Martin said in unison.

Standing up, Noah smiled with a certain amount of enthusiasm. "Shall we meet here at, say, four thirty?

"What about the search warrant," Lily quietly remarked.

"Don't worry about that, leave it to me."

Slowly they all made their way out of the office. Jack left to relieve Dixon outside the rectory, while the others returned to the hotel. They were leaving

Noah to telephone Brentwood and arrange the search warrant.

Looking back Archie said. "See you in the morning, bright and early." He turned and left with Lily.

Noah nodded. "Yes, see you in the morning."

Archie and Lily walked along North Street as the setting sun cast long shadows on the ground, giving the sky a warm orange glow.

"This is beautiful," Lily snuggled into Archie. "I can't think of anywhere else I would rather be or with anyone else."

Archie stopped and looked around. "Yes, this is perfect and I'm with the perfect person."

The foyer was bustling with people down for the Easter weekend holiday. Tomasz was booking several couples into the hotel and noticed Archie and Lily as they walked past him.

"Archie," he called out then quietly said.

"Noah has phoned, the ballistics report on the shell casing in De Villiers-Blyth's murder has come in and he also said everything is sorted out for tomorrow."

Taking Tomasz to one side, Archie asked. "Are you free first thing tomorrow morning?"

"What time?"

"Four o'clock."

Tomasz's inquisitive nature took over. "Yes, it sounds intriguing. What do you want me to do?"

Archie explained about the morning's raid and at

the same time kept him up to date with all that had happened during the day. Tomasz handed him a small scrap of paper. "I wrote down the inspector's message just in case I got it wrong."

Thanking Tomasz, Archie took the note and joined Lily in the lounge.

"I've got you a whisky, what did Tomasz want?"

"Thank you, the ballistics report has come in."

"What does it say?"

Archie straightened the crumpled paper. "Let's have a look. That's interesting. The casing is from a pistol used by the Soviet Armed Forces. It's from a TT-30, commonly known as the Torkafev, a semi-automatic pistol."

Archie sipped his whisky, deep in thought, and glanced at his watch. "It's getting late. Shall we eat? You must be starving."

"I thought you would never ask," a broad smile came across Lily's face.

The dining room was quiet as Archie and Lily ate their meal. Lily took Archie's hand. "You're very quiet. What are you thinking?"

"A Russian pistol, an execution. Our spy is already here, but who and where, at the moment I can't think who it could be.? Also, I must remember to telephone the major and keep him in the picture."

Lily reflected. "What about this Isenberg character? We saw him in Ball Road not far from the shooting."

Archie nodded. "Yes, we must speak to him, but

tomorrow will do. Shall we go to the lounge and have a nightcap, we have an early start?"

Forty-One

Friday 15th April (Good Friday)

The sound of the alarm woke Archie with a start. He rolled over and hit the bells on top of the clock to stop the noise. He checked the time, three thirty. *Time to get up*, he thought to himself.

Tomasz, Lily and Brentwood's men were waiting in the hotel's foyer.

Henry was at the reception desk and a very excited Maisie was jumping up and down trying to get Lily's attention.

Archie, doing his jacket up, came dashing down the stairs. "Am I late?"

"Not at all, in fact, we're a little early," Lily said.

"Down old girl, not this morning, Dotty will take you for your walk later. We have a very busy day ahead." Maisie had turned her attention on to Archie hoping to be taken for an early walk.

"Good morning Dad."

"This all looked very intriguing, what are you all up to?"

Ushering the group out of the front door, Archie turned to Henry. "I can't explain now, but no doubt you will hear all about it later."

"Be careful."

"We will."

Outside the early morning air was crisp and clear as they made their way to the police station where they found Tom outside, clapping his hands together to keep warm.

"Good morning, the others are inside waiting for you."

"Good morning Tom, are you joining us?"

"I'm waiting for Jack, he's a bit late. It's not like him."

Archie looked up and down the road to reassure Tom he said. "He did have a late night, he's probably overslept. I shouldn't worry, he'll turn up."

The front counter was bustling. Noah, shrouded in smoke, was talking to Sergeant Whiting and Private Keeling. There was an air of anticipation mixed with a great deal of excitement.

Noah bangs on the desk. "Can I have your attention please? Good morning everyone, thank you for coming."

The room fell silent as Noah explained how he wanted the raid to be carried out.

Looking at Dixon. "Right, can you and Martin go straight around the back and cover the rear of the house? Tomasz can you check the potting shed and any other outbuildings, Whiting go with him? The rest of us will go into the house, Archie and Lily you check upstairs, Martin and Tom you're with me downstairs."

Tom, who was standing half inside the main door, remarked, "What about Jones, sir?"

"He was up late watching the place, so he is going to meet us there and will guard the front door to make sure no one sneaks out. Do we all know what we are doing, and are you all armed?"

They unanimously nodded their heads in agreement, and with tense excitement, left the police station.

There was an eerie silence as they proceeded along River Street toward Church Street. No one said a word, there was a nervous energy that was quite tangible. Soon they were staring up the long driveway that led to the rectory. Jack had already arrived and was waiting by one of the large gate pillars.

Noah turned and faced them. "Are we ready? Then let's go."

Dixon and Martin headed straight for the back of the house, while Tomasz and Whiting went to the outbuildings. After giving them time to get into place Noah thumped on the large heavy main door.

"This is the police, open the door."

A light came on in one of the upstairs rooms and the sound of someone moving about could be heard.

"If you don't open this door we will break it down, now open up."

An upstairs window opened. "Who is it?"

"The police, open this door."

"Hold on."

"Right, I've waited long enough, Tom let's get this

open." Noah said after waiting some time.

As Tom was just about to put his shoulder to the door it creaked open.

Florence Ward peered through the crack of the partly opened front door, clearly surprised "What do you want at this hour?"

"I have a warrant to search these premises, now move aside."

Her jaw dropped, eyes widening in disbelief. "Why, what are you looking for?"

Pushing their way into the house. "There have been reports of someone else staying here. With your husband still missing we have to follow up on every report. Mrs Ward, is your husband staying here?"

"No, for the last time, there is no one else staying here. I don't know what else to say."

Archie and Lily proceeded upstairs, guns at the ready, while Tom and Martin went straight into the kitchen.

They made their way cautiously along the corridor that led to the bedrooms, Archie opened the door to the first room and slowly went in. After checking the wardrobes and under the bed and finding nothing moved on to the next room. In each room, they drew a blank. "No one here and nothing out of place."

Lily looked at Archie. "What about the attic?"

"Just what I thought, can you pass me the chair behind you?"

Archie stood on the chair and opened the hatch. He carefully peered into the dark void. "Pass me the torch would you, it's as black as the ace of spades up there."

Shining the light into the dark space, Archie heaved himself up into the attic.

"Do be careful, Archie."

"There's nothing up here but cobwebs, it doesn't look like anybody has been in here for years."

Archie lowered himself back down and joined Lily on the landing. "Well, we've checked everywhere and there's certainly no one staying up here."

Downstairs, every room in the house had been turned inside out, but there was no sign of anybody staying there.

"Nothing upstairs," Archie said, as they came down the stairs.

"Let's wait and see whether Tomasz has found anything outside," Noah said.

Several minutes later Tomasz came through the front door. "We didn't find anything outside."

An indigent Mrs Ward scowled at Noah. "I hope you're satisfied. I said no one was staying here. Now, can you leave me in peace and concentrate on finding my husband?"

Noah looking puzzled turns to face Mrs Ward. "Mrs Fishwick? You said she visited you on Wednesday evening. Was she a ghost?"

"What do you mean?"

"Mrs Fishwick died several years ago, so can you-?"

She interrupted Noah. "That's the name she gave

me, I've never met her before and they don't attend church. She just wanted to know what was happening over Easter, that's all I can tell you."

"Can you describe her?"

Mrs Ward thought for a while. "She was pretty ordinary, I can't think of anything that comes to mind, She was about my height, slim and had dark hair. Oh, yes she had a slight accent."

"What accent, can you remember?"

"I'm not good at accents, but if I had to guess I would say German. Does that help?"

"Thank you, it may. I'm sorry for troubling you, but we have to investigate every report. Your husband is our priority; you must understand."

"Yes, I'm sorry. I'm so worried about John. I keep thinking the worst."

Archie looked across at Lily and then at Mrs Ward. "Can you remember what she was wearing?" he asked.

"I don't take much notice of that sort of thing. But saying that, I think she had a blue dress on and oh yes, it had white spots on it."

"Thank you, Florence. We won't disturb you again."

As there was nothing else they could do, Archie suggested they all head back to the hotel for breakfast.

Returning to the hotel Noah pulls Archie to one side. "I don't understand, how could we have got it so wrong."

Archie thought for a moment. "I think we were

short on suspects and we were grasping at straws and possibly seeing things that weren't there."

"Yes, you're probably right. So it's back to square one, two bodies and a missing vicar. But are they somehow connected and where do we go from here?"

"Breakfast first," Lily, who had caught them up, said with a smile.

Taking Lily's arm in his, Archie agreed. "You're right, we need to take stock and I always think better on a full stomach."

Forty-Two

Ruth was setting the tables for the breakfast service and being so early the room was empty.

"Good morning Ruth, there are ten of us for breakfast, is that okay?"

When Ruth saw Archie and the others, her face lit up as she caught Benjamin Martin looking at her, and she smiled. "Yes, I think we can manage that."

The room became full of noisy chatter and a smokey haze filled the restaurant. When they had finished eating Noah returned to the police station with Tom and Jack. Brentwood's men went back to their rooms to change, while the major's men returned to Parkhill Garrison. Archie and Lily went to their rooms to freshen up.

They had all agreed to meet in Emily's lounge later that morning.

***

There was a knock on Archie's door. "Are you ready to go down?"

Archie recognised Lily's voice. "Yes, I won't be a jiffy, I'm just coming."

Making their way down the main staircase, Archie

noticed Isenberg at the reception desk.

Starting to hurry he pulled Lily by the arm. "We need to talk to him before he goes out."

"Mr Isenberg, can we have a word?"

"I'm very busy and I don't have time at the moment."

"This won't take long, just a few minutes."

Isenberg was becoming a little irritated. "No, I'm sorry, I'm too busy.

Archie grabbed Isenberg's arm. "It's not a request, now come with us,"

Archie and Lily led a complaining Isenberg through to the back office.

"Take a seat, Mr Isenberg."

Lily sat opposite him while Archie stood behind her.

"What right do you people have to question me, who are you working for?"

"We are attached to the police and have full authority here in Pewsey. Tell me, Mr Isenberg, what are you doing here in Pewsey and what were you doing in Ball Road on Tuesday evening?"

"I've nothing to hide. I am working for the government, implementing the Countryside Protected Act."

Archie looked a little puzzled. "Countryside act, I haven't heard of that, what is it?"

Isenberg quoted the act word for word.

"The 1949 Act's main provisions are national parks, areas of outstanding natural beauty and national nature reserves; for public rights of way to be formally mapped and managed; long-distance routes (now known as national trails); and improved public access to open country."

"What is your part in this?" Lily asked.

"I'm mapping public rights of way and the public's access to the countryside. Something that is not popular with some farmers. So I keep myself to myself."

Archie looked at Lily.

"Thank you, Mr Isenberg, we will have to check your story. What department do you work for?"

"The National Parks Commission."

"Where are they located?"

"3 Chester Gate, Marylebone, London."

Lily Stood up. "One thing Mr Isenberg, did you see anything or anybody in Ball Road that evening?"

Isenberg thought for a minute. "Yes, a man was walking toward the pub and there was also a woman walking the same way.

Lily sat back down. "Can you describe them?"

"From what I can recollect he was quite tall and upright, that's all I remember of him. The only thing that comes to mind about her was that she was short. Other than that I can't help you anymore, that's all I can recall."

"Thank you, Mr Isenberg, sorry to trouble you," Archie said, opening the office door. "Oh, by the way, don't leave Pewsey until we say so."

Isenberg, leaving the office, shrugged his shoulders

and grunted. "I won't."

Watching Isenberg, shoulders hunched, shuffle out through the main door. Archie turns to Lily.

"Coffee and biscuits in the lounge before the others get here."

"That sounds nice."

The lounge was deserted and stale smoke from the previous night was suspended in the air. Knowing Lily's aversion to smoke, Archie quickly opened all the windows to clear the air.

"Thank you, Archie."

Settling back into the large comfortable armchair, Lily asked "Could the tall man be De Villiers-Blyth."

"I can't help thinking that it could be, but who is this woman and is it just a coincidence?"

"We don't believe in coincidences," Lily cut in.

"No, we don't," Archie said with a broad smile.

The sound of rattling cups takes Archie's attention.

"Coffee," Ruth said, entering the lounge.

"Thank you, Ruth. Just pop it down there."

Lighting his pipe and sipping his coffee, Archie mused. "We need to find this woman, she may have nothing to do with anything. But we need to rule her out of our investigations."

Just then Dotty pops her head around the lounge door. "Archie, Noah's on the telephone for you."

"Thank you, Dotty, I'm just coming."

Archie made his way to the hotel office. "Hello Noah, how can I help?"

"I wanted to speak to you before we all met up.

I've just had a call from Special Branch. They say that Salvatore Buccafusca and Alfio Rizzuto are not Valentino's men. Their informant confirms that they have been hired by Luciano Bagarella to eliminate Valentino. Bagarella is a member of Valentino's mob and believes he has grown weak and has the support of other mob members to take over. These people have no respect for the law and are capable of anything, so let's be vigilant."

"Hmm, we need to find Buccafusca and Rizzuto before they cause any trouble," Archie pondered.

"Yes, but at the moment we have to carry on as normal with our investigations. Special Branch said they have informed Devizes Police Headquarters and if we need them they will send some extra men over. Keep this to yourself for the moment, at least until we know more."

A very pensive Archie returned to Lily in the lounge and explained what he had learnt from Noah. The two sat silently, trying to make sense of it.

"As if we don't have enough on our plates, we don't need an inter-gang warfare here in Pewsey," Archie said.

A thoughtful Lily took Archie's hand. "I still can't put the pieces of this jigsaw together. Are they connected?"

"I'm just not sure. Noah said he has sent Jack to the station to keep an eye on anybody strange coming from London. Oh and he also said he would be a bit late to the meeting."

The clock struck ten-thirty and Les Whiting and George Keeling popped their heads around the door. "Ah, there you are Archie, just to let you know we're back."

"Can you make your way up to the lounge, we'll be right behind you."

Archie and Lily noticed Dixon, Martin and Tomasz were making their way up the main staircase toward Emily's room. As Archie and Lily reached Emily's lounge, Tom's voice came from behind them.

"Room for one more."

"Always room for you Tom," Archie replied with a smile.

Entering the room, they were greeted by the others.

When they were all settled Archie apologised for Noah being late and recapped on what had occurred earlier that morning.

"I know it was disappointing and it appears we are back at square one. But it was a case of eliminating a possible suspect, so we need to move on. Tom, any sightings of Buccafusca and Rizzuto?"

"No, they've gone to ground somewhere. But I've told people to keep an eye open for any strangers in the area and if they spot anyone, that on no account are they to approach them."

"Thank you, Tom."

"We must make these two our priority, it's of the utmost importance that we find them as soon as possible," Archie said.

A few minutes later Noah hurried into the lounge.

"I'm sorry I'm late, but I've just received the analysis on the tyre track from the field where we found De Villiers-Blyth's body. Interestingly enough they believe it comes from a Morris Traveller. There can't be many here in Pewsey, our focus is on finding that car and the two Italians."

Les Whiting looked across at Noah. "Are they connected?"

"We're not sure, but we have to keep an open mind, especially with everything that's going on."

Lily suggested they search every empty house, garage and building, including farm and commercial ones in the area. Also, to go in pairs, with at least one being armed.

Noah agreed with Lily and assigned pairs to search designated areas.

"Dixon, you and Martin search the area around Strong's Farm and Everleigh Road. Whiting and Keeling along Ball Road and up to Kepnal. Tom can find some spare maps and point you in the right direction."

"There are several on the desk in the foyer Tom, Dad won't mind if you take a few."

"Thanks, Archie, are you and Lily happy to look around Wilcot Road and the area surrounding the hospital? Tom and I will look around the village center."

They all agreed, but before they set off Noah advised. "Remember, take care and don't take any risks, have you all got your guns, good, we'll meet back here when you've finished."

Having been given their orders and maps, they filed quietly out of the lounge and headed off to their allotted locations.

Knowing Lily would be hungry, Archie popped into the kitchen and got Sam to make sandwiches for them.

Forty-Three

The dappled sun shown through the trees as Lily and Archie made their way along Wilcot Road.

Staring up the road, Archie pondered. "We mustn't forget the cemetery chapel, they could be hiding anywhere."

They searched house by house and every garage and building and found nothing. Finally, they entered the cemetery. Archie had a bad feeling.

"I don't like this, there's something not quite right."

He drew his gun and cautiously he and Lily made their way to the small chapel.

Lily whispered. "The door has been forced open."

"This is the police, we're coming in."

Tentatively Archie pushed the large oak door open and with his gun held in front of him, entered. There was a strong smell of dampness in the dimly lit chapel. They carefully made their way through the dusty pews to the altar.

He turned to Lily. "There's nothing here."

As they were leaving, Lily noticed something half hidden behind one of the pillars.

"What is it?"

"Someone has been staying here."

Empty packets of food and cigarette ends littered the place.

"Whoever it was has long gone. It could have been a tramp or possibly the Reverend Ward, although he would have had a key. I think we should be heading back, there is nothing out here."

As they made their way back along Wilcot Road, Tom came running toward them.

"Archie, I'm glad I've found you.

"Dixon and Martin have found a body in some old building on Everleigh Road. Noah has already gone there and is waiting for you both."

Archie, Lily and Tom ran quickly back to the hotel. They found Henry bringing a barrel of beer from the cellar.

"Dad, can I borrow your car? There's been an incident in Everleigh Road and we need to get there."

"Yes, of course, help yourself." Henry reached into his jacket pocket and tossed Archie the car keys.

Soon all three were racing toward the scene and were soon driving up the narrow lane that led to the building. When they arrived and exited the car, they found a strange air of tranquillity. The afternoon sun bathed the derelict building and gave it warmth and a sense of peace.

Peering through the broken wall Archie noticed the body. It was lying almost hidden under a pile of stones that were taken from the walls. Noah was removing some of the stones from the body to see if he could identify who it was.

He looked up and saw Lily. "Lily, have you got your camera? Silly question, of course you do."

Lily rummaged through her handbag, pulled out her camera, and started taking photographs of the scene.

After removing several more stones, Archie noticed a copy of Paese Sera beside the body.

Archie rubbed the back of his head. "Where have I seen that before?"

Lily peered over his shoulder. "Let me have a look. On the train, in Valentino's briefcase. "

"You're right, we need to ….."

"Archie, it looks like we have found our missing vicar."

The three stood over the body. "Yes, I think you're right. Any idea how he died?" Lily asked.

Noah bent down and examined Ward's body. "Nothing obvious, there's no blood or apparent wounds. By the look of him, he has been here quite a while, but we will have to wait for Dr Stagg to be sure."

"I thought we had searched this area, how could we have missed him?" Archie pondered.

Stepping back and looking around Noah stated, "I suppose he would be quite easy to miss under all these stones."

The sound of ringing bells could be heard in the distance as the ambulance raced toward them, closely followed by Dr Stagg.

In no time at all they were pulling into the lane.

"What have you got for me this time," the doctor said, with a rye smile, as they got out of the car.

"It's the Reverend Ward, this way," Noah led him to the body.

Dr Stagg examined him. "Well, because of the advanced stage of decomposition and depending on factors such as temperature, humidity, and the presence of insects or scavengers. I would suggest he's been dead for anything from eight to twelve days. But it is only a guess and that's the best I can do for now."

"Do you have any idea how he died?" Archie asked'

"There's no blood and no obvious wounds. I can't really say at the moment. I'll know more when we get him back to the morgue."

"That is most helpful, thank you doctor. It gives us a rough window to work with. Someone will have to inform Mrs Ward, and bring her to the morgue to officially identify the body." Noah thanked him as the men put the Reverend's body in the back of the ambulance.

As he was leaving Dr Stagg wound down his window. "I'll prioritise my report and see if I can get it to you before the day is out."

"Thank you, doctor, I'll appreciate that."

Archie looked at his watch. "We'll go and break the news to Mrs Ward before going to see Valentino. Shall we bring him straight to the police station when we get back?"

Noah turned to Archie, "Yes, that's probably the best idea. I'll see you there later, although I may be late. I need to pop to the hospital first and I'm not sure how long I'll be."

"We'll manage, see you later." Archie and Lily set off to the rectory.

Pulling up outside the rectory, they waited for a few minutes to compose themselves. Archie rang the front doorbell after a moment Mrs Ward's head peered through the opening.

"Hello Florence, can we come in?"

There was a moment of hesitation.

"Yes, of course, come in. Is there a problem, have you found John?"

"Perhaps it would be a good idea if you could sit down."

The colour drained from her face and she fell back into the chair.

Archie continued, "We have found a body on the Everleigh Road and believe it to be your husband John."

Florence Ward slumped forward in her seat and held her head in her hands.

"When you feel up to it we need you to formally identify the body, which is in Marlborough Hospital.

Lily took Florence's hand, "Can we contact anybody for you? Would you like me to take you to the hospital and stay with you?"

"Thank you Lily, but I will telephone my sister in Woking and ask her to come."

247

"Will you be alright on your own," Archie asked.

"Yes, I have been expecting bad news and have prepared myself for the worst. I know you are both busy and need to find out how he died, so do feel free to go."

Archie and Lily stayed with Florence for a short time. Eventually Archie checked the time.

"Four-thirty. We do need to speak to someone today. So if you're sure you will be okay we will be going."

Florence Ward stood in the half open door and watched Archie and Lily disappear up Church Street toward Everleigh. Twenty minutes later they were pulling up beside the guard house at Parkhill Garrison.

Forty-Four

Getting out of the car they heard the familiar sound of the drill sergeant barking orders, ringing out around the parade ground. Entering the calm of the guardhouse, Sergeant Cooper greeted them.

"Hello, sergeant, can you telephone Major Osborne and tell him Freestone and Miss Forester are here to see him and Valentino?"

"Yes sir, straight away."

"Has Mr Valentino been behaving himself, sergeant?"

"On the whole, sir, although he does have a very loud voice. I believe the whole camp knows he's here."

Archie smiled. "Yes, we have had that experience, I'm surprised the whole of Wiltshire hasn't heard him."

"I'm not sure who he is, but he would like us to think he's someone very special."

"He is just a low-life gangster from London," Lily said.

In no time at all Major Orsborne appeared in the doorway.

"Freestone, good to see you and of course you Miss Forester. Come this way."

Major Osborne led Archie and Lily along the narrow dimly lit corridor that led to the cell where Valentino was being held.

"It all seems quiet, major."

"Yes, I'm not sure what happened, but there were one or two complaints about the noise. Apparently, a couple of my M.P.s visited him and since then he's been very quiet," Osborne said with a knowing smile.

They opened the cell door and found Valentino slumped on the floor in one corner. He lifted his head and saw Archie.

"Freestone, you're a dead man," he hollered.

"Come Mr Valentino, that's no way to speak to a representative of the law." the major calmly said.

Archie looked a little surprised. "You're a bit of a mess old chap, did you walk into a door by any chance."

Valentino's face went pale. He gritted his teeth and spat out his words. "You won't get away with this, you're way out of your depth."

"We have two murders, your wife and Reverend Ward. At the moment everything points to you. You can either decide to help us or we can just leave you here, it's entirely up to you."

"You can't pin anything on me, you don't have any evidence."

"We have plenty of evidence."

Running out of patience, Archie pushed Valentino against the cell wall. "Are you at all interested in who murdered your wife?"

"We sort out our own problems. We don't need local plods getting in the way."

"Do the names Salvatore Buccafusca and Alfio Rizzuto mean anything to you?" Lily cuts in.

"No."

"We are informed they have been hired by Luciano Bagarella, who you are familiar with, to kill you. Do you have anything to say?" Lily continued.

Valentino appeared stunned and stared thoughtfully at the floor.

Archie persisted. "Do you know the Reverend Ward?"

"I have nothing to say."

"Why were the contents from your briefcase found near the body of Ward?"

Valentino, still staring at the floor, remained silent.

"Right major, we are obviously not getting very far here, so we'll leave him with you."

"Would you like a couple of my men to have a word with him, I'm sure they can find a way to get the necessary answers you require?"

"I'm very tempted, I'll give it some thought."

Archie, Lily and the Major left the cell and were locking the door.

"Freestone," there was a different tone in Valentino's voice.

"We need to talk," he said quietly.

Archie hadn't seen this side of Valentino and wasn't sure whether he was being genuine.

"Major, can we use an office?

"Yes, I think the Provost Marshal's office is free."

Major Osborne called two M.P.s to escort Valentino to the office.

"Would you like my men to stay with you?"

Archie carefully weighed up the situation. "I think it would be well advised to have your men posted outside the office door. Thank you, Major."

In the Provost Marshal's office, a large table was placed under a picture of King George Vl and papers were neatly stacked beside a typewriter. Valentino sat opposite Archie and Lily.

"Do you have a cigarette?" Valentino asked.

"No, I'm sorry we don't smoke, I'll check if either of the guards do."

As Archie leaves the room, Valentino stares coldly at Lily, who stares back.

"I've dealt with bigger villains than you, you don't frighten me, Mr Valentino."

"There you go," Archie said, returning to the office and handing him a cigarette that was already lit.

Archie leans forward in his chair. "Right, let's start at the beginning. Why did you come to Pewsey?"

"How do you know Bagarella hired Buccafusca and Rizzuto to take me out?"

"I'm asking the questions. Now why-?"

"If I'm going to help you, I need to trust you first."

There was a short silence. Archie looked at Lily. "Well, I don't suppose it will hurt; it's not as if you're going anywhere. I can only tell you what I know. Special Branch has a man working inside your organisation, and he has tipped his boss to what the plan is. At the moment, they have both disappeared, but don't worry—we are the only ones who know where you are, and they won't be saying anything."

"Thank you for being honest. Right, where do I start? I'm not the best husband, I'm probably very hard to live with. I got wind that my wife was leaving me and heard she was in a small Wiltshire village, why Pewsey, I've no idea."

"How did you find out she was in Pewsey?" Lily asked.

"It was sheer chance that one of my men saw her leaving by the back door of our house. She was wearing some kind of disguise but my man still recognised her and followed her. She went to Paddington and bought a ticket."

"Was she on her own?" Archie asked.

"Yes, she got on a train and my man went to the ticket office and enquired, with the help of a pound note, where she was going and it was Pewsey."

"Why did you follow her down here?" Lily asked.

"It's a matter of honour, she's my wife and should be with me in Whitechapel. I came to take her back."

"Did you kill her?" Archie came straight to the point.

"Why would I?"

"Where were you in the early hours of Tuesday the fifth?" Archie continued.

"Tuesday, early. I was in bed at the hotel"

"Can anybody confirm that," Lily pushes him.

253

"I was on my own, so, no I can't."

"I suggest you met her by the bridge, she wouldn't go with you, so you cut her throat," Archie said.

The colour drained from Valentino's face and he dropped his head and mumbled. "Is that how she died?"

"Yes, I'm sorry I thought you knew."

"No, I didn't. Did Buccafusca and Rizzuto murder her?"

"We'll be back in a minute."

Archie and Lily left the office briefly to discuss what Valentino had said, they both agreed he did not kill his wife.

"It was obviously a shock, I think we can rule him out," Archie whispered as they made their way back to the office.

"To answer your question, it's possible, but we're not sure, we have several leads that we are looking into, but nothing concrete yet."

"Mr Valentino, can you explain why your briefcase and contents were found near the body of the Reverend Ward," Archie changed the subject.

"I don't know a Reverend Ward, why would I kill him? And I've already told you I lost my briefcase on Monday last week."

Lily sat back in her chair. "Why are you still here?"

"She was my wife and whoever killed her will pay. I will not leave until I have cut the heart out of the murderer."

"I think we need to take a break. Would you like a coffee, Mr Valentino?"

"Yes, if you don't mind."

The two M.P.s came into the office and stood behind Valentino while Archie and Lily left to speak to the major.

Forty-Five

The major was in the outer office, feet up on the desk reading some documents.

"How did it go," he enquired, sitting up.

"Well I think we can rule him out of murdering his wife, as to the vicar, as yet, I'm not sure," Archie answered.

"Do you trust him?" the Major asked.

Archie thought for a moment. "He certainly looked surprised when we told him how she was murdered, so, yes I think he was telling the truth. But if it's alright with you we would like to continue interviewing him."

"Yes, take as long as you like, I don't have to be anywhere. Do you think he is connected to De Villiers-Blyth?"

"Now, that's another thing, again I'm not really sure. We are keeping an open mind."

Having finished their coffee, Archie decided it was time to go back in. "I think it's time we carry on with the interview," he said.

When they returned they found Valentino sitting quietly between two very large M.P.s. Archie and Lily sat opposite him.

"What's the interest in communism?" Lily said,

hoping to catch Valentino off guard.

"What do you mean?"

We found a copy of Wage-Labour and Capital by Karl Marx and an Italian left-wing newspaper in your briefcase."

"Oh that, yes of course. I've always been interested in the German philosopher and sociologist Karl Marx, as you probably know my mother is Russian and my father is Italian. She used to tell me stories about the Bolsheviks and Lenin who led the October Revolution in Russia. I'm not a communist, I just find Russian Revolutionary Red Army tactics fascinating."

Archie leaned forward, " What do you mean?"

"They terrorized and intimidated their opposition. I've taken a leaf out of their book and it's something that has worked for me and something we are good at."

Archie stood up and stared out of the window and turned to Valentino.

"That's not doing you any good now."

"What do you mean?"

Archie had grabbed Valentino's attention. He sat back down and lit his pipe, drawing on it sending plumes of smoke into the room.

"I'm informed that whilst you left the security of your patch Bagarella has taken over and has the support of your mob. He has also, along with others, put a contract out on you. So the way I see it, going back is not an option, your reign is over and they want you dead. Also, you are facing charges for assault and battery against a police officer, plus resisting arrest, these carry long prison sentences."

Valentino sat forward, his head dropped. He sat silently, trying to take it all in. For the first time, he had nothing to say.

As bad as he was, Lily was starting to feel sorry for him. He had lost his wife and all the people he knew and trusted had turned against him.

It was getting late so Archie decided to call it a day and get back to Pewsey.

"Can you escort Mr Valentino back to his cell and we-"

"Freestone, before you go, can I have a word?"

Archie turned to Valentino. "Go on."

"I find myself in a bit of a corner, so can we make a deal?"

Archie sensed a change in Valentino's mood. "What do you have in mind?"

"It sounds like a lot of people would like to see me dead. People in prominent positions, judges, high-ranking police officers, ordinary bobbies on the beat and plenty more. I can give you all their names, what they're involved in, who they're connected to. But I need something in return."

Archie's attention was captured.

"Go on."

"I need you to drop the charges against me, give me a new identity, and the money to make a new start somewhere nobody knows me."

Archie considered everything Valentino had

requested.

"That's asking a lot. I can't promise, I will have to speak to Inspector Jackson. But you will have my support."

"Thank you." Valentino's demeanour had become more reserved and thoughtful.

Archie left him in the office and joined Lily who was in the outer office along with Major Osborne.

"He wants to turn king's evidence, he is prepared to give us names, other mob members involved in the Leman Street nick and all the high-ranking officials he knows."

"No wonder they want him dead," Lily said.

"We need to keep him safe and hidden. After De Villiers-Blyth, I'm not sure who we can trust."

"Leave it to me, I will put two of my most trusted men to watch him. No harm will come to him, you have my word."

"Thank you, Major, I know I can trust you. As it's getting late we will have to be getting back to Pewsey."

Before leaving Archie went back to see Valentino. "We're leaving now. You will be safe and no one will know you are here. I will do everything I can to get you what you want."

"Thank you, Freestone, you're okay. I wish I had someone like you in my mob, someone I could trust."

Archie gave Valentino a sideward glance, "I don't think that is going to happen."

Valentino smiled back at Archie. "Who knows, a

different time, a different place."

Leaving Valentino and quietly smiling to himself Archie rejoined Lily and the Major in the outer office.

"Thank you Major for all your help, but it's time we were going."

Leaving the garrison Archie and Lily hurried back to Pewsey. It was nine-fifteen when they pulled up at the back of the hotel.

"I hope we can get something to eat, I'm starving."

Archie looked at Lily "I'm sure Sam can rustle something up for us."

The bar was heaving, the sound of clinking glasses and the constant hum of people engrossed in conversation filled the air. Henry and Tomasz were busy behind the bar, while Ruth was on the reception desk.

"Hello Ruth, is Sam still here?"

"Yes, I think he's still in the kitchen."

Archie left Lily talking to Ruth while he went to find Sam. Several minutes later he returned with two plates of sausage and mash.

"Oh, that looked marvellous," Lily said,salivating.

The dining room was deserted.

"I like having the place to ourselves, it gives us time to talk," Lily remarked.

"I know a lot has happened over the last few days, but we need to talk about our wedding. Everytime I see Mum there is a barrage of questions. When would you like our special day to be."

Lily thought for a while. "If I had my way

tomorrow would be perfect," she thoughtfully considered her answer. "Do you know what I would really like, a Christmas wedding in St John the Baptist here in Pewsey."

Archie's face lit up, reaching across the table he took Lily's hand. "That sounds perfect. Christmas it is."

When they finished eating they retired to the lounge for a nightcap before calling it a day.

"Well, it's been quite a day, I must telephone Noah before going up, there's quite a lot to tell him."

Archie disappeared into the back office, leaving Lily to enjoy her single malt and wait for him to return.

"Well that's interesting, some new information has come to light and it doesn't look good for Valentino. As it's late, Noah will explain in the morning when we see him."

"Oh dear, I was just starting to feel sorry for him and to trust him. We will have to wait and see what Noah has discovered." Lily sighed.

"Strangely enough I was just getting to like him too. But we will hear what Noah has to say before making any judgments."

It had been a long day and they were feeling tired and decided to finish their whiskies and retire to their rooms.

Forty-Six

Saturday 16th April (Easter Saturday)

Six-thirty and Archie's alarm was scratching at his door. "Coming old girl, go and wake Lily."

Archie could hear the patter of Maisie's feet running down the hallway towards Lily's room. He was first downstairs and was talking to Henry when Lily and Maisie came dashing down.

"Are we late, there's so much to do before going out?"

"No, not at all we were just talking."

Outside the sun had just risen and shone softly on the houses and streets, it brought a flurry of early morning activity around the village. Archie and Lily with Maisie squeezed tightly between them strolled down the High Street toward Ball Road, as they rounded the corner, a voice rang out.

"Good morning, Archie and Miss Lily and of course you Maisie."

The familiar voice of Jacob came from one of the cottages that lined the street.

"Good morning, Jacob. What a wonderful morning," Archie said, struggling to hold Maisie back.

"Yes, it is. I hear you've found the Reverend Ward up on the Everleigh Road."

Lily turned to Archie. "How does he know?"

"Small village, news travels quickly around here," Archie said quietly with a smile.

"Do you know how he died?"

"No, we are still waiting for the autopsy report."

"Sad business, I liked the man," Jacob sighed.

After chatting for a while they left Jacob to his milk round and arm in arm headed toward Green Drove.

"It is such a beautiful morning it seems a shame we have to go back to the hotel. Do you know what time we are seeing Noah?" Lily asked.

"Yes it is beautiful, it's hard to believe what is going on here at the moment." Archie replied, "He's meeting us at the hotel at ten thirty. Why so late I've no idea."

Snuggling closer to Archie, Lily said. "I'm sure he has his reasons."

"Well, at least it gives us a chance to have breakfast and get changed. Maisie, come back," Archie shouted as Maisie spots a rabbit and heads into the fields. After coaxing her with several treats they managed to get her back on the lead.

"Good girl, Maisie, it's time we were going home."

"Don't forget to pop in and see your Mum. You can tell her what we have decided."

"I will, I won't forget"

***

Archie puffing on his pipe looked at the dining room clock.

"Nine-thirty, it's time we were making a move."

He and Lily left the dining room and headed upstairs. After changing out of his walking clothes Archie headed to Emily's room.

"Hello darling, where have you been hiding? Have you fixed a date yet? Are you getting married in Pewsey? Has Lily told her parents? Have you found the Reverend Ward?"

He kissed his mother on the cheek before replying to her many questions. "Slow down, we've been very busy and yes we have found him, unfortunately he is dead."

"Oh dear, that is so sad for Florence, how is she?"

"Very upset, that's all I can say at the moment. You will be pleased to know we have set a date for the wedding and-"

"When?" Emily interrupted, excitedly.

"Christmas, at St Johns, here in Pewsey."

Emily welled up and was unusually lost for words. "Perfect."

"I have to go and meet Noah in the lounge. But I will call in and see you later and answer all your questions."

Lily was talking to Tomasz while waiting for Archie in the foyer.

"Have you seen Noah yet?" Archie asked.

"No, Tomasz said he is already in the lounge with a strange man and they're expecting us."

The smell of stale tobacco permeated the air in the empty lounge. Noah stood up as they entered the room and called them over. He then introduces Archie and Lily to an overweight man who was sitting with him.

The gentleman had a pointed nose which supported a pair of tortoiseshell glasses. Archie was surprised to see that he was wearing a shabby dark suit.

"This is Cannon Kingsley who runs a women's rescue centre in Spitalfields London. I'll let him explain what he is doing here."

"Mr Freestone, Miss Forester, nice to meet you. Where to start, Reverend Ward has been working at a centre for vulnerable women in Spitalfield, London, for the past two years. He has been using seminars at Deans Yard as a cover, no one knows what he's been doing, not even his wife. Last September a young woman came to the centre, she was very distressed and wanted help, Ward developed a close working relationship with her. Over the next seven months, he devised a plan to help her escape a dangerous and brutal husband."

"Do we know who she is," Lily cut in.

"Isabella Valentino the wife of Leonardo Valentino the head of the Whitechapel mob, a particularly vicious man. Ward and Isabella had planned that she would go in disguise to Pewsey and wait for him to join her; he would then get her to a safe house in Truro, Cornwall."

An uncomfortable silence fell in the room as Archie and Lily considered the situation.

"This doesn't look good for Valentino," Archie sighed.

"What do you mean?" Noah enquired.

Archie did what he always does when he is deep in thought, reached into his jacket pocket, got out his beloved pipe, filled and lit it, drawing on it and sending up rings of smoke. He told Noah about the deal Valentino had put to him and that he and Lily weren't convinced that he murdered his wife.

"What makes you think that?"

"It's only a feeling, but when we told him how his wife was murdered he looked genuinely shocked and upset. But we obviously have to reconsider that he may have actually killed her."

Noah thought for a while. "We still need to talk to him, where have you got him hidden?"

Archie pulled Noah to one side. "The fewer people know where he is the better. All you need to know is he won't escape, I can promise you that."

Noah didn't push Archie for an answer, he trusted his decision.

While Noah and Archie were talking Lily turned to Cannon Kingsley and asked him why he came to Pewsey.

"We were due to meet at the centre last Thursday when he didn't turn up. I tried telephoning his home.

Mrs Ward answered and told me he had gone missing. Knowing the plans he had made regarding Mrs Valentino, I thought I needed to come down and speak to the police."

"Knowing the severity of the situation, why didn't you come down yesterday or telephone the police?"

"I wasn't sure who to trust, Valentino has some high-powered connections, so I didn't telephone. Also, Easter is a very busy time for the clergy and I already had commitments I couldn't get out of, so I came at the very first opportunity."

"Has the Inspector told you we found his body early yesterday morning?"

"No he hasn't. Oh dear, that is so sad. Do you know how he died?"

"We are still waiting for the autopsy report, but it looked like foul play."

"I must go and offer my condolences to Mrs Ward and explain his involvement with the centre in Spitalfield and offer some comfort."

"Yes, I think she would appreciate that, she never questioned his work at Dean Yard."

"Where would you like this?" Ruth said, entering the lounge and balancing a large tray of coffee and biscuits.

"Just pop them on the table, thank you, Ruth," Archie said.

There was an uncomfortable silence as Noah poured the coffee and handed the cups around. The silence was broken by Tomasz popping his head around the lounge door.

"Sorry to butt in, but I thought you should know, Jack has just telephoned the hotel and wanted to speak to the Inspector. I told him you were in a meeting, so he left a message. He said he had found something, he didn't say what but as he was talking the line went dead. It's probably a fault at the telephone exchange and nothing to be concerned about."

"Thank you, Tomasz," Noah said.

Lily glanced at Archie. "I don't like the sound of this. How often does the exchange have a problem?"

"Not very often in my experience," Archie said, concern evident in his voice.

"Tomasz can you check whether there was any trouble at the telephone exchange during the morning?" Noah asked.

"Yes, of course, I will talk to them straight away."

"Where was Jack," Archie asked.

Noah thought for a moment. "Tom sent him out to check garages around the High Street"

"I'm sorry but I must go and speak to Mrs Ward. Can you point me in the right direction?" Cannon Kingsley said, looking at Noah.

Noah directed the Cannon to the rectory. Before he left the lounge he turned to Noah, "I will pop in and see you before going back to London."

"Thank you for your help, Cannon."

"Where's Dixon and Martin?" Archie enquired.

"They are still out looking for Buccafusca and Rizzuto."

A hazy atmosphere due to the lingering smoke from Noah's cigarettes and Archies pipe was slowly filling the room.

Henry stuck his head around the lounge door. "Sorry to disturb you but there's been a message left at the reception desk. I don't understand it. Ruth took the message."

"What did it say?" Archie asked.

"We have your boy, we need Valentino, we will contact you later and give you instructions. If you want him back alive you will do as we say."

There was an unspoken tension as if the air had been sucked from the room. The colour had drained from Noah's face as they stared silently at each other. Archie jumped into action.

Forty-Seven

"Right, we need Dixon and Martin back here. Lily, can you telephone Tom at the police station and find out where Jack was searching? Noah, can you contact Major Osborne, explain the situation, and get Whiting and Keeling back to Pewsey? Tomasz, can you check around the village and see if you can find Dixon and Martin and send them back here? Also, ask around and see if anyone has seen anything?"

"What about Valentino?" Noah asked.

"We have more important things to think about at the moment, he can wait," Archie said, forcefully.

"Tomasz, you don't need to go to the exchange. I'm going to check to see if they know where the telephone call came from. Dad, can we use the back office?"

"Of course, anything to help. Is there anything else I can do to assist?"

"It would be helpful if you could man the telephone in case they call back and we are not here. Also in case we need to liaise with each other."

They all agreed to meet back at the hotel and in no time the lounge was empty. Noah and Lily went to the back office to make their telephone calls. Tomasz was heading out of the main door along with Archie, who was on his way to the telephone exchange.

Outside the newsagents in the High Street, Tomasz bumped into Dixon who was coming out of an alley that ran alongside the shops.

"George I'm glad I've caught you, we need you and Benjamin back at the hotel, something cropped up. Where is Benjamin?" Tomasz said, looking around.

"I'm not sure, he went to check something out about fifteen minutes ago and I haven't seen him since."

Whilst they were talking, Benjamin Martin appeared from round the corner and headed toward them.

"Hello you two, what's going on?"

Tomasz explained the situation. They returned to the hotel leaving Tomasz to continue looking for the Italians.

Arthur Hewit the newsagent had just come out of his shop and was standing on the pavement, as normal, a cigarette was stuck to his lip with a long trail of ash hanging from it, ready to drop off.

"Arthur, I'm glad you're here, you are aware of most things that happen around here, have you heard anything about two Italians in the village from anybody?" Tomasz asked.

"Two Italians?" he thought for a moment. "No nothing. I'm sorry I can't help."

"That's okay, I'll just keep looking. If you do hear anything, can you let the Inspector know."

"Of course."

As Tomasz sets off Arthur calls to him.

"Tomasz, there is something. It may not be important, but one of my paperboys said he saw a light in Thaddeus Feelmore's cottage."

"Is that important?"

"Well, he's away in France at the moment. I didn't take much notice, boys have vivid imaginations and come back with all sorts of tales."

"Where does he live?" Tomasz asked curiously.

"Southcott Villas along Southcott Road you can't miss it, it's the big house with a garden full of tulips."

"It may be nothing, but I'll take a look anyway. Arthur, can you do me a favour?"

"Yes, anything to help."

"Can you telephone the hotel and tell Archie where I've gone."

"I'll do it straight away, Tomasz."

Tomasz thanked Arthur and headed off to Southcott Road.

The occasional barking of faraway dogs broke the afternoon's silence as Tomasz made his way cautiously toward Southcott Villas.

***

At the hotel, Archie and the others had returned and were gathered in the lounge discussing how they had got on.

"Did you find out where the telephone call came

from?" Noah asked Archie.

"Yes, it was at the telephone box on the High Street opposite Ball Road. How did you get on with Major Osborne?"

"Whiting and Keeling are on the way and should be here in about ten minutes."

"Lily, what did Tom say?"

"He had asked Jack to check garages on River Street and along the High Street."

Noah and Archie started to devise a plan to retrace Jack's route when Henry called back into the lounge.

"Archie, Arthur from the newsagents is on the telephone for you."

"Thank you, Dad, I'm just coming."

***

Reaching a short distance from Southcott Villa, Tomasz decided to go into the field that lay behind the villa. There was a small gully that ran along the field that was lined with an overgrown hedgerow. He crouched down and made his way along, hidden by the hedgerow he could get a good look into the villa without being seen. Parting the bushes he peered into the house, there was somebody in there, he thought to himself.

To get a better look he crawled from the field on his stomach to a small log pile in the back garden, hoping to see more clearly into the room. Reaching the pile of wood, he stretched forward to get a better

273

look, in doing so he knocked a log off the top which clattered onto a petrol can lying beside the pile, making a loud noise. The back door flew open and Rizzuto stood at the back door, stepping into the garden, his gun in his hand, he studied the surrounding area.

Tomasz ducked behind the pile of logs, hardly daring to breathe. He could hear the crunch of footsteps getting closer, frozen to the spot, Tomasz couldn't help thinking that this was the end. Rizzuto stopped just short of the log pile and turned his back on Tomasz. An uneasy silence filled the air broken by the ringing of a telephone from somewhere in the house.

Forty-Eight

Tomasz's heart pounded in his chest as he squeezed tightly into the logs, a voice rang out.

"Alfio, ci stanno addosso, dobbiamo andarcene da qui."

Alfio, they are onto us, we need to get out of here.

"Cosa faremo con il poliziotto?"

What are we going to do with the policeman?

"Sparategli, non ci serve a niente adesso."

Shoot him, he is no good to us now.

Tomasz's understanding of Italian was fairly good, he understood exactly what was being said. Noticing a small iron bar beside him he picked it up and with an almighty swing smashed Rizzuto on the back of the head, he sank to his knees and crashed face-first onto the ground, knocking over the small petrol can.

"Stai bene Alfrito?"

Are you alright Alfio?

Tomasz, caught by surprise, managed to reply in his best Italian accent.

"Sì, tutto è pinnato."

Yes, everything's fine.

There was a strange silence and time seemed to stand still as Tomasz edged his way to the back door. Peering through the open door, he could see a

275

reflection in the mirror of Jack on his knees with a gun pointed at the back of his head.

***

Archie along with Lily, Whiting and Keeling were working their way cautiously along the hedgerow toward Southcott Villa's. Suddenly there was a loud bang sending crows scattering into the sky.

The colour drained from Archie's face and he turned to the others.

"That was a gunshot and it came from the villa."

Drawing their pistols they ran toward the house.

"Whiting, Keeling take the front of the house, Lily you're with me around the back."

There was an eerie silence as Archie and Lily inched their way along the side of the house. Archie peered around the corner.

"It all seems quiet."

"Be careful," Lily said.

"I will."

Archie crouched down and crawled under the kitchen window toward the back door, which he noticed had been forced open. He could hear voices coming from inside the house so he made his way to where the sound was coming from.

As he reached the door he noticed Rizzuto's overweight body, with his wavy red hair lying face down on the ground beside a log pile. Standing to one side of the door Archie composed himself and peered around the corner into the kitchen. All he could see half hidden behind a table, was a body lying on the floor that had a pool of blood surrounding it.

Archie took a deep breath and burst through the door, pointing his gun in front of him, shouting

"This is the police, put your weapons down."

"Archie, it's me, we are both okay," Tomasz calls from the backroom.

Carefully entering the room Archie was confronted by Tomasz holding Buccafuscam's gun, Jack with his head in his hands, was sitting on a kitchen chair.

"What happened?" Archie enquired.

A cold sensation came over Archie, the sensation of someone standing behind him.

Rizzuto, had come too and managed to stagger to the house, he had come up behind Archie gun in hand and said.

"Vieni qua con l'altri due, eh! Andiamo."

Come here with the other two, eh! Let's go.

Archie looked at Tomasz.

"Do you know what he said?"

"I'm not fully sure but I think he said, he wants you to join us over here."

Archie turns slowly and sees Rizzuto pointing a gun at him and decides to move closer to Tomasz and Jack.

"I'll take that."

Lily had been waiting for the all clear from Archie, when he didn't call, she decided to check things out. She saw Rizzuto staggering to the back door and followed him in.

Rizzuto felt the cold barrel of Lily's gun in the back of his neck, but like a flash of lightning turned and knocked Lily to the ground and grabbed her gun.

"Eh, va a stare con l'altro, capisci?"

Get with the other, understand?

Rizzuto said, gesturing with his gun for Lily to join the others. As she passed him, Lily grabbed a saucepan from the table and swung it at Rizzuto who ducked and lost his balance. Archie lunged forward in an attempt to grab him but was overpowered and felt Rizzuto's gun barrel pressed against his temple, he was just about to pull the trigger.

"Ah, non lo farei, eh? Metti giù la tua pistola, capisci?"

I wouldn't do that, put your gun down, understand?

The reassuring voice of Keeling, who was fairly fluent in Italian, came from behind them, along with Whiting who was also pointing his pistol at Rizzuto's head.

Rizzuto looked around and after considering his options decided to throw his gun on the floor.

"Sulla tua ginocchia, adesso, picia!"

On your knees, now! Keeling shouted.

Rizzuto dropped to his knees and put his hands behind his head.

"Good show Keeling, perfect timing." Archie, looking across to Jack, asked.

"Jack, have you got your handcuffs on you?"

Jack was still shaken.

"Yes, always."

"Restrain him."

"It will be a pleasure, sir."

Tomasz explained everything that had occurred, how he understood they were just about to shoot Jack and had to act quickly.

"I had no option, I didn't want to kill him, but he left me no choice."

"You did the right thing Tomasz. Plus, I'm not sure how we would have managed if anything had happened to Jack. And, besides, his mother is expecting him home for his evening meal," Archie said with a smile.

The relief in the room was tangible as Archie turned to Lily.

"Are you all right, did he hurt you?"

"Just my pride, I should have hit him."

"He was very quick. I had the chance to grab him, but I was too slow."

Archie went over to Buccafusca's body, putting his finger against his neck to check for a pulse, as he thought, there were no signs of life, he was dead.

"Tomasz, can you telephone Dr Stagg and explain the situation and that we need him here. Also an ambulance to take the body away."

"Right away, Archie."

Forty-Nine

Keeling and Whiting dragged Rizzuto out of the front door where they were met by Noah, who had just pulled up at the front door of the Villa.

"What have we got here," Noah said, getting out of his Land Rover and stubbing a cigarette out on the drive with his foot.

"Archie is inside, I'll let him tell you everything. Can we put this man into your car?" Whiting asked.

"Go ahead, but I suggest you handcuff him to the seat and stay with him."

Noah made his way into the villa expecting the worst, but was greeted by an excitable Jack Jones who was bursting to explain all that had happened that morning. How he was making a telephone call in the High Street, when he felt a gun being pushed into his back and was forced to go to Southcott Villas.

"They received a telephone call, I couldn't understand what was said, but after it, the Italian made me kneel down in front of him." Jack took a deep breath.

"I thought he was going to shoot me, there was a loud bang, nothing happened for a few seconds. I thought he had missed me, then there was a thud next to me and it was the Italian lying beside me covered in blood. I almost cried when I looked up and saw Tomasz, I just wanted to hug him."

He went on. "As I was talking to Tomasz, to our relief Archie appeared in the doorway. Unbeknownst to us the other Italian crept up behind Archie and pointed a gun at his head, making him drop his gun on the floor. He pushed Archie toward us, he was going to shoot us, then Lily appeared behind the Italian, it was just like a film."

Jack went on to describe how the others had restrained the man and dragged him off.

While they were discussing what had taken place, Dr Stagg arrived.

"They certainly mount up when you're in Pewsey," the doctor said, giving Archie a sideward glance.

"He's over there," Archie pointed to Buccafusca's body.

"Doctor, can you take a look at Jack, he's had a bit of an ordeal and I want to make sure he's okay?"

"Yes, I'll take a look at him first."

The sound of the ambulance's bells could be heard coming up Southcott Road. There was a small crowd of spectators starting to form outside the villa. Close behind the ambulance and rushing to the villa was Tom along with Dixon and Martin.

Inside, Archie pulled Noah to one side.

"Someone telephoned to warn Rizzuto and Buccafusca that we were coming, it could have been fatal. They have an inside man, what do we know about Dixon and Martin? I can't think of who else it could be."

"They come recommended by Superintendent Brentwood, I trust his judgement, but, does he know his men?"

"I'll get him back to the morgue and let you know what he died of," Dr Stagg said, from the other room, finding a difficult situation slightly funny.

"Jack's fine, just a bit shaken. I'll keep an eye on him over the next few days."

"Thank you, doctor. I look forward to your report."

"What would you like us to do, sir?" Tom appeared in the doorway.

"Ah, Tom, can you and Dixon move the crowd on outside the villa and secure the scene when they've gone?"

Noah glanced across to Archie, "We'll carry on with our discussion later on this evening."

Archie nodded in agreement as he, Lily and Tomasz made their way to the front door.

"Come on you lot, move along there's nothing to see," the raucous voice of Tom soon had the crowd moving.

"We are off now Tom, are you, Martin and Dixon free to meet later at the hotel?"

"Yes Archie, what time?"

"Shall we say eightish?"

"We'll be there."

Fifty

The hotel foyer was relatively quiet as Archie, Lily and Tomasz made their way through to the dining room. Emily was writing in a book at the reception desk and looked up when they entered.

"Hello darling, what sort of day have you had, busy I imagine, is it true there's been another body found, do you know who it is, what-?

"One question at a time, Mum."

Archie, discreetly recounted some of the day's events to Emily, being careful not to be too precise about what happened, but satisfying her curiosity.

"We need to eat, it's been a long day. I'll let you know if anything else happens. Mum, is your lounge free for a few hours?"

"Yes, I'm looking after the reception desk until ten o'clock. Go straight up when you're ready"

"Thank you, Mum, you're a treasure."

Archie kissed his mother on the cheek then left her to join Lily and Tomasz in the dining room. Whilst they were eating Noah appeared in the doorway, Archie beckoned him to join them. They discussed what their next step should be while they ate, then made their way up to Emily's lounge having asked her if she would send the others up when they arrived.

283

"Yes, of course, darling."

Soon everybody was gathered in Emily's lounge.

There was a contemplative mood as they considered how different the day could have gone, if it wasn't for Tomasz who followed his instincts and quick thinking, things may have ended in tragedy. They all congratulated a very embarrassed Tomasz who's face turned a dark scarlet.

"Right, we need a plan of action," Noah said, who was missing his incident board.

"Can I make a suggestion," Archie enquired.

"Go ahead."

"We need to get Valentino back to Pewsey. He has a lot of questions to answer. Also there are a number of other questions that need answering and I believe Rizzuto is the key to them. Tom can you double check if anyone knows anything about the woman seen on the bridge the morning Mrs Valentino was murdered. We also need to find the Morris Traveller; it is an important element to solving the De Villiers-Blyth's case."

Looking at Noah, Archie asked. "Did Jack say what he had found?"

"No, I sent him straight home. It was quite a traumatic day for him. I'll check with him in the morning," Noah said.

Archie deep in thought said. "I will arrange to have Valentino brought here first thing in the morning. Keep this to yourselves, I believe his life is in danger."

"What are we going to do with Brooks and Haynes?" Lily asked.

"Nothing at the moment, we will just leave them to sweat in their cells and deal with them once these cases are resolved," Archie replied.

Noah thoughtfully asked. "I know it's Easter Sunday tomorrow and you would like to be with your families. This case is complicated with lives being at risk. We are not sure what we are dealing with and if any of you want to be with families I fully understand and you are free to go."

Noah looked up to gauge their reactions. Everyone was of one accord; they thought that staying was more important, that it was a case of life and death. Noah thanked them and decided to call an end to the day. Slowly they all made their way out of the lounge, Tom and Noah to their respective homes, Whiting and Keeling back to Parkhill Garrison while Dixon and Martin went to the hotel bar.

Archie and Lily choose to have a nightcap in the lounge. As Tomasz was on night duty he relieved Emily at the reception desk.

Fifty-One

Sunday 17th April (Easter Sunday)

Six thirty soon came around for Archie, the scratching and whimpering of Maisie woke him up with a start.

"Coming old girl."

Maisie sat patiently outside Archie's door waiting for him to come out.

"Hello Maisie, have you woken Lily yet?"

At that Maisie dashed off down the hall and greeted Lily who was up and on her way downstairs.

"Wait for me," Archie shouted from down the hall.

"We need to get off early and bring Valentino back to Pewsey. We'll give Maisie a short walk before going, but first we must have breakfast." Archie said as they headed to the dining room.

***

Archie was waiting by his father's car in the hotel car park as Lily came out through the back door. "I thought we would use dad's car, I can't see Valentino fitting in mine," he grinned.

The journey to Parkhill was fairly quick, when they

arrived Major Osborne was waiting for them outside the guardhouse.

"Good morning Major, how is everything?"

"Good morning Freestone, Miss Forester. He's in the office, ready for you."

The major escorted Archie and Lily down a narrow corridor to the rear of the building. Valentino was sitting in a small metal chair handcuffed to the table, he looked round as they entered the office. There were two very large guards hovering over him, although the thought of escaping was the last thing on his mind. Archie and Lily sat down opposite him. Archie pulled his chair close to the table and, leaning on it, lit his pipe.

"I've spoken to my boss, he has agreed to your deal, in principle that is. He needs some names as a gesture of goodwill from you before he will agree. For the time being we need to take you back to Pewsey. I know it's dangerous but we will protect you."

"Do I have a choice?" Valentino asked, leaning back in his chair.

"Not really. Can you give me any names?"

Valentino sat quietly deep in thought.

"Chief Superintendent Booker at Leman Street nick was on my payroll, along with Detective Sergeant Brooks, who is one of his men. That's all for now. I like you Freestone and I think you're an honest man, I trust you."

"Thank you, you can trust me. I'll try not to let you down."

"Do we have your word you won't attempt to escape?" Lily asked.

"You have my word, besides where would I go. I'm in your hands," a tentative Valentino replied.

Archie asked one of the guards to remove Valentino's handcuffs.

"Thank you, Major, for all your help."

"Freestone before you go, do you have any information on De Villiers-Blyth's murder. We have nothing this end?" Major Orsborne asked, shaking Archie's hand.

"We are following up on several leads. A set of tyre tracks from a Morris Traveller were found near the body, we are also looking for two poachers who may have seen something. As things unfold we will keep you in the picture."

"Thank you Freestone, oh, do you still need my men?"

"Yes, is there any chance of having Whiting and Keeling travel back with us?"

"Yes of course, I'll get Corporal Higgins to fetch them and have them meet you at the main gate."

Archie and Lily led Valentino out to their car, putting him in the back seat and they drove to the main gate. Whiting and Keeling were waiting when Archie pulled up, they climbed in, seating themselves either side of Valentino.

There was an uncomfortable silence as they drove back to Pewsey.

Breaking the silence Archie looked at Keeling in

the car's mirror. "When we get there, I want you and Whiting to guard Valentino, keep him safe."

"We will."

Pulling up at the rear door of the police station Archie gets out and studies the surrounding area.

"All clear."

The four gathered around Valentino creating a shield and led him towards the station door.

"This doesn't feel right," Archie's intuition of possible danger kicked in.

Cautiously they entered through the backdoor, Archie going first.

"It's too quiet, where's Tom?" Archie said, drawing his gun.

The others following him into the building hesitated, just then a shot rang out, the bullet ricocheting past Lily's head sinking into the backdoor.

They quickly ducked down and surrounded Valentino. Archie lifted his head slightly to see where the shot had come from, a second shot was fired from deeper inside the police station, missing them all.

Whiting ushered Valentino back outside, while Keeling stood with his gun close to his chest in the doorway, looking back into the room.

Then a third shot rang out, standing in the doorway was the slim well dressed figure of Benjamin Martin. Archie and Lily stood up, only to be confronted by Martin, who lifted his gun, to her horror Lily realised he was pointing the gun at them and was about to shoot.

Archie moved quickly in front of Lily to act as a shield. Martin, with finger on the trigger ready to shoot, suddenly sank to his knees and fell face down on the floor.

A bemused Archie looked at an ashen faced Lily, then at the body of Martin laying in front of them, blood starting to ooze from the bullet hole in his back.

"Is everyone alright?" The reassuring voice of Noah came from behind the fallen body of Martin. Holding his gun in front of him, Noah cautiously advanced into the room.

"What happened?" A relieved Archie asked.

Noah bent over the body to check for signs of life and found none.

"I wasn't meant to be here, but by sheer chance I popped into check with Tom to see if the autopsy report on Reverend Ward had arrived. The place seemed strangely quiet, as I passed my office I noticed Tom lying on the floor. I checked to make sure he was okay, he had been knocked out. Then I heard a gunshot, I saw Martin pointing his gun, he fired again. The rest you know."

"Glad you could make it, old chap," Archie said, with a reassuring smile.

"No trouble, anything to help."

Whiting led Valentino back into the police station, as they passed Martin's body, Valentino stopped.

"Ben Martin, I thought I could trust him, he's one of my boys. Thank you, Freestone, I knew I could trust you. I'm now ready to tell you everything I know."

"Before you go to your cell, did you kill your wife?" Archie asked, hoping to catch Valentino off guard.

"No, you may not believe me but I loved Isabella."

Archie thanked Valentino, then Whiting led him to a cell away from Brooks, Haynes and Rizzuto. "I'll phone Dr Stagg and explain what has happened," said Archie.

"I'll just check on Tom, to make sure he's alright, Keeling, can you stay with Valentino?" Noah asked as he left the room.

Archie and Lily watched Keeling and Whiting escorting Valentino to one of the back cells. George Dixon appeared in the doorway and looked at Martin's body lying on the floor.

"What's been going on here?"

Archie explained what had happened.

"I am shocked, we didn't even consider him being corrupt. The Superintendent will be devastated, we thought we could trust him."

"We must be careful who we trust. I think we need to speak to Rizzuto and find out what he knows about Mrs Valentino's death and see ...."

"Archie, Lily can you pop in here?" Noah calls from his office.

In the office, Tom was sitting holding his head while Noah was waving a piece of paper in the air.

"I phoned Dr Stagg, he can't get away right now, so he is organising an ambulance to pick up the body." explained Archie.

"Okay, thank you Archie. I think you will find this very interesting. Stagg's autopsy report on Ward makes interesting reading. At first he couldn't find any means of death, but on further investigation he found a small puncture mark at the back of his neck.

He sent a blood sample to the forensic laboratory in London, who discovered he was poisoned by a drug called curare. It's the preferred poison used by Russian agents. The poison causes weakness of the skeletal muscles and, when administered in a sufficient dose, eventual death by asphyxiation due to paralysis of the diaphragm. Apparently a very nasty death."

"Why would a Russian agent want to murder a village vicar?" a puzzled Lily asked.

Fifty-Two

In the office, a thoughtful atmosphere permeated the room. No one spoke as they considered all the relevant facts that surrounded all three cases. Eventually, Archie broke the silence.

"We need to eliminate suspects one by one and see who we are left with. Firstly we need to speak to Rizzuto and find out where he fits into the scheme of things. Dixon, can you and Whiting fetch him and bring him to the office?"

As they leave, considering all the facts Lily asked, "what do they all have in common? We have Mrs Valentino's murder, De Villiers' murder and now the Reverend Ward's murder?"

"I have come to the conclusion that Valentino's murder has nothing to do with the other two and that her death was gang related. We need to separate the cases."

There was a knock on the door.

"Where do you want him, sir?"

"Can you take him to the interview room," Noah said.

The solitary figure of Rizzuto sat silently handcuffed to the table as Noah, Archie and Lily entered the room. Archie stood behind him while the others sat opposite.

Noah started, "Unless you cooperate with us you will hang, be sure of it."

"I-a don't-a comprendere, capisce?"

"In British law, a kidnap carries the death penalty. Do you understand?"

"My English, eh, it's-a not so good, you know?"

Archie persists, "Did you murder Mrs Valentino on Tuesday 5th of April?"

"Perché dovrei, eh? Non la conosco manco un po'. Lei non significa niente per me, capito?"

"English please," Noah insists.

"I think what he is saying is, why would he, she means nothing to him" Lily roughly translated.

"We need Tomasz here to translate," Archie suggested.

"Good idea, I'll telephone the hotel," Noah said.

They decided to stop the interview and wait for Tomasz to arrive. In no time at all Tomasz arrived at the front desk and Archie explained the situation to him.

Can you ask him, what were he and Buccafusca doing on the bridge near River Street early on Tuesday the 5th?"

Tomasz begins, *"Cosa stavate facendo tu e Buccafusca sul ponte vicino a River Street martedì 5 presto?"*

"Non siamo stati noi, capisce?"

"He said, it wasn't them."

"Tell him, they were seen crossing the bridge.

What were they doing there?" Noah insisted.

"Sei stato visto attraversare il ponte, cosa stavi facendo lì?" Tomasz continued.

Rizzuto sat silently and motionless.

"Remind him he will hang if he lies."

"Ricordategli che se mentirà verrà impiccato."

After a minute or so Rizzuto leaned forward in his seat.

"Stavamo seguendo la signora Valentino ma l'abbiamo persa vicino al fiume ma l'abbiamo persa di vista e abbiamo deciso di tornare in albergo. Lungo la strada abbiamo visto una donna che si allontanava dal ponte. Questo è tutto quello che posso dirti."

"What did he say?" Noah asked.

He said. "They were following Mrs Valentino but she vanished near the river and lost sight of her so they decided to go back to the hotel. On the way we saw a woman walking away from the bridge. That is all he can tell us."

Archie, not satisfied with the answer continued "Ask him, why were you following her and how did you know it was her?"

"Ci è stato detto che aspetto aveva, cosa indossava e speravamo che ci portasse Valentino."

We were told what she looked like, what she was wearing and hoped she would lead us to Valentino."

"Can he describe the woman?" Lily asked.

"Puoi descrivere questa donna?" Tomasz questioned.

Rizzuto thought for a moment and continued.

"Era una donna alta e snella e l'unica cosa che ricordo era che indossava una giacca a doppio petto. Questo è tutto quello che posso dirti."

"She was slim and tall, the only thing he remembered was that she was wearing a double-breasted jacket. That is all he can tell us."

"Ask him why they wanted to find Valentino?"

"Chiedergli perché volevano trovare Valentino?" Tomasz asked.

"Per ucciderlo." Rizzuto said coldly.

"They wanted to kill him."

"Didn't you know he was staying at the hotel?" Tomasz asked.

"Non sapevi che alloggiava in albergo?"

Rizzuto thought for a moment.

"No, non l'abbiamo visto, capire."

"No, they didn't see him." Tomasz translated.

There was a moment of silence as they reflected on what was said. Smoke was steadily filling the room, so Archie suggested it was time to finish the interview.

"Whiting, can you take Rizzuto back to his cell?" Noah shouted out.

"C'era qualcos'altro, incontrò un'altra donna all'angolo della strada," Rizzuto said as he was being led from the room.

"What did he say?" Achie said looking at Tomasz.

"Ha detto che c'era qualcos'altro, ha incontrato un'altra persona all'angolo della strada."

"He said, there was something else, she met another person on the corner of the street."

"Ask him what did they look like?"

"Che aspetto avevano?"

"Tutto quello che riesce a ricordare è che questa persona era più bassa della donna. Poi è passato un camion agricolo e quando se n'è andato erano scomparsi."

"All he can remember is that this person was shorter than the woman. Then a farm lorry passed and when it had gone they'd disappeared."

"Era un uomo o una donna?"

Tomasz asked, was it a man or a woman?

"Potrebbe essere stato l'uno o l'altro, non saprei."

"It could have been either, he couldn't tell."

"Take him to his cell," Noah ordered.

Rizzuto was led away by Whiting.

Archie refilled his pipe and lit it.

"Do you believe him?" Lily asked, as they walk along the narrow corridor that leads to the office.

"I'm not sure, he has no reason to lie," Archie pondered.

Turning around to Noah. "I didn't know kidnapping was a hanging offence," Archie said.

"It isn't, I just wanted to scare him."

"I certainly think you managed to do that," Lily said, smiling.

In Noah's office they considered the morning's events and reflected that it could have been much worse. Noah suggested they stop for lunch, which

Lily thought was a marvellous idea.

Noah glanced across at Tom, who was looking a little groggy. "Tom, I think you need to get yourself to Dr Staggs and get your head checked out."

"I'm alright, sir."

"That wasn't a request, that was an order."

"Yes sir." Tom mumbled quietly under his breath, as he left the room.

"Keeling, Whiting can you stay and guard the prisoners, Dixon will you man the front desk for the rest of the day?"

Dixon disappeared to the front desk, Whiting sat by the door at the entrance to the cells.

Noah thanked Tomasz for all his help and suggested they meet back at the police station after lunch. While they were talking, the ambulance pulled up in front of the station to collect the body of Benjamin Martin and take him to the morgue in Marlborough.

Fifty-Three

Back at the hotel, although they were late for lunch Sam managed to rustle up a hearty meal for them, much to Lily's delight. Archie sat back in his chair and contentedly puffed on his pipe, life felt good as he contemplated his up and coming wedding to Lily.

"We need to call in and see your mother," Lily said, breaking Archie's concentration.

"Yes, we must, time is racing by and with all that is going on it's too easy to forget everyday life."

Emily was lounging in her large comfortable armchair with one leg resting, as usual, on a pouffe and clutching a small sherry.

"A bit early for that," Archie jokes.

"It's my one guilty pleasure," Emily bantered back.

Archie and Lily spent some time filling Emily in on all that was going on, but leaving most of the details out, which seemed to satisfy her.

"We have to go, Noah is expecting us. We will pop in later and have a drink with you."

Arm in arm Archie and Lily made their way back to the police station. The warmth of the late afternoon sun filled them with contentment that life for them was good.

At the police station Noah was sitting in a cloud of

smoke, with his back to the door studying the incident board that hung behind his desk.

"What are you thinking," Archie asked as they entered the office.

"Hello you two, I was thinking what are we missing! I can't help thinking we've missed something or somebody."

Archie opened the small office window and pulled a chair close to Noah's desk.

"Why, why was Isabel Valentino murdered? Buccafusca or Rizzuto didn't do it nor her husband. So why, who wanted her dead?

Noah stood up and scratched Valentino's, Buccafusca and Rizzuto's names off the board. He added Brooks and Haynes to the list of suspects.

"I can see them trying to kill Valentino, but his wife? I just can't see it," Lily said as she shuffled closer to the desk.

"No, I think you're right, There is no reason for them to kill her," Noah agreed.

Archie stood up and rubbed the back of his neck.

"One of them could have done it, if they needed Valentino out in the open, it could have been a message, a warning, to keep his mouth shut."

"Whiting, can you put Brooks in the interview room and stay with him?" Noah shouted out."

"Yes sir," Whiting's voice came from down the corridor.

"Before we see him, have we had any come back on the Morris tyre tracks yet?" Archie asked.

"No, although I do need to talk to Jack, to find out if he discovered anything important."

As they made their way to the interview room the sound of a disturbance was heard coming from the room. Taking his gun from his holster, Archie burst into the room, to find Brooks lying face down on the floor with Whiting's foot on his back.

"This one's a feisty one," Whiting said with a broad smile.

Noah and Whiting lifted Brooks off the floor and handcuffed him to the table.

"Who the hell do you think you are Jackson, you'll be lucky to be walking the beat when we've finished," Brooks vehemently shouted out, turning purple with anger.

Noah grabbed him by his tie and pushed him onto a chair.

"Chief Superintendent Booker will hang you out to …"

"Chief Superintendent Booker is being arrested by Special Branch as we speak. So I suggest you come clean and help us or I will throw the book at you, starting with assaulting a police officer."

Brooks turned pale as the colour drained from his face, he sat in stunned silence.

Eventually after giving it some thought Brooks opened up.

"What do you want to know?"

Noah sat opposite Brooks.

"Did you kill Mrs Valentino?"

"I don't know Mrs Valentino why would I kill her. I only know Leonardo Valentino."

"Do you know if Haynes killed her?"

"He has been with me all the time since we got here, so no, he didn't kill her."

"Where were you early morning on Tuesday the fifth?"

"Tuesday the fifth? We were in Leman Street nick, there were plenty of witnesses. So I can't help you there."

"What are you both doing in Pewsey, " Archie asked.

"We were told to pick up Valentino and bring him back to London. That's all I know."

Noah lifted his head and looked at Archie and Whiting.

"Take him back."

Whiting grabbed Brooks by the back of collar and dragged him back to his cell, mumbling.

"No one likes a bent copper," he muttered quietly to himself.

The three silently sat in Noah's office studying the incident board.

"Of course, we mustn't forget, we may have a Russian spy in the area. He or she could hold the key to what's been happening." remarks a thoughtful Archie.

Noah scrubbed Hayne's and Brooks's names off the incident board and added a question mark to represent the possible spy. Archie did what he did best when faced with a problem, he filled and lit his pipe, drew on it and sighed.

"We need to know who this woman on the bridge is and was there a connection between her and Mrs Valentino? Also we need to find the Morris Traveller and who was this second person there on the fifth. Can we take it that the De Villiers-Blyth murder was an execution by this Russian agent, but it doesn't explain why the Reverend Ward died from a preferred Russian poison."

Lily got up and moved toward Noah's desk. "Have we forgotten Mrs Fishwick, who is she and where did she go. Was she the woman seen talking to De Villiers-Blyth in Marlborough? Can you remember the description Mrs Ward gave of her?"

"From what I can bring to mind she was quite ordinary and had an accent of some kind. Oh and had dark hair," Archie said.

Noah scratched his head and lit another cigarette.

"We need to find her, if she is still here, that is, in the meantime, I'll pop in and see Jack, he may have found something."

As it was getting late Noah suggested they call it a day and meet the following morning. Whiting, Keeling and Dixon volunteered to stay at the police station and guard the prisoners overnight.

***

For a Sunday evening the bar was packed, smoke

hung close to the ceiling, the constant clinking of glasses and the hum of people talking filled the room. Bob and Henry were working hard behind the bar. Archie and Lily were propping up one end of the bar when their attention was drawn to a familiar voice coming from somewhere in the room.

"These are on me, ducks," the sound of her cockney accent drifted in the air.

"Where have we heard that voice before?" Lily asked.

Archie thought for a while.

"On the train, coming here. The woman opposite us reading." Archie pondered for a moment. "The Daily Sketch."

"Yes, you're right. Where is she?" Lily said, scouring the room.

Archie and Lily wandered through the busy room trying to find her.

"Over there, that's her going out of the door," an excited Lily cried out.

"Come on, let's see where she's going?"

As the women disappeared through the main door Archie and Lily pushed their way quickly through the crowded room, they soon had her in their sights.

Fifty-Four

The blanket of darkness from the night sky gave Archie and Lily adequate cover as they followed the woman along North Street. Keeping their distance making sure they weren't seen, they continued around the corner into Wilcot Road but, to their surprise she had vanished.

"Where did she go?" Lily asked.

"I'm not sure, she could be anywhere," Lily could hear the disappointment in Archie's voice.

"If she's here, we will find her," Lily said, trying to lift Archie's spirits.

"You're right."

They decided to carry on walking along Wilcot Road hoping to catch sight of her. After half an hour or so, they gave up the search and walked slowly back to the hotel.

"Could she be the other person Brooks said he saw? We need to know who she is and if she has been staying here, if so, where." There was a change of mood and an air of excitement was now in Archie's voice.

Arriving back at the hotel Archie decided to ask his father about the woman and who she was sitting with.

"Hi dad. There was a woman in here earlier, she

spoke with a London accent, do you remember seeing her?"

"Yes I do, she was a young woman, very smartly dressed, I think she had dark hair. I realise that sounds like half of the women who were in here tonight, I'm sorry, that's not much of a help."

"That's okay, Dad, I know the bar was busy, could you see who she was sitting with."

"Sorry, no I didn't."

"Never mind, I'll telephone Noah and arrange for somebody to keep an eye out for her."

"Good evening Noah, sorry to trouble you at home, but we have a bit of a coincidence going on here and you know we don't believe in coincidences."

Archie explained about the woman to Noah.

"Can you describe her?" Noah asked.

Archie thought for a moment. "I'll hand you over to Lily, she has a much better eye for that sort of thing."

"Hello Noah, we didn't get a good look at her in the bar. But from what I saw, she was a smart young woman. If my memory serves me, she wore a double breasted jacket and trousers when we saw her on the train. I hope that helps."

"Can you remember the colour of her hair and was it long or short?"

"I think she was a brunet and I can't remember what length it was. I'm sorry."

"No, not at all. I'll get Tom and Jack to keep an eye out for her. If she's in Pewsey they'll find her."

Back in the bar Archie sipped his whisky while Lily devoured another packet of crisps.

"What are you thinking?" she asked Archie.

"I didn't notice who she was speaking to, there were too many people milling around. I don't suppose you noticed?"

"No, I had the impression she was talking to two men. But, I may have imagined it."

"Archie, I know it's getting late, but can you call in and see your mother, you know she hates being left out of things?" Henry shouted from the bar.

"We're on our way, Dad."

An eager Emily lifted herself up in her armchair as Archie and Lily came into the room. Maisie managed to lift one eyebrow but soon fell back to sleep.

"What's been happening, you promised to call in and see me. Are you both safe? Someone said there were gunshots heard coming from the police station, were you there, was anyone hurt?"

"Yes we are both safe and yes there was a gunshot, someone was hurt it's ….."

"Who?! Do I know them?"

"No one you know, Mum. You shouldn't worry so much about us, we can look after ourselves." he said gently, noticing the concern on her face.

"You will take care," Emily said, her voice trembling with emotion.

"Yes, we will be extra careful. Sorry mum but we have to go, we have a busy day tomorrow."

Fifty-Five

Monday 18th April (Easter Monday)

The sound of Maisie snuffling outside Archie's door woke him with a start. He looked at his clock, six-thirty, he thought to himself how does she always know what time it is.

"Maisie, go and wake Lily up."

"I am awake," Lily's voice came from outside Archie's door.

"I'm sorry, I didn't know you were up. I'll be down in a jiffy, see you in the foyer."

"Come on Maisie, we'll see Archie downstairs."

When Archie arrived in the foyer he found Lily talking to Henry while Maisie sat patiently waiting by the main door.

"Good morning Dad, another beautiful day."

"Yes it is, what are you both up to today, anything exciting?"

"Not sure at the moment. I would like to call and see if Mrs Ward is okay, other than that we've nothing planned."

In no time Archie and Lily found themselves walking along the High Street toward Ball Road.

"Good morning Archie, Miss Lily, looked like it's

going to be another beautiful day again today. It's days like today I wish I didn't have a shop and could just lounge around in the garden," Arthur Hewit said, with his cigarette hanging from his lip.

"Yes it is, I don't envy you being stuck indoors. Anyway have a nice day"

"And you."

"Oh Arthur, has a stranger, a young woman, smartly dressed, who may have had a cockney accent, been in your shop over the last few days?"

Arthur thought for a minute.

"There have been a number of young women in here, but none had a cockney accent. I'm sorry I can't help. There was a young lady, but she had a foreign accent."

"Could you make out where she was from?"

"I'm not good at accents, it could have been German."

"Would you recognise her if you saw her again?"

"I'm not sure, I'm sorry."

"That's okay, we'll find her."

Lily snuggled into Archie as the dawn chorus of birdsong drifted in the air. Archie sighed with contentment. The couple wandered happily down Green Drove with Maisie stopping and sniffing every minute or so as they headed back toward the hotel for breakfast.

After they had eaten, Lily went to her room to change, while Archie called in to see his Mum.

"Hello darling, did you have a nice walk?"

"Yes thank you, it is beautiful around here, where else would one rather be than in Pewsey."

"Yes, it is rather nice. Archie, it's so lovely to have you back home and especially with Lily."

"I'm a very blessed man, mum."

Archie and his Mum chatted, they were soon joined by Lily and the subject of the wedding became the main discussion.

"Do you have any dates, yet, are your parents happy that you are getting married here, have you heard about a new vicar …?"

"No date yet, but it will probably be around Christmas and Lily's parents are very happy that we are getting married in Pewsey. Mum, I'm sorry but we have to go, I would like to pop in and see Florence and make sure she is okay. Also check whether she has thought of anything else that may help us before we meet Noah."

"Yes of course, darling, be careful."

"We will," Archie said, giving her a kiss on the cheek as they leave.

Making their way through the foyer Henry called Archie.

"Sorry to bother you, but can you give me a hand with a barrel in the cellar, it won't take a minute?"

"Yes of course, Lily, why don't you go ahead and I'll be right behind you?"

"I'll see you there, don't strain yourself will you," Lily said, with a smile.

"I won't, it's Dad I'm more concerned about at his

age."

"Less of the old age, I can still give you a run for your money."

Archie and Henry made their way down the narrow stairs that led to the cellar, while Lily left through the main hotel door. It only took Archie and his Dad a couple of minutes to sort the problem out and Archie was soon on his way.

It was another beautiful day as he strolled along Church street and up to the rectory, happily whistling to himself.

Ringing the front door bell Archie looked around and admired the gardens, the door creaked open and Florence's head appeared in the opening.

"Hello Archie, can I help you?"

"Is Lily still here?"

"Lily, no, I haven't seen her."

"She was coming to see you, to see if you were okay."

"I've been in all morning and no one has come to see me. Would you like to come in and use the telephone, she may have gone back home?"

"No, thank you, I would have passed her on the way here. She probably got waylaid and is chatting to someone. I'll let you know."

"Thank you, Archie if you could. If she does turn up I'll get her to telephone you."

"Thank you Florence."

Archie tried hard not to show his concern as he left Florence, who was equally concerned especially after

John her husband had disappeared and ended up murdered. He made his way slowly along Church Street and River Street, checking every garden and doorway back to the hotel, but there was no sign of her. Perhaps she went straight to the police station, he thought to himself.

Tomasz was on the reception desk as Archie entered the hotel.

"Have you seen Lily?" he asked him.

"No, but I've only just come on duty, so she may have come in earlier. I can telephone Emily to see if she's up there with her."

"Would you?"

"I'm going to telephone Noah and see if she is with him." Archie dashed into the back room and dialled the police station.

"Good morning, Hopkins here, how can I help you?"

"Ah Tom, is Lily with you?"

"No, she's not with the Inspector and I haven't seen her. Why, what happened?"

Archie recounted what had taken place earlier.

"I'll put the Inspector on the telephone for you. In between time I will send Jack out to do a door to door around the area. I'm sure she's fine and probably having coffee with someone."

"Thank you, Tom."

Noah could hear the anxiety in Archie's voice, he knew this wasn't like Lily.

"Don't worry old chap we'll soon have her back,"

he said, trying to reassure his friend.

Archie thanked Noah, they arranged to meet straight away at the hotel.

"Keep this to yourself for now," a worried Archie said to Tomasz.

Archie stood in the foyer, frozen to the spot, his chest feeling like it was being crushed and staring around without focus.

"Archie, what is it?" Henry, who could see the tension in Archie's demeanor.

"It's Lily, she's gone missing and I'm not sure what to do. I was supposed to be …"

As Archie was talking, Noah along with Tom and Dixon burst through the main door into the lobby.

"Have you heard from Lily?" Noah enquired.

"No nothing."

"Can you remember what she was wearing?"

In all the confusion Archie hadn't given it much thought. He reflected for a moment.

"She was wearing a pretty red floral dress and, let me think, yes, she had a, what do they call them, light blue cloche hat, you know the sort, like an upturned bucket with a small red bow on it."

Fifty-Six

Archie knew Lily was trained to handle difficult situations and thought that whatever position she found herself in, she would have some degree of control.

"Right, here is what we are going to do," Archie lifted his head, shaking himself out of his stupor, he looked at the others, taking control of the situation, he continued.

"Tom, can you and Dixon check every house, gardens and out buildings along River Street. Noah, you and I will search Church Street. You all know what she was wearing and can describe what she looked like, she's been missing for about an hour, so she can't be too far away."

As they were in the foyer before leaving the hotel, Noah turned to Archie.

"Archie, whilst I think of it. Jack said he saw a green Morris Traveller being driven by a woman coming out off Ball Road, just before he was kidnapped. Unfortunately he didn't recognise the driver. I'm not sure if that helps or not."

"We will have to see," Archie replied, impatiently wanting to get going.

Before they got outside Tomasz called from the

reception desk.

"Can I help?"

"If that's okay with Dad."

"Yes of course, go on Tomasz. We can manage here."

"Thank you Dad. Tomasz can you go and find Jack and help him, he's started checking the area around the Everleigh Road?"

Outside, Pewsey was bustling, people were taking advantage of the warm spring holiday weather and enjoying a mid morning stroll.

Henry, unbeknownst to Archie, had telephoned around and arranged several groups of people as search parties. Sam hotel chef, Jacob, Dotty and her son Arthur, Flynn Watkins landlord of The Coopers, John Strong, Arthur Hewit and around a dozen others were waiting in the hotel car park.

Henry had overheard Archie telling Noah what Lily was wearing and relaid that to the group that had assembled. He arranged them into groups of three and sent them around the village, warning them to be extra vigilant.

"Thank you for your help, especially on a bank holiday. We're not sure what we are dealing with, she could be in danger. Knock on every door, check everywhere, talk to everyone you see and don't do anything silly."

There was a tense uneasy atmosphere hanging over Pewsey as the groups set off. On the corner of Church Street and Swan Road, Archie stood with his hands on his hips staring into the distance. Noah came around to join Archie.

"She can't be far, I think we need to go and talk to Mrs Ward, that was the last place Lily was headed, and see if she has heard anything."

"Yes, that's a good idea." Archie agreed.

Walking back along Church Street they saw Tom running toward them, Archie's heart sank.

Fifty-Seven

"Inspector, I'm sorry to bother you, I had to pop into the police station. Superintendent Brentwood has telephoned and left a message. He said he has arranged with Special Branch for a Black Maria to pick up Haynes, Brooks, Valentino and Rizzuto later this evening. Can you be at the station?"

"Thank you, Tom. Any news of Lily?"

"No, I'm sorry there's been no sign of her so far, from anybody."

Tom left Archie and Noah to continue searching, as people were starting to return to the hotel. The village had been turned upside down in a vain attempt to find Lily. Archie was starting to feel desperate as he and Noah made their way along the rectory drive. On ringing the doorbell, Florence appeared from around the side of the house.

"Sorry to trouble you again Florence, but this is the last place Lily was meant to meet me. Have you heard anything?"

"I haven't, I'm sorry."

"Florence, would you mind if I came in and had a glass of water? I'm finding the whole thing a bit of a strain."

Florence hesitated for a minute.

"Yes, of course, come in."

Inside Noah asked, "Would you mind if I used your toilet, it's been a long afternoon?"

"It's the second door on the right at the top of the stairs."

Archie scoured every room on the way to the kitchen to see if there were any signs that Lily had been there. Likewise Noah opened every door upstairs checking for her. But there was nothing to suggest Lily had ever been there.

Thanking Florence for the drink they left the rectory, as they were walking down the drive, he turned to Noah excited, something had caught Archie's eye as they were leaving the house.

"She's been there, I noticed stuffed behind the hall settle Lily's blue cloche hat, she would never leave it behind. We need to get the others up here straight away. Can you go and find Dixon, Tom, Jack and Whiting, we will need them here and I think they need to be armed?"

"Will you be okay on your own, you won't do anything silly, will you?" Noah asked before he left to get the others.

"No, I'll wait for you to get back."

Time was of the essence, Archie realised every second would count in finding her. His heart was thumping, as he worked his way through the bushes that surrounded the rectory. Stopping at the back of the property he noticed several branches had been placed over a large tarpaulin. Carefully removing the branches and brushing away the leaves he lifted one corner of the tarpaulin to reveal a green Morris Traveller. His heart was now pounding and his impatience was over taking him.

Crouching outside the lounge window he peered in only to see Florence reading a newspaper. Where is she? It all looked normal, he thought to himself. Just at that moment Noah appeared at the side of the rectory, waving his arms to attract Archie's attention.

Archie crawled under the kitchen window and joined the others to the side of the building.

Keeping out of sight, Archie gathered the group close to him and spoke quietly.

"She must be in there somewhere. Whiting can you and Jack go around to the back? Tom, guard the front door and make sure nobody leaves. Noah and I will search the house thoroughly."

Archie cautiously tried the front door handle and pushed it gently open, only to be confronted by Florence blocking their way.

"What are you doing here Archie?" an indignant Florence shouted.

"We need to search your house, out of the way."

Florence was becoming more angry by the minute.

"There's nothing here. You wasted your time looking for John and seeing how that ended up and now you're doing the same thing with Lily. I told you, she's not here. But go ahead and find her."

Archie pushed past Florence, followed by Noah.

"I'll go upstairs, can you check down here?"

Archie said to Noah.

Archie worked his way along the landing trying every door and came to one that was locked.

"Have you got the key to this room?" he shouted down the stairs.

"Which one? None of the rooms are locked."

"It's the one on the right at the end of the landing."

"I'm not sure, it shouldn't be locked," Florence thought for a moment. "I don't have any keys for the bedrooms."

Running out of patience Archie put his shoulder to the door and forced it open. He scoured the room, hoping to find some evidence that Lily had been there. There was an unmade bed in the corner and an empty jug of water on a small side table, but no sign of Lily.

Disappointingly he walked back down the hall, looking up and noticed the loft hatch. Grabbing a chair he carefully lifted the hatch and peered in.

"Have you got a torch?" he shouted down to Noah.

"No, but I'm sure Mrs Ward has one," he said, looking at her.

"Yes, it's in the kitchen on the shelf."

Noah handed Archie the torch, he stuck his head into the dark void. Shining the light around the loft there was no sign of Lily or that she'd even been there.

"Nothing up here," he handed the torch back to Noah.

For the next hour Archie and Noah turned every room upside down but found nothing. There was a heavy air of disappointment as they congregated back in the rectory hallway.

Archie turned to Florence. "Where is the blue hat that was stuffed behind the settle?"

"Blue hat?" Florence looked confused.

"Yes, there was a blue cloche hat behind your settle."

"Oh, that old hat. Yes it was mine. I was throwing it out, why?"

"No reason. Sorry to trouble you, Florence. We have to go."

Fifty-Eight

As they were leaving Jack came round to the front door and pulled Archie to one side.

"Archie, I know this may be silly and you've probably thought of it. But what about the church, it's not being used at the moment and it's a perfect place to hide someone?"

"Jack, you are a genius! I hadn't thought of it."

Archie went back into the rectory and faced Florence.

"Can I have the keys to the church?"

"I haven't got them, I had to give them to Cannon Kingsley when he was here. Apparently the Bishop told him to pick it up for safe keeping, at least until they find a replacement for John."

"Do you know if there is a spare somewhere, with the church warden perhaps?"

"Not to my knowledge, John looked after that sort of thing."

Archie thanked Florence and met the others at the rectory gates.

"The only place we haven't searched, thanks to Jack, is the church, we need to get in there."

Archie started to devise a plan. There were two doors that led into the church, the main door and a small side door. He sent Dixon and Whiting round to the side door, while Archie and the rest to the main door. Archie tried the handle, but Florence had said it was locked. He examined the lock.

"Piece of cake," he got out his trusted lock picking case, "you never know when you may need one," he smiled.

In no time the lock was picked and the large main door creaked open. The familiar smell of damp filled the air, there was an uneasy silence as they made their way through the sanctuary. Much to Archie's disappointment it was empty.

"Nothing, in there …"

"Did you hear that?" Noah grabbed Archie's arm.

They stood silently straining to hear any noise that was out of place.

"There it is," Jack said, pointing to the narrow staircase that led to the crypt.

Whiting had managed to force the small side door open and was coming up the stairs.

Oh, it's you, we thought we heard something," Noah said.

"That wasn't us, we heard a noise coming from the crypt."

Archie's heart was thumping as he gestured to Whiting and Dixon to stand either side of the door.

"If you come in here I will kill her," a voice resounded from the crypt.

"We are coming out. I have a gun to your friend's head and I will use it if you try to stop me, throw your guns down."

Archie detected a slight accent coming from a woman's voice deep in the crypt.

"Come out we won't try anything," Archie said, feeling relieved that Lily was still alive.

A figure half hidden in the shadow appeared in the doorway. Archie could make out that it was Lily, then he saw the glint of the barrel of a gun pointed at Lily's head.

"Let them through," Noah shouted.

The woman ordered everyone to go back into the main body of the church but she hadn't noticed Whiting crouching out of sight behind the door. In the light of the church Archie recognized the woman as the one that had seen on the train. Noah, Archie and the others threw their guns on the floor and backed off.

In a split second Whiting jumped up and pushed the barrel of his gun into the back of the woman's head.

"Drop it! Now!" He ordered.

She hesitated.

"You wouldn't."

"Try me."

The woman reluctantly lowered her arm and dropped her gun on the floor. Lily stepped away from her, relief written on her face.

Archie kicked the gun away, "Handcuff her," he said, there was an air of relief in his voice now that Lily was safe. At last, perhaps they could wrap these cases up, he thought.

There was a click from a gun being cranked from behind them. The ground sank beneath Archie's feet and the air was sucked from the room.

"On the contrary, put your gun down whoever you are."

Fifty-Nine

Without turning around Archie recognised the voice that came from behind him.

"Drop your guns. All of you."

"Do as she says," Archie said, staring in disbelief at the women holding the gun. "Why Florence?"

"You wouldn't understand, now get over there, I want you all back in the crypt, one false move, and be in no doubt, I will shoot you."

Waving her gun in the air she gestured to Lily.

"Lily with me, you're my insurance, I don't trust you Archie."

The other woman picks up her gun and pushes past Noah to join Florence, while Lily moves slowly toward the two women.

"No, take me," Archie pleaded with her.

Florence pondered the situation for a few minutes.

"I'm fond of you Lily, I think I will take Archie, he is probably more important. Archie, get over here."

Archie beckoned Lily toward him.

"No tricks," Florence said, pointing her gun at Lily.

The atmosphere could be cut with a knife as Archie considered the situation. He was not going to let anything happen to Lily nor was Florence going to get away with it.

"We don't need anybody. He will just slow us down, why don't we shoot them all and get going. The plane will be waiting for us and we will be out of the country before anybody finds them." The other woman said.

Florence thought for a moment, that made sense.

"Archie, get back with the others."

Archie moved slowly towards the others, when suddenly Tom made a dash for the door, hoping to cause a distraction.

Seeing Tom move, the woman raised her gun to shoot him and in all the confusion Lily, who was trained in Defendu, managed to kick the gun out of her hand before she shot. Then Lily swung round and with her heel kicked the woman in the stomach and sent her flying to the floor. Florence turned quickly and started randomly shooting, Dixon grunted, grabbing his leg as he went down, blood blooming on the thigh of his trousers.

Whilst Florence was distracted, Archie took advantage, leaping at her and wrestling her to the ground.

In the struggle there was the sound of another gun shot that resounded around the church and Jack, who was standing by the crypt door, fell to the ground.

Archie struggled with Florence and finally managed to subdue her, holding her arms behind her and forcing his knee into her back.

The other woman, who was winded, lay on the

floor gripping her stomach, with Lily holding one arm behind her back.

"Whiting, check what's happened to Jack. Tom, give me your handcuffs then go over to the rectory and phone for an ambulance."

Jack was slumped against the crypt door with a trickle of blood running down a small gully that had formed on the old flagstones.

"It doesn't look good for him, he's been hit in his side, and losing a lot of blood, and he's unconscious," a concerned Whiting looked at Noah.

"Stay with him, and keep pressure on that wound," Noah said as he handcuffs the two women, then storms out of the church.

"Where's that ambulance?" he shouted, as he pounds up and down outside.

By the crypt, Lily relieved Whiting and knelt down beside Jack, keeping the cloth they had found on a pew tightly pressed against his side to stop the flow of blood, she gently stroked his hair. Although knowing he was unconscious, Lily, with tears in her eyes, spoke to him.

"It will be fine, Jack, just hang on, think of your Mum, she'll be expecting you. The ambulance will be here soon."

The atmosphere was quite charged as Archie gathered his thoughts. In no time the ambulance men were running through the church toward Jack and Dixon.

"Don't worry about me, see to him," Dixon

pointed to Jack.

One of the ambulance men bent down to check Jack's pulse.

There was a long agonising silence as the ambulance man held his fingers on Jack's neck.

"It's not strong and he's lost a lot of blood. But he's still alive, we need to get him to hospital straight away."

They carefully lifted Jack on a stretcher and carried him to the waiting ambulance.

"On second thoughts, can you go with him Tom and I'll meet you at the hospital later," Noah said, having come back into the church.

"Yes sir, I'll take Dixon with me."

"Good idea, Tom."

Noah stood with his hands on his hips and watched the ambulance, with bells ringing, racing off toward Marlborough.

The group slowly made their way back to the police station. Archie with his arm around Lily to comfort her, Noah and Whiting, escorting the two handcuffed women, through a small crowd that had formed.

"Let us through, there's nothing to see here," Noah ordered the crowd, who moved aside.

Sixty

There was a Black Maria along with two police cars waiting outside. Special Branch had come to pick up the prisoners Tomasz had been guarding, and take them back to London.

Introducing themselves and showing him their warrant cards, Noah took them to where Haynes, Brooks and Rizzuto were being guarded by Tomasz, in their cells.

"Come on you three, we've arranged a nice little trip to London for you," Noah said.

Cuffed and complaining, Rizzuto was dragged from his cell. He suddenly stopped and stared at the two women sitting in the corridor.

"Quella è la donna, sul ponte l'altra mattina, sì, proprio lei," He said staring at them.

Noah looked at Tomasz. "What did he say?"

"I think he said, 'That's the woman he saw on the bridge.'"

"Ask him, which woman?"

"Quale?"

Rizzuto stepped forward and pointed to Mrs Ward. "Quello."

"He said, that one, sir."

Florence sank her head into her hands and sighed.

Once Haynes, Brooks and Rizzuto were safely chained in the back of the maria, one of the Special Branch men turned to Noah.

"I thought we were picking up four people, where's Valentino?" he asked.

"He's not with us any more, you don't have to worry about him," Archie said.

Soon they were watching Special Branch's Black Maria and squad cars disappear up the High Street towards Hungerford and on to London.

"I'm glad they've gone, we need the cells. Whiting, can you bring Mrs Ward to the interview room?"

There was a tense atmosphere in the room as Archie, Lily and Noah entered. Florence was waiting handcuffed to the table.

Archie sat beside her while Noah and Lily sat opposite, a single light swung gently above the table, lighting up the room, which soon started to fill with smoke as Archie puffed on his pipe and Noah lit another cigarette. Lily stood up and went to the small barred window and opened it.

"Would you like a drink?" Noah asked Florence, in an attempt to relieve the tension.

"Yes, that would be welcome, thank you Inspector."

"I'll get that, sir," Whiting offered.

The four sat silently, Florence looking at the floor while Archie studied her, hoping to see some form of emotion.

"There you go," Whiting placed the cup of tea in front of Florence, she picked it up with her left hand.

Archie instantly noticed. "Why did you kill Miss Hunt?" he abruptly asked.

"I loved John, I really did. I couldn't bear the thought of him being with another woman. You see, I had already telephoned Dean's Yard earlier in the week and they told me they hadn't seen him for months."

"What happened?" Lily interrupted.

Florence with a vague expression on her face, stared in front of her, her voice lacked emotion.

"I went to meet him off the train and when I turned the corner into the station, I saw him talking to another woman and holding her arm, they looked close. I felt betrayed. I watched them and after a few minutes turned to go home when something caught my eye on the other side of a low wall. It was a briefcase, so I picked it up and took it home with me."

There was a brief period of silence, interrupted by Archie.

"What did you do with it?" he asked.

Florence picked up her tea and took a sip.

"Do you have a cigarette?" she said, looking at Noah.

He handed her a cigarette and lit it for her.

"Thank you."

"The briefcase." Lily said, feeling a little impatient.

Florence took a long pull on her cigarette and

looked at Lily.

"It wasn't locked so I emptied it onto the kitchen table, there was a book."

Florence thought for a minute.

"I think, yes, it was Wage-Labour and Capital by Karl Marx, one of my hero's, and a pistol along with some papers.

Florence stopped and looked toward the window as though in a dream.

"I first met John at Oxford University in a debating society, we shared the same ideologies. We immediately became friends and soon fell in love, that was a lovely time," Florence sighed deeply.

"Shortly before we left university a mutual friend introduced us to a woman and we developed a close relationship. We shared the same political socialist ideals. Unbeknownst to us she was a NKGB agent who eventually recruited us as sleeper agents."

Archie leaned back in his chair, an awkward silence fell in the room as they looked at Florence.

"What was her name?" Archie asked.

Florence shuffled her feet and smiled.

"She is the woman who was staying with me for the last two weeks. You nearly caught her when you came the other day, Archie."

"What is her name?" Archie repeated.

"Gerda Muller, she was from East Germany who became our handler. During our time at Oxford John and I had spent our time being trained in espionage and in covert methods of elimination."

The air of disbelief filled the room, despite what was being said, the atmosphere was relatively calm. Florence continued.

"When John came home, I questioned him about the women, but he denied even talking to her. I pretended it didn't matter and carried on cooking the evening meal. Whilst he was eating I crept up behind him and injected him in the back of his neck with a lethal dose of curare. When I saw him reeling in agony on the floor and then eventually dying, I had a sense of satisfaction and peace."

Archie looked at Lily and then back to the emotionless face of Florence.

"Where did you get the poison from?" he asked.

"We have a small safe hidden in the kitchen, which you missed when you searched the house, that contains new passports, pistols and several poisons along with a hypodermic syringe.

"What did you do next?" Archie continued.

"With Gerda's help we managed to put him in the back of my car and take his body to that derelict building on the Everleigh Road. We covered his body with some stones and scattered some things from the briefcase I found around him. Later that night I took John's ration book along with the briefcase and hid them in some bushes near Strong's farm."

"Before we have a break, Mrs Ward, did you murder Miss Hunt on Tuesday the fifth April?" Noah asked, abruptly.

Sixty-One

"Yes," the answer was cold and lacking emotion.

Noah continued, "Can you be more explicit."

Florence suddenly stood up and knocked her tea over.

"Sit down," Noah shouted.

Sitting back down, Florence picked up her cup and calmly put it back on the saucer.

"I couldn't sleep and wanted to clear my head, so I went for an early morning walk. As I was passing the River Hotel, by pure coincidence the woman John was talking to came out of the hotel and brushed past me. I was so incensed I followed her.

"She turned off River Street and headed toward the river. It was a chilly morning so I was wearing a jacket that happened to have a cut throat razor sewn into the lining, for emergencies, you see.

"I'm not sure how but the razor was in my hand and she was standing just in front of me. It wasn't hard, I grabbed her by the hair, pulled her head back and cut her throat, she didn't make a sound. She fell back against me and I managed to push her into the river."

Lily leaned forward on the table and asked, "Did you speak to a Cannon Kingsley?"

"Oh him, I just didn't believe him, they always stick together, that lot. They're all a bunch of hypocrites, say one thing and then do the opposite "

"We telephoned the local police near to the refuge center, who confirmed that John did in fact spend a lot of time helping Cannon Kingsley," Lily continued.

"Well, it's too late now, John should have told me, it's all his fault, you must realise that there are always consequences to people's actions." Florence shrugged her shoulders and sounded very matter of fact.

The room was getting warm, smoke was clinging to the ceiling, the atmosphere was tense. There was a knock on the door, breaking the tension.

Tomasz's head appeared around the corner of the door.

"I'm sorry to disturb you Noah, but Tom is on the telephone from the hospital for you, it sounds urgent."

"Thank you Tomasz, I'll be right there. I think we need a break."

Noah hurried from the room and picked up the receiver in his office.

Sixty-two

Noah could hardly speak, he didn't want to hear any bad news regarding Jack.

"Tom, what news?"

"He is still in surgery, the doctor said he has lost a lot of blood and it's touch and go whether he will pull through or not. I think it would be a good idea if someone could go and pick up his mother, she needs to be here."

It wasn't the news that Noah was hoping for.

"Yes, I'll get Tomasz to fetch her and explain the situation. Let me know if there are any further developments. Thank you, Tom. Oh, by the way, how is Dixon."

"He is fine sir, just a flesh wound, he is waiting here with me."

"That's good news at least, well done Tom."

Noah lit another cigarette and made his way along the narrow corridor to join the others. Archie and Lily had left the interview room to meet Noah.

"It's not good, I'm afraid."

The colour drained from Lily's face expecting the worst. Noah relaid what Tom had said and not to lose hope.

"He's in good hands, they got me through it when I

was shot," he said, trying to reassure them.

"Tomasz, can you collect Mrs Jones and explain what has happened and take her to the hospital."

"Use my car," Archie said, handing him his keys.

It was getting late but they all agreed to carry on and rejoined Florence in the interview room where she was still handcuffed to the table, quietly humming to herself.

"Thank you Whiting, can you mind the desk?"

"Yes sir."

Noah and Lily sat opposite Florence while Archie sat next to her. The room had cleared of most of the smoke, Lily stared Florence in the face.

"Tell me Florence, what was Gerda Muller doing here?"

"You need to ask her," Florence began to sound dismissive.

"I'm asking you, what was she doing here?" Lily insisted.

Florence stared back at Lily and then turned her head away and started humming again.

"I'm very fond of you and Archie, you've always been fair with me." There was a change in Florence's attitude, her shoulders dropped as she sighed then she began to open up.

"She had information that someone in her network was working as a double agent, and feeding her false information. It was a chap called De Villiers-Blyth, he worked on one of the camps around here. I was to eliminate him.

"She had met De Villiers-Blyth in Marlborough and had told him that a plane had been arranged to take him to a safe place somewhere in France.

"The plane was to leave RAF Avon. Gerda was to meet him. My assignment was to eliminate him and dispose of the body."

There was a knock on the door.

"Sorry to bother you, sir, but can I have a word?" Whiting interrupted the interview.

Noah stood up. "I'll be back in a minute."

"There's a lady from the hotel waiting at the front desk."

"What does she want?

"To speak to you, Sir."

Noah made his way to the front desk and found Dotty waiting.

"Hello Dotty, how can I help you?"

"Tomasz came to the hotel and said that you were working late and you haven't eaten since lunch time, so I've brought some sandwiches and cake for you all."

"Thank you Dotty, that's extremely kind of you and I know Lily will certainly appreciate it."

Noah took the sandwiches into the interview room, much to Lily's delight. As they were eating Florence carried on.

"Gerda had arranged for him to meet her on the north perimeter of the camp on Monday morning. My part was to wait in a small copse just outside the camp. When he appeared I approached him and explained the plane was delayed and he was to wait with me. When he turned his back on me, I took out my pistol and shot him twice in the back of the head. Gerda was waiting with my car, so we had to act quickly. We picked up his body and put it in the back of the car, then took it to a field just the other side of Kepnal."

"Did you meet him in Devizes?" Lily interrupted.

"Devizes? Oh, the man I was talking to, no he was a man asking for direction. I never met De Villiers-Blyth till that morning."

"Why didn't Gerda shoot him and why did she stay after giving you your assignment?" Lily persisted.

"She is just our handler, she has not been trained to kill, it's not her job."

"But why did she stay in Pewsey after she had contacted De Villiers, why didn't she leave?" Archie cut in.

"The assignment needed two people, I couldn't handle his body on my own, so she stayed around to help."

"Why dump De Villiers-Blyth's body at Kepnal?" Archie asked.

Florence shuffled in her chair and looked into the distance.

"I need to go to the toilet." There was no emotion in her voice.

Noah called Whiting back into the room.

"Can you escort Mrs Ward to the toilets?"

Leaving the room Florence turned around and

looked at Archie and Lily.

"I meant it, what I said, I am very fond of you both. Very fond. I'm sorry."

After she had gone, Noah lit another cigarette, stood up and stretched, then turned to Archie and Lily.

"That's a lot to take in, how did we miss so much?"

We didn't, she is a very clever woman and has been trained to lie," Archie said, while drawing on his pipe.

"Archie, she's been gone for a rather long time. I think I'll go and check on her."

"Good idea," Archie said.

Walking down the corridor Lily felt a cold shiver run down her spine. There was a strange empty atmosphere as she approached Whiting, who was waiting outside the toilets.

"She's still in there," he said.

"Do you know if there are any windows she could escape through?" Lily asked.

Whiting hesitated. "I'm not sure, I've not used those cubicles before."

Sixty-Three

Lily carefully pushed the cloakroom door open.

"Florence, are you in there?" she called out.

There was uneasy silence as they entered the room. Two of the cubicles were closed. Lily called her again, but there was no reply.

"What's that smell?" Lily said, as she tried to push the door open.

"Can you give me a hand, Les."

They struggled to get the door to open wide, something was jammed behind it. With a lot of effort they eventually managed to force the door open enough to enable Lily to peer into the cubical. Florence's body was lying on the floor blocking the door.

Lily looked at her body, shock evident on her face. "Cyanide," she could smell the familiar aroma of bitter almonds and noticed her complexion was pink.

"Les, can you go and get Noah and Archie and then telephone Dr Stagg and ask him to come here?"

Whiting disappeared down the corridor while Lily tried to open the door wider. She knelt on the floor and managed to take Florence's hand.

"Oh, Florence, what have you done?" There was a sadness in Lily's voice.

Archie stood in the doorway and looked down at Lily. There was a look of disappointment on his face.

"Why?" Archie said, as he moved into the room.

"She had nothing to live for, she knew she would hang and probably thought there was no other choice."

After a short while Noah appeared with Dr Stagg, who pushed his way into the room.

"Where's the body?" he demanded.

Lily moved out of the way so he could get a better look at Florence.

"This won't do, any chance of getting this door off? How do you expect me to examine the body if I can't get to her?" Dr Stagg moaned. He was obviously not in the best of moods.

Archie and Noah wrestled with the door and eventually managed to remove it from its hinges.

"Cyanide poisoning," I'll need to get her to the morgue to tell you more. Has anyone telephoned for an ambulance?"

"It's on its way, should be here in about ten minutes," Noah said.

"There's not much more I can do here, I'll bid you goodnight and send you my report when I've completed my autopsy." The doctor shrugged and hurried out of the police station.

"I would say he got out of the wrong side of the bed, if it wasn't the middle of the night," Archie said with a smile.

Archie, Lily and Noah made their way back to the

interview room leaving Whiting to guard the body.

The hour was getting late and although there was an air of satisfaction at solving the murders, it was tainted by the events of the evening.

"I think we're all a bit tired, it's been a very long day. I'll wait for the ambulance to arrive, why don't you two head home, we can continue in the morning."

"Are you sure, I don't mind staying," Archie suggested.

"Someone needs to stay with the prisoners, I'll send Whiting back to Parkhill. Plus I wouldn't sleep knowing Jack's life lies in the balance."

Lily, can you search Muller and make sure she hasn't any suicide capsules on her or any other means of taking her own life?"

Archie waited outside Muller's cell while Lily thoroughly searched her.

"I have nothing on me. Can I speak to Mrs Ward?"

Lily explained what had happened. The colour drained from Muller's face, she appeared genuinely shocked.

"That is sad, she was a fine woman and a valued member of my group."

Leaving the cell, Lily turned around and faced Muller.

"Your English is very good."

"I was trained to have a very good cockney accent," Gerda said to Lily.

"Yes, we heard you, ducks." Lily looked back with a knowing smile.

She joined Archie by the front desk, they said good night to Whiting and Noah and arranged to meet at ten thirty, later that morning.

There was a chill in the air, as Archie and Lily made their way back to the hotel, a full moon lighting their way.

"What a day, how are you feeling Lily, being kidnapped, threatened, then finding Mrs Ward's body is a lot to deal with."

"I'm fine actually, I think I am so tired, the enormity of the situation hasn't really hit me yet." She had started to shake however. Archie put his arm around her to support her as they walked slowly home.

"I think a stiff drink is in order don't you."

"That would be lovely, thank you Archie."

Sixty-Four

Tuesday 19th April

Six-thirty came too early for Archie, but Maisie was becoming quite insistent. Despite Archie only having a few hours sleep, he dragged himself out of bed.

"I'll be there in a jiffy, old thing."

Archie left Lily sleeping whilst he took Maisie for her morning walk. Henry was on the reception desk when they returned and Lily was up and having coffee in the dining room.

"Good morning Dad."

"Hello Archie, Lily tells me you had quite a day yesterday and you didn't get to bed until the early hours of this morning. You should have left a note and I would have got Dotty to walk Maisie."

"Thank you, Dad, but I needed to clear my head before meeting Noah later on."

Archie joined Lily in the dining room.

"How did you sleep?" Archie asked.

"To be honest not very well, I can't help thinking that there is more to this case than meets the eye."

"Yes, I agree, It kept me awake as well, but I can't quite put my finger on it."

After breakfast they walked arm in arm to the police station.

"Good morning Tom, how are you? Have you heard how Jack is doing?"

"Good morning, I'm doing well thank you, a bit tired. Good news about Jack, he made it through surgery and had a comfortable night. He's out of danger and should make a full recovery, although it will take time."

"That's really good news, what about Dixon?"

"I'm very well thank you," Dixon's voice came from the small office behind the front desk.

They had left the hospital late last night and had relieved Noah to give him a break.

"The inspector is waiting for you in his office."

"Thank you, Tom."

Noah was lighting another cigarette as they entered his office.

"Good morning, did you manage to sleep at all?"

"Good morning Noah, no not really. We both felt we may have missed something, but we are not sure what."

"Yes, I know what you mean. Tom, can you take Muller to the interview room?"

"It seems an open and shut case, Mrs Ward has confessed to the murders, we should be happy with the outcome." Archie said, lighting his pipe.

Tom led Gerda Muller along the narrow corridor to the interview room, where Noah, Archie and Lily were waiting. The small dark room was already filling with smoke, the single light bulb above the table had not been switched on, making the room even darker.

Tom opened the door and guided Muller in, seating her opposite Noah and Archie.

"Tom, can you turn on the light before you go?"

The small bulb hardly made any difference to the darkness, it only managed to cast soft shadows around the room. The atmosphere felt more like a smoky Soho jazz club than a police interview room.

Facing Muller, Noah speaks.

"Gerda Muller I am charging you with the kidnapping of Lily Forester and carrying a firearm with the intent to cause bodily harm. You do not have to say anything but anything you do say will be taken down and may be given in evidence, do you understand?"

"Yes."

"Can you state your full name and address?" Noah opened the interview.

"I will only give you my name and address and nothing more. My name is Gerda Muller and my address is one hundred and two Hooper Street London."

"Where is Hooper Street," Lily asked.

"Off Leman Street, Whitechapel. That is all I am saying."

Archie and Lily looked at each other, their interest piqued.

"Do you know Leonardo Valentino?" Noah continued.

"I have nothing to say, you can not ask me any more questions," Muller said, turning her head away in defiance.

"It's not a difficult question, do you know him or not?" Archie pushed for an answer.

Muller smiled, "I have nothing to say."

"Why are you in Pewsey?" Lily asked, changing the subject.

"I will give you a telephone number, I suggest you call that number. Westminster 1616 extension 2."

Archie stopped, turning to the others he whispered, "I know that number. It was my old MI6 HQ at Century House, in London, before I went to the Home Office."

"What are you doing with that number?" Archie asked, sounding surprised.

Muller stared silently at the wall behind Archie.

Noah suggested, as they weren't getting anywhere, that they would stop for a coffee break and called Tom in to stay with Muller. Archie and the others made their way to Noah's office, Lily went straight to the window and opened it.

"I'll give my old HQ a call and see what this is all about."

Archie left to use the telephone on the front desk.

"Hello operator, can you get me Westminster 1616, please?"

"Yes, hold the line and I'll connect you."

After waiting a few minutes, the phone crackled, and a women spoke.

"Westminster 1616, how can I help you?"

"Can I have extension 2, please?"

"Who shall I say is calling?"

"Archie Freestone."

Archie waited.

"George Graham here," Captain Sir George Graham was head of MI6, "how can I help you Freestone?"

"Good morning sir, we are holding a prisoner here called Gerda Muller, who has given us your name. Can you explain why?"

There was a long silence. Archie could hear voices in the background.

"Freestone, you are still bound under the Official Secrets Act that you signed when you joined the department. What I am about to tell you is for your ears only, you can not share this information with anyone. Do you understand?"

"Yes sir."

"Gerda Muller was a member of MGB, the Ministry of State Security. Last March she defected and came across to our side. She has been extremely helpful in closing down many Russian networks in Britain. She is too valuable to have her cover blown. I am giving you a direct order, you have my authority to release her straight away. Do not question her, do you understand Freestone?"

Archie thought for a few minutes, although not being particularly happy, he had no choice.

"Yes sir, she will be released as soon as I have

finished this call."

"Good chap, Freestone."

"One thing sir, can you tell me why she was in Pewsey?"

"The only thing I can tell you is that things didn't really go to plan. That's all I can say, goodbye Freestone."

Archie stood for a while pondering the consequences, he wasn't satisfied with the outcome, but had no choice. Lighting his pipe he went back to Noah's office, where he found Lily and Noah chatting and drinking coffee.

"Not good news I'm afraid, we have to let Muller go and I'm sorry but I can't say why."

Noah looked quizzically at Archie.

"That's okay old chap, you have your reasons and I trust your judgment. Do you want me to release her or would you like to do it?"

"I'll do it, if you don't mind."

A contemplative Archie, made his way along the corridor to the interview room.

"Thank you Tom, you can leave us." he said, entering the room.

He sat opposite Gerda puffing on his pipe.

"I've spoken to Captain Sir George Graham who has explained your situation, we have agreed to release you. You are free to go."

As she was leaving the room Archie looked up.

"Can I ask you one question? Do you know Valentino?"

Gerda Muller looked back at Archie.

"He is a good man, he trusts you. That is all I can say. Goodbye Archie Freestone."

Gerda brushed past Tom on her way to the main door. Lily and Noah watched as she left the police station and headed off toward the hotel to collect her things.

"That just leaves Valentino. By the way, Archie, what have you done with him." Noah asked.

Sixty-Five

A few days before Lily was kidnapped Archie had secretly taken Valentino to the MI6 safe house in Milton Lilbourne and left him on his own, unguarded. They had formed a mutual trust with each other, so Archie felt confident Valentino would not make a run for it. Archie explained to the others what he had done and decided to collect him after they'd had lunch.

The hotel dining room was packed, all the usual people were there, Jacob was in deep conversation with Arthur. Ruth was running around like a headless chicken while Dotty remained calm and in control.

"I've kept your table, Archie," Dotty said.

Archie thanked her. He and Lily enjoyed their meal in peace, instead of grabbing something while they were on the move. Because Lily had signed the Official Secrets Act as well, Archie was able to divulge what he had been told.

"So, she's going to get away with it," Lily sounded a bit disappointed and rather angry.

"Yes, it looks like it." A frustrated Archie replied.

Once they had eaten, they made their way back to the police station to meet Noah, who would then be going on to Milton Lilbourne to collect Valentino. Tom was on the desk when they went in.

"The Inspector is around the back waiting for you."

The drive to the safe house was quiet, as Archie was unable to tell Noah why they had to let Muller go without charging her.

"Here we are, I'll go and get him," Archie said, as he pulls up outside the safe house.

Archie felt something wasn't quite right. He walked up to the door, turned around and beckoned the others to join him. Archie pushed the front door cautiously open.

"Leonardo, are you here? it's Archie."

There was no answer, there was a strange silence as they made their way further into the house. Noah went upstairs while Archie and Lily searched the ground floor.

"All clear up here," Noah shouted down.

Archie and Lily went into the kitchen, propped up on the table was a note addressed to him next to a pile of papers. He opened the envelope and read the content out loud.

Archie,

I'm sorry I think you will understand why I had to leave. I know I'm not a good man and have done some terrible things. My wife dying the way she did brought me to my senses. I regret the way I treated her, but it is something I have to live with for the rest of my life.

You kept your word and trusted me, something I'm not used to. I have left a detailed list of the names and addresses of most of the people connected to the Whitechapel Mob. There are some very high-profile names on the list, there are other names operating with several other mobs, which is why I have to disappear and make a new start, within the law, of course. I am prepared to turn Kings evidence if required. I trust that you will know what to do with the list. Trust no-one..

Thank you and Lily for your trust.
Leonardo.

Glancing at the names on the list, Archie smiled to himself among them was Gerda Muller.

Noah had joined them in the kitchen, he peered over Archie's shoulder to see what it was that Archie was studying.

"It's a list of names, people connected to the mob and apparently there are even more names he hasn't told us about," Archie said.

Noah scanned the list, "There are some very influential and powerful names here, people I knew personally and trusted. Considering who's on this list, Valentino will be a hunted man. People will want him dead, who can you trust to keep him safe? We need to give him time to get as far away as possible and a chance to make a new life wherever he's gone."

Archie agreed, putting the list inside his coat, the three made their way back to Pewsey deep in thought. Noah felt let down by the names Valentino had written on the list.

When they arrived back at the police station, Keeling was on the front desk.

"Inspector, Superintendent Brentwood has telephoned, can you call him back?"

"What does he want?" Noah said.

"I imagine he wants to know where Valentino is," Archie suggested.

Noah was cautious about who he would share information with at the moment. In his office Noah telephoned Brentwood.

"Jackson here, sir."

"Jackson, I didn't give permission to let Valentino go, what's going on down there, where is he?"

"I'm sorry, sir, I thought you knew, when I told Special Branch he wasn't with us anymore, that's because he was shot and killed."

There was silence.

"How and who shot him?" Brentwood spluttered out.

"He was caught in the crossfire when Martin tried to shoot Freestone. We were bringing Valentino through the back of the police station, when he was hit from a ricocheting bullet that caught him in the chest. He died before we could get him to a doctor."

"Where's his body and the autopsy report?" Brentwood insisted.

"He was cremated, I will get a copy of his death certificate to you as soon as I can. Is there anything else I can help you with sir?"

"No, just get me that death certificate, Jackson."

"I will, sir."

Archie and Lily were listening to the conversation Noah was having with Brentwood. After he had put the telephone down Archie turned and faced Noah.

"You're a good man, Noah. What about the death certificate?"

"Don't worry about that, this is a small village as you know, we all look after each other."

Noah thanked Whiting and Keeling for all their help, before they left.

"Thank you Inspector, it's been quite an

experience, anytime you need help in the future, you know where to find us."

When they had left to make their way back to Parkhill.

"Well, there's not much we can do here, so I think we will go back and have lunch," Archie said.

There was a sense of disappointment as Archie and Lily walked arm in arm back to the hotel. Clutching the list close to him he reflected on the names, these were some of the people he knew personally and had respected.

"This is going to open a can of worms, I think for the time being I'm going to hang on to it until we decide what to do," Archie said.

Noah and Dixon had followed Archie and Lily back to the hotel. When they arrived they found them waiting in the foyer.

"Lets go into the office Noah, we need to talk in private."

Lily made straight for the chair next to the open window, closely followed by Dixon, knowing the room would soon be full of smoke.

Archie and Noah had wanted to share some of the names on Valentino's list with Dixon. After studying the list, they thought that it would be advisable for Dixon to stay on in Pewsey to help out, at least, while Jack was laid up.

"I think it's best if we keep these papers locked up in the hotel safe."

"Good idea." Noah agreed.

Henry was on the reception desk when they came out of the office.

"Ah, Dad, can we put these papers in the safe?" Archie asked, handing the sheets of paper to him.

"Yes, of course, I'll do it straight away. Are you both okay?" Henry asked, bending down to unlock the safe.

"Thank you Dad, yes we are fine, just a little tired. Is Mum upstairs?"

"Yes she is, I know she would love to see you both."

"We will pop up after we have all had lunch."

They settled down in the dining room, there was a quiet pensiveness about the four, as the thought over what they had discovered.

"I suppose, for now, life must go on. I'll check on Jack when we get back to the station, and advise Tom what we have decided."

"Yes, it's hard to consider what will happen now, but life does go on and we have a wedding to plan." Archie mused. "But for now, we must pop up and see my mother."

"Give Jack our love, and hope he gets better soon." Lily said as Noah and Dixon turned to leave.

"Will do, thank you both for all your help, we couldn't have managed without you."

"You're welcome. I don't think any one of us could have managed this alone, it was a team effort. Let us know how Jack is, won't you." Archie said.

Noah and Dixon sauntered back to the police

station. People were going about their daily chores, oblivious of what had just taken place in their village. They looked at each other and smiled.

**

Emily was eagerly waiting for them. Maisie, who was sleeping on the settee, raised her head as they came in. On seeing who it was, ran straight to Lily and rolled onto her back for a tummy tickle.

"Where have you two been? I've been waiting to hear all your news. Have you had a nice day, have you decided on a date yet, when are you going to Hastings, how is Jack I heard he was-?"

Archie smiled and looked at Lily.

"Slow down, Mum, it's been a good day, Jack is on the mend and we are going to Hastings on Thursday to see Lily's parents, and no we haven't set a date."

"I have some news," Lily says, turning to Archie.

"I've sent my letter of resignation to my department head, to take effect immediately."

"That's wonderful! Archie go and get a bottle of something special. Call your dad, we have to celebrate."

Archie's face lit up, he pulled Lily close to him and whispered.

"Lily Forester, I love you."

The End.

Epilogue:

A half-hidden figure crouched suspiciously beneath the open window of the hotel office, straining to hear what was being said by Archie and the others, who were discussing what to do about the names on the list that Valentino had left for them.

"Can I help you?" the voice of Dotty, the hotel housekeeper, echoed around the rear hotel car park.

Startled, the person staggered as they struggled to stand upright and fell back against the wall, but quickly recovered.

"I've lost some papers. I was just reading my notes when the wind blew them out of my hand."

"Can I help you."

The answer was short and sharp. "No, no, thank you. I'll find them. Don't worry, plus, you must be busy and have far more important things to do."

"If you are sure."

"Yes, thank you." The eavesdropper sighed in relief as Dotty moved away, keeping up the pretense they started to search around the parked cars.

Dotty made her way through the back door of the hotel, and thought no more about it.

Footnotes:

A sleeper agent, also called a sleeper cell, is a spy placed in a target country or organisation not to undertake an immediate mission, but instead to act as a potential asset if activated.

A.W.O.L: means **Absent Without Leave**. It is used to describe someone who is absent from their assigned duty or location without proper authorization, primarily in a military context.

The People's Commissariat for State Security (NKGB) was the Soviet Union's secret police, intelligence, and counter-intelligence agency from 1941 to 1946. In 1946, the NKGB was renamed the Ministry of State Security (MGB). In 1954 after the deaths of Joseph Stalin and Lavrentiy Beria. The KGB, or Committee for State Security, replaced the Cheka, NKVD, and MGB, which were earlier Soviet secret police agencies.

Turning King's Evidence:

Evidence for the prosecution given by someone who is also accused of the crime being tried. People often turn King's evidence for a reduced sentence or immunity from prosecution.

About The Author

Graham Hardy, BA, was born in Bournemouth and spent a significant part of his childhood travelling with his father, mother, and brother. His father was in the British Army, attached to the SIB, Special Investigation Branch and was connected to counter-terrorism in Cyprus, working alongside the Greek Cypriot authorities. The turmoil in Cyprus left a lasting impression on Graham, and memories of his father carrying a shoulder holster hidden under his jacket form part of the inspiration for this book. In later life, Graham and his wife moved to Pewsey and spent a number of years living in Wiltshire and the surrounding area with their dog Archie. A fine art graduate from Exeter University, he has dabbled in writing most of his life, but this is his first published work.

Also Available

London 1949.

At the height of the Cold War, highly sensitive information is being passed beyond the Iron Curtain from somewhere near the sleepy village of Pewsey. Archie Freestone is sent undercover from the War Office to investigate.

Within twenty-four hours, the body of a man is discovered in a roadside ditch on the outskirts of the village.

Archie teams up with an old friend, local police inspector Noah Jackson, to solve the murder.

Meanwhile, a mysterious woman checks into the hotel, demanding an interview with the inspector.
Who is she, and why is she here?

A gripping who-done-it in this, the first of the Archie Freestone mysteries.

Printed in Dunstable, United Kingdom

67882071R00214